THINGS I CAN'T EXPLAIN

ALSO BY
MITCHELL KRIEGMAN

BEING AUDREY HEPBURN

THOMAS DUNNE BOOKS ST. MARTIN'S PRESS NEW YORK

THINGS I CAN'T EXPLAIN

MITCHELL KRIEGMAN

This is a work of fiction. All of the characters, organizations, and events portrayed in this novel are either products of the author's imagination or are used fictitiously.

THOMAS DUNNE BOOKS.
An imprint of St. Martin's Press.

Printed in the United States of America. For information, address St. Martin's Press, 175 Fifth Avenue, New York, N.Y. 10010.

www.thomasdunnebooks.com
www.stmartins.com

Illustrations by Demi Anter
Courtesy of Soft Reality LLC.

Designed by Anna Gorovoy

The Library of Congress Cataloging-in-Publication Data is available upon request.

ISBN 978-1-250-04654-3 (hardcover)
ISBN 978-1-4668-4679-1 (e-book)

Our books may be purchased in bulk for promotional, educational, or business use. Please contact your local bookseller or the Macmillan Corporate and Premium Sales Department at (800) 221-7945, extension 5442, or by e-mail at MacmillanSpecialMarkets@macmillan.com.

First Edition: November 2015

10 9 8 7 6 5 4 3 2 1

TO THE NOW AND FUTURE T.K.

You have to be prepared to take a spill.

—SHAUN WHITE

If a black cat crosses your path, it signifies that the animal is going somewhere.

—GROUCHO MARX

THINGS I CAN'T EXPLAIN

CHAPTER 1

Was it Malcolm Gladwell who said, "Where you're standing now is not where you're going to be"? Maybe it was Lady Gaga. All I know is that it's true. Whatever you think your problems are now, by the time you solve them you're in some new place with new problems. I think Einstein tried to adjust for this with his theory of relativity and Heisenberg had some special principle about it, but I don't think anyone has ever explained it.

Where I'm standing now is on an Upper East Side sidewalk, shaking off the residual effects of another pointless job interview, thanks to Lou at the Unemployment Office, who, if you ask me, is lucky he has a job. They should really think about changing the name of that place to something more upbeat, like the "You Will Be Settling into Your Own Cozy Little Cubicle Any Day Now" Office. Otherwise simply tag it "The Unenjoyment Office," because that's what it is.

Like a lot of people my age, in my situation, burdened with college debt and overqualified, I prefer *not* to think of myself as "unemployed." What I really am is an aspiring, highly trained journalist—whatever that means in the age of BuzzFeed. Sooner or later, some editor in chief or web czar is going to recognize me for what I can do. I'm hoping for sooner.

This afternoon's interview was more miserable than most; they were considering me as the faculty advisor for the school paper at a private academy for overprivileged and underdisciplined girls. The headmistress, Mrs. Rippington, really seemed to like me. Although this job is not exactly a career booster, a paycheck of any kind is an urgent priority, so I was thinking I'd sign up for this gig. Besides, it might be amusing, catering to the pampered progeny of the 1 percent while trying to catch up on my back rent. But that thought lasted about twelve seconds. That's when I heard fourteen-year-old Marissa, the seventh-grade, ahem, head editor, whisper to her sportswriter and BFF, Gwenyth, that as soon as she got her braces off she was planning to bop and drop handsome Mr. Lithicum, their twenty-something science teacher. I still have enough Ohio in me to be appalled by this. Exactly how much extra credit in biology is brace-face hoping to earn here? I flash back to my own seventh-grade science teacher, who wore a toupee and smelled perpetually of formaldehyde.

Mrs. Rippington was just opening her mouth to offer me the position when I overheard Miss Metal Mouth's bestie propose in a fast-talking addy rant that they make the little independent study in science a three-way, with a very specific graphic description of the contours of Mr. L's anatomical assets. How do they know that much detail?

I couldn't help myself. I thought the headmistress would appreciate knowing what's going on behind her back, so I ratted out the little Lolitas, thinking it might actually endear me to the woman by showcasing responsibility and moral fortitude, but apparently, headmistresses at posh Upper East Side girls' schools prefer to be ignorant of such sordid scandals—even those that threaten to become statutory, if you know what I mean. Who knew?

Guess who's still out of a job?

Now do you blame me if I'm in need of a little comfort? And for me, in New York City, comfort is spelled c-o-f-f-e-e.

I head to the downtown subway because that's where the coffee is. Not all of it, of course, but the kind I'm jonesing for right this minute. I don't have full-blown trainophobia, which is a fear of subways and other trains (not to be confused with trannyphobia, which I also *don't* have), but I admit, however, that in eight years I've never become quite comfortable with speeding underground on a rickety train through a pitch-black tunnel filled with electrical wires, water pipes, and rats, while enormous skyscrapers hover overhead.

Back home in Ohio we commuted at street level with plenty of available oxygen circulating among the minivans, punch buggies, and SUVs. But since the subway is the most expedient means of getting from "where I am standing now" to "where I would like to be," I plunge. Mr. Gladwell would be proud. Lady Gaga would probably want to know why I hadn't worn taller stilettos.

The subway seemed so exciting to me when I arrived in the city. At first it was such a novelty, but eventually it began to wear on me. Taking the 6 train, I find it calming to imagine I'm on a ride at Disney World *simulating* a New York subway. I note the cartoonishly authentic details that include metal-against-metal screeching noises, shaky train cars, lights flashing randomly on and off, and even an old deserted City Hall Ghost Station.

Like the seasoned eye-contact-avoiding New Yorker I have become, I slide past my fellow subway riders and gingerly take a seat. To my immediate right there is a man eating the world's smelliest falafel (a Disney cast member in disguise?). I may also be sitting on gum, but I overcome those lingering concerns. I'm the last one to endorse all that princess Disneyana of Disney World, but you've got to admit they know how to make a good ride. I marvel at how good Disney is at this authenticity stuff.

As the doors open and the speakers fzzt and schzzt, garbling every word from Subway Announcer Lady, reality sets in and I know it's not a theme park ride. Besides, if it was actually a ride at Disney World, I would have exited into a gift shop and bought a bracelet made of antique subway tokens for a souvenir. But no matter, I am on a quest for the dark roasted steaming beverage I've come to think of as nothing short of liquid manna.

In my opinion, the best coffee in Manhattan can be found in the lobby of the *Daily Post*. That's where I used to work. The *Post* was the reason I came to New York City in the first place. It was my dream job, the answer to an aspiring journalist's prayers. But like a lot of old-school newspapers (the kind with news actually printed on paper) the *Daily Post* was forced to close up shop many months back, resulting in my present career-lite condition.

That hasn't stopped me from returning here. I guess it's like visiting the graves of deceased loved ones. Maybe communing with the ghosts of grizzled old newspapermen and -women and listening to the echoes of breaking stories hot off the presses inspires me, even though the concept of old-style news is totally obsolete—like developing film in a dark room or sending a postcard. Maybe I'm a nostalgia junkie or even, despite my precocious early video-game-making experience, a Luddite at heart, but I still like to turn the pages of a newspaper made with wood pulp and ink.

The fact that the best cup of joe in the entire city can be found at the coffee cart in the *Daily Post* lobby is what I call a major perk.

I should also add that the operator of said coffee cart and I have been involved in what I call a micro-relationship for quite some time. For those of you who live outside the city that never sleeps, let me define my terms:

> **micro-relationship** (n.) the sense of being incidentally connected on a very small scale, 1968. *micro* meaning "small," comb. form of Greek *mikros* "small, little, petty, trivial, slight" (see *mica*) with *relation + ship*, 1744, "sense of being related," specifically of romantic or sexual relationships by 1944. *micro + relation + ship* interpersonal connections that develop in bustling metropolitan areas, as a result of frequent exposure, 2007. A stranger who happens to appear in one's sphere of experience on a regular basis and with whom it becomes necessary to interact usually in a positive manner. Not to be confused with "meaningful relationship" or "unconditional love."

New York totally lends itself to these drive-by friendships. And they're more important than you might think, because in a city like this, you can really start to feel disconnected and alone.

I do have actual friends here in Manhattan. Like my old friend from Thomas Tupper High back home, model-perfect BFF Jody Dicippio. Then there's my childhood pen pal Piper Henderson (who knew that a juvenile pen pal could become a real bud?), and hard-core New York native Penny Rodgers. I mean, Rodgers. God, she'd smack me upside the head if she heard me call her Penny.

At one point last fall I had more of Piper's clothes in my closet than my own. I am not afraid to call Rodgers at three a.m. (I have) or to borrow Jody's Apocalips lipstick (currently in my bag). I like to think that we are an equal-opportunity mix of personalities, career choices, and cup sizes, which is precisely why I love them. These are my girls. My peeps.

Still, you can't underestimate the importance of those New York City relationships of the micro kind. They give NYC a face. The little relationships we all have are the ones that keep you from simply giving up and dropping into an open manhole on purpose. Here is a sampling of my vast, ever-evolving inventory of micro-relationships.

MY MICRO-RELATIONSHIPS

The Grumpy M15 Bus Driver. Despite his ever-present scowl, he always gives me extra time to find a seat before he puts the pedal to the metal. This courteous gesture protects me from the dreaded "bus lurch," which occurs when the articulated bendy bus hiccups out from under you before you're seated and causes you to land uninvited on the lap of some businessman, or (worse) to spill your coffee.

The Pakistani Newsstand Guy. This fast-talking guy makes a point to say hello, even on windy days when his inventory is being blown uptown in a tiny *New York Times–* and *New York Post–*fueled microburst tornado.

The Lady Power Walker in the Chartreuse Jogging Bra. I see her when I jog the bridle paths in Central Park. We pass each other every Sunday morning and exchange the ever-popular "incline your head and keep moving" quasi-greeting. I know she'd be there for me if I ever got caught in a mugging.

The Voluptuous Latina Nanny. I see her from time to time at the fountain in Washington Square Park. She pushes a double stroller that is more spacious than my apartment. No matter how loudly her charges are screaming and how far they throw their sippy cups, she always has a beautiful smile and an "hola" for me that brightens my life.

And last but definitely not least:

The Cute Coffee Guy. On my second visit to his cart long ago when I worked at the newspaper, I christened him with his nickname, and when I mentioned him to Jody, she abbreviated it to CCG. This is typical Jody. She talks so fast she only has time for abbreviations and half words. "Whatevs" is her fave, for examp. Rodgers and I have to create a full-on glossary on occasion to follow what she's saying. But sometimes her shortcuts say it all.

Ah, my CCG. I used to see him multiple times a day while I was interning for Hugh Hamilton, famed columnist, muckraker, and Pulitzer Prize–winning reporter at the *Daily Post*, because Hugh was a coffee addict. The guy had more caffeine than blood in his veins. If he could have walked around attached to an IV bag filled with Green Mountain blend, he would have. Hugh's hands were so jittery that for the first three months of my internship I thought he was actually trying to say something in sign language. Still, CCG and I never really conversed beyond small talk. In fact, once he memorized Hugh's beverage of choice and mine, too (which I thought was very micro-sweet of him), I didn't even have to place an order anymore. He saw me coming.

I've grown so used to referring to him as CCG that even though I've continued to patronize his establishment on a daily basis following my premature retirement from the newspaper biz, I still don't know his actual name.

That's because, among the many complicated criteria for a micro-relationship, there is the primary imperative that neither party knows the other's name. Ever. Under any circumstances. If a person had to learn and remember the name of every one of her micro-acquaintances, her head would explode. But it mostly has to do with emotional investment. The minute you know someone's name, you venture out of the micro-zone into a whole new scary level of intimacy.

If you actually knew the name of everyone you encountered, wouldn't you be obligated to say hello every time you saw him or her? That would require more memory space and oxygen than any New Yorker could realistically afford. And if you forgot, which is inevitable, the repercussions could be enormous.

Anonymity is salvation in New York. Speaking for anonymous people everywhere, I know that if *I* stopped to consider that every one of those zillions of faces I pass on the street has a complete backstory featuring dysfunctional families, overdue library books, foot fetishes, nut allergies, and so on, I'd be overwhelmed with wonder, joy, disgust, and dread. And that's just on the three-block walk from my apartment to the South Street Seaport.

All I really need is the occasional welcoming face to nod back at me in mutual recognition of our respective humanity. In my mind I make up shortcut names like "Falafel Dude" and "Cop Who Ate Too Many Krispy Kremes" and "Jimmy Choos for Every Day of the Week Lady," and I'm good.

But the truth is that my micro-affair with CCG is a bit more important than the others. He holds a special place in my heart and I always feel a little less alone and a little more positive when I see him.

The subway regurgitates me a block from the old *Daily Post* building and I make my way to my former place of employment.

I shuffle through the glass wedge of the revolving door and as it spits me out into the tiled lobby, I'm struck with abject panic.

Although it's just as busy as always—the lobby seems emptier.

The invigorating aroma of roasted beans wafts heavily through the air, piercing the foggy midafternoon with the smooth, rich scent of Colombian ground as usual.

And yes, the coffee cart is there, thankfully.

But CCG—my most significant micro-other—is . . . nowhere to be seen.

CHAPTER 2

Okay, he was here yesterday. I know because I was going to tell him I really liked the Sex Pistols song that was playing on his vintage mini boombox, but since that felt outside the realm of micro-appropriate chitchat, I resisted.

I take in the familiar gleam of the stainless-steel carafes and the espresso machine that look like something Jules Verne might use to travel to the center of the earth. I once heard CCG telling the customer in front of me that he cobbled it together himself using parts from a bunch of obsolete Italian espresso makers. He called it "Frankensteam," which I thought was mocha clever.

I glance at the stacks of beige cardboard cups emblazoned with the little establishment's name: WHERE HAVE YOU BEAN ALL MY LIFE? I think as I always do that the name is too long. My alternative shorter, simpler name is "Where Have You Bean?" which is what I think it should be called. I repeatedly say it to myself like a prayer or like someone with a compulsive disorder because the only question going through my mind is, "Where the hell are you *now*?"

CCG is MIA and there is a ridiculously skinny girl with a fluffy white-blond bob haircut dispensing java in his place.

What happened? Did he get a job at another coffee cart

elsewhere in town? Did he return home for a family crisis? Does he even have a family? And why didn't I ever ask him? Why did I have to be so damn faithful to the rules of micro-interaction? If I'd taken the time to investigate I might have a clue as to where he is and why he's gone and why I have to be ordering my coffee from a macro-stranger with dandelion fluff for hair.

I approach the cart at a march, determined to get answers.

She looks up at me, smiling through her orange lipstick. "Coffee, tea, decaf, espresso, or latte?"

"Where's CCG?" I blurt mindlessly.

"Um . . ." She fiddles with her wispy white bangs, which have snagged on her eyebrow ring. "I'm not sure. Is CCG that marketing company on the fourth floor, or is it the modeling agency on the twenty-fifth?" she replies with airhead innocence. And as she smiles at me, she reveals a metal stud the size of a garbanzo bean lodged in the center of her tongue.

Okay, first of all: ouch.

And second of all: I understand piercing is a rite of passage, a celebration of survival, and a sexual turn-on for some, but I have enough trouble keeping track of my earring backs. What if you lose the one to your tongue stud? Can you say "choking hazard"? But none of that is important right now, is it?

"The guy who usually works here," I explain to Fluffy, my new default barista, to whom I have taken an immediate dislike. "Is he around?"

"Oh, him." Fluffy bobs her bob. "Yeah, he's here. He just stepped away to make a phone call. I'm filling in."

I let out a sigh of relief so great I scatter a stack of unbleached paper napkins. The girl looks at me funny, so by way of explanation I fib: "He owes me money."

"No way!" She looks at me suspiciously. I don't blame her. Why did I say that?

Then I see him, making his way back to the cart from the opposite side of the cavernous lobby—CCG, in all his espresso-scented splendor. I take in the familiar shape of his broad shoulders beneath his thousand-times-washed WHERE HAVE YOU BEAN? T-shirt (see, it definitely works better shortened) that fits him perfectly; as always, his tousled hair looks . . . well, tousled, but in a manner that is more about careless style than unkempt laziness.

When CCG sees me standing at his cart, he smiles in that shy way of his. He selects a chocolate-almond biscotti from a tray and hands it to Fluffy. I can't keep myself from thinking puppy treats. "Thanks for covering, Clem," he says.

I can tell this slender little pincushion of a girl is half in love with him. She bats her blue mascara-ed lashes and giggles. "Anytime."

I think I might be sick, but hold myself together.

She lingers a moment, gives me a quizzical look, and finally turns, heading for the elevators.

"Clementine works for some accounting firm on the eighth floor," CCG explains, plucking a cup from the cardboard tower. I don't know why I'm startled by his soft voice. "It's slow up there, so I call her whenever I need to sneak off for a bit." He nods toward the tray of cookies. "I pay her in biscotti. Works for both of us."

It occurs to me that although I've probably purchased two thousand cups of coffee from CCG, this is more than he's ever said to me at one time. It's a clear violation of the micro-code, but today I'm thinking, *Screw it. I really like his voice, especially when he says whole sentences.* I like that even though he's super shy, he's making an effort to look me in the eye and actually succeeding. And those soft indigo eyes . . . why didn't we attempt this fifteen hundred cups ago?

"Gotta love a good old-fashioned barter system," I say. CCG positions the small cup under the spigot and presses the handle. The carafe releases a stream of fresh coffee. I inhale deeply as he hands me the cup.

Feeling a tingle of warmth rush through me that has nothing to do with the hot beverage I'm clutching, I make a decision.

Today is the day I'm going to kick this up a notch.

After all, if some snotty little seventh-grade slut-ling can put the moves on her science teacher and Miss Fluffy can bat her eyelashes for biscotti, I can certainly get my flirt on with Cute Coffee Guy, right? I reach into my knock-off Birkin for the $2.29 and hand it over. As I'm doing this, I purposely let my fingers brush against his. It's a calculated maneuver, but it surprises the heck out of him. The good news is that he doesn't withdraw, he actually blushes and grins.

Hah. Now I'm feeling downright cocky. I made the coffee guy blush.

"Thanks," I say in a breathy murmur (take that, seventh grader, and you, too, Clementine). Then I press my lips softly to the rim, and in a dreamy kiss-like way, I take a cautious sip. I'm careful not to be obvious, keeping the maneuver subtle so that it whispers: *See this cup? This could be you. Your lips, your earlobe, or the body part of your choice.*

CCG seems very interested as he watches my lips make contact with the cardboard cup. And why not? There's a reason why this stuff works. This move is right out of *The Flirty Girl's Handbook*.

But apparently, he's read a page or two of *Boy Talk for Beginners*. Because the next thing he says is: "So . . . you're a writer, aren't you?"

It's my turn to be surprised because our micro-status never allowed me to tell him what I did for a living. But I do realize that since he'd seen me scuttling across the lobby after Hugh a zillion times, it wasn't much of a leap for him to arrive at this conclusion. Still, the fact that he noticed is very encouraging.

"Yes. Yes, I am." I smile and take another, less prudent sip, and stifle a scream, pretending that the Colombian Breakfast Blend isn't scorching my throat on its way down.

Then something even more amazing happens. Without warning, this shy coffee peddler with the scruffy jaw and silky indigo eyes takes the notch-kicking entirely out of my hands and into his own.

"So what's your name?"

Whoa. Please refer to Rule 1.0 of the Micro-Relationship Code. No names! That's how it works. That's *why* it works! Distance, anonymity, mystery.

Anything less would be . . . well, something completely different. Which is exactly what I was moving toward, but I'm a little thrown by the fact that he's leap-frogged so far ahead of me. Thrown, yes. Displeased . . . not even a little bit.

CCG is still waiting for me to introduce myself. So I open my mouth and say . . .

"Clarissa!"

Wait a minute. That's definitely the correct response, but that's not my voice providing it. Who could be calling my name here?

"Clarissa!"

I know that voice. Oh boy, do I know that voice.

I whirl away from CCG, hot coffee inadvertently splashing from my cup onto the marble floor in what seems like slow motion. Mental alert: It's always bad luck to spill. What will result from this ominous event? Only misfortune, I fear, but I don't have time to do anything about it. I turn and there they are: Marshall and Janet Darling, the revolving door spinning behind them. The two people to whom I credit my existence, the Official Sponsors of my X and Y chromosomes.

Too weird.

My parents.

Shit.

CHAPTER 3

"Surprise!" my father hollers across the lobby.

Gee, ya think?

CCG looks from me to these two strangers who are charging toward us, then back to me. To say that seeing my dad and mom, aka Marshall and Janet, in New York is surreal would be an understatement for a couple of reasons:

REASONS WHY SEEING MARSHALL AND JANET IN NYC IS SURREAL

1. They live in Ohio.
2. They never called, e-mailed, texted, or sent out a homing pigeon with a note banded to its leg to tell me they had plans to visit.
3. My parents aren't exactly what you'd call spontaneous. Or at least they didn't used to be.
4. And finally—they're not *together*, and by that I mean, they're *separated*. As in legally. You know, like Splitsville, "taking a trip to Reno," which basically entails paying some guy with a law degree to draw up papers stating that they can no longer stand the thought of living under the same roof.

And yet, here they are in New York City, unannounced and, unless my eyes deceive me, *together.*

I pounce on the together part and feel a surge of hope. That has to be good, right?

Unless they're here to share the burden of informing me that the legal separation has evolved into a full-fledged divorce. That would *not* be good.

"Hi, Mom," I sputter as she arrives at the cart and flings her arms around me.

"Dad, hey!" He leans in to kiss my cheek.

"Hi, Sport!"

I blink at them and go with the approved response to this situation and usually good for close encounters of an unexpected kind: "What are you guys doing here?"

And as I think of it, I'm astonished that they stumbled upon me at one of my random-but-regular coffee runs. I know Sigmund Freud said we always act according to our greatest desire and that there's no such thing as coincidence, or was that Suze Orman, the Freud of the Spreadsheet, talking about forbearance and student loan debt versus the desire to pay them off? I forget. The point is, it's pretty unbelievable that they're showing up here in this particular lobby, the scene of my former employ, as I happen to be working my flirt on CCG.

"We came to see our journalist daughter," my mother offers brightly.

Oh no. I'm putting it together as they speak . . . *oh shit.*

"It's been so long since we've seen you," she bubbles on. "We just couldn't wait for you to find time to invite us, so we planned our own visit."

Visit. Ambush.

Tomato, tomahto . . .

"We've heard so much about where you work," my father says. "We were dying to see it. Impressive building architecturally, by the way." He nods toward the enormous pillars and marble-tiled walls. "This lobby just screams big-city newspaper excitement!"

No, he didn't just say *that*.

As stunned as I am, I admit I'm feeling encouraged by the fact that Mom and Dad appear to be operating as a parental unit again. I don't care how old you are, or how independent you pretend to be, when your parents tell you they're considering a divorce, you turn into a terrified little child. When my parents first told me, I didn't sleep for two full weeks. I was so confused and afraid. All I wanted to do was crawl into their bed, like I used to do during thunderstorms or after waking up from a nightmare. The only problem being that I was in New York and their bed was in Ohio.

And they weren't in it.

"You know what would be nice?" Dad says, draping his arm over my shoulder. "If you took us upstairs and showed us the newsroom bullpen where all the action happens!"

I couldn't agree more. It *would* be nice . . . if all that big city newsroom action were still there.

I shift a quick glance to CCG, wondering what he might be making of this conversation. He knows that the *Daily Post* is no more, but to his credit he doesn't throw me under the bus, subway, or coffee cart by pointing out this inconvenient truth to my parents.

"Yes," says Mom. "That's *one* of the reasons we came." She holds up a few shopping bags and I see Marshall's holding two as well. Dad smiles painfully. "But sweetie, we were really hoping you could give us a tour of the *Daily Post*."

"They do allow tours, don't they?" Dad asks eagerly.

Um, sure . . . to potential renters, who want to move into a vast empty office space?

The problem is, since the news of my joblessness had come hot on the heels of the news of their separation (and some equally distressing news about my younger brother, Ferguson, which I can't even think about beginning to explain right now), I made an executive decision to keep my parents out of the employment debacle loop. It was dishonest, I know, but I had saved up a little, and at that time I wasn't behind on my loans or my rent (my, how times change) and I really just wanted to spare them the additional stress.

In fact, given that things are about in the same place, and my stress level is a tad higher, I still do.

"Well, you know I'd love to!" I fudge. "Especially since you came all this way to . . . uh, surprise me—but the office is closed. What a drag, huh?"

Not a lie, exactly. It *is* closed at the moment, and will remain thus for every moment following, ad infinitum, ad nauseum. Fortunately they never heard the old newsroom saying "The news never sleeps." In the case of the *Daily Post*, the news seems to have fallen into an artificially induced coma.

I sneak another peek at CCG, who is watching me closely. I mean, unless he's a complete idiot he's already figured out my little scam. But so far he doesn't seem to be judging me harshly for it. He even looks amused. There's this tiny smile on his face, which, even in the throes of this pending catastrophe, I can't help but notice is awfully sexy.

"That's a shame," my mother says, crestfallen.

"And we're leaving tonight, so we won't be able to see it tomorrow," Dad says, and I can tell he's wallowing in it. Come on, Dad, get over it.

"You're leaving tonight? That *is* a shame," I say shamelessly, hoping I don't sound as unashamedly relieved as I feel.

"Yeah, your mother can't stay," says Dad. "She's got an R and D meeting tomorrow with the Chinese Defense Department and I . . . well, you know . . ." He trails off and I know it's because he really has nothing to do besides fix himself waffles at the Make Your Own Breakfast Bar in the crummy hotel he's been living at during the separation.

Heartbreaking as that is, my survival instincts kick in. "Well, there's always next visit. In the meantime, let's see about finding you two crazy kids a cab to the airport."

Mom laughs. "Clarissa, we just got here. We don't have to leave that fast."

"You don't?" I gulp.

"Not without taking you to dinner," Dad chimes in. "Besides, if we can't see that corner office of yours overlooking the Big Apple, at least we can meet that terrific entrepreneur boyfriend you've been bragging about."

Wait, so now there's a terrific boyfriend? I lied about having one of those too? It takes a second for the synapses in my brain to spark before I realize that when I told Mom and Dad I had a boyfriend, it actually wasn't a lie. I did, at one time, have a boyfriend. The "terrific" part, not so much—just a case of delusional behavior and poor character judgment on my part.

Norm. My parents are talking about Norm.

I flick yet another look at CCG, curious to see how the mention of a "terrific boyfriend" is sitting with him. I mean, three seconds ago I was making out with a coffee cup in an attempt to entice him. Now this revelation. I try to meet his eyes, hoping to see devastation, or at least disappointment. But at the moment, he's attending to an aging female corporate warrior wearing a bright red Elie Tahari business suit who has sidled up for an herbal tea, so I can't get a read on his reaction.

Here's another confession: In addition to not telling my parents that the *Daily Post* was no more than a journalistic memory, I'd also neglected to tell them that the guy I'd gushed about before as My One and Only had been demoted to My Ex with Serious Stalker Tendencies.

Frickin' Norm. Let me take a moment here to give you the low-down on that failed entanglement:

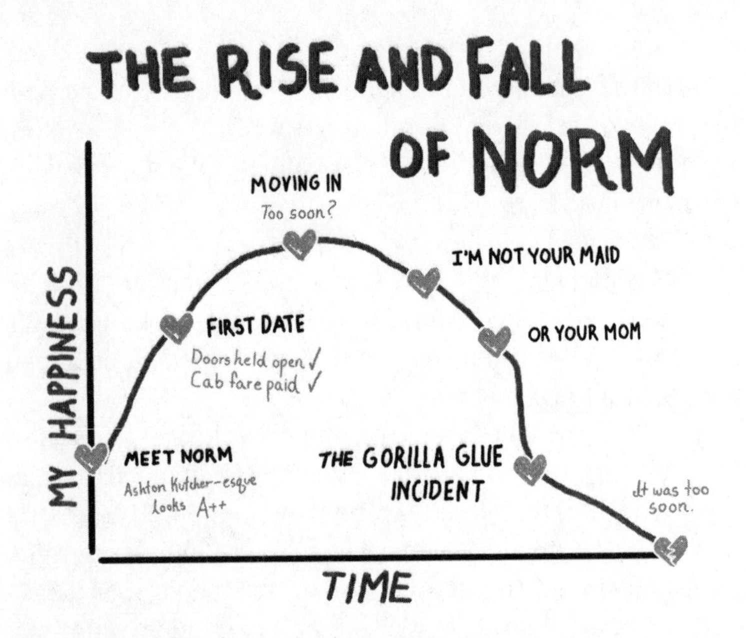

Met him. Loved him (mostly his looks, which are Ashton Kutcher–esque), dated him, moved in with him, realized it was a ginormous mistake, and dumped him. Norm seemed great at the beginning, but once I made the commitment to him he became an emotional and financial parasite. In three short months he went from holding doors open for me to wordlessly leaving his dirty socks on the kitchen counter to wash.

The "entrepreneur" part to which my father is referring would be All Decked Out, the custom skate deck company Norm dreamed of establishing.

He got as far as pulling together seven layers of veneer and mixing a bucket of Gorilla Glue in the middle of our apartment. I rolled up my sleeves to dig in and help, but when his left hand and right foreleg got stuck in the wooden layers sopping with fast-drying glue, I knew we were in trouble. My foot almost got caught in the sticky stuff when I tried to pry him off. It was like a bad game of permanent Twister. Ripping the hair off the side of his right leg almost hurt me as much as it hurt him, especially when I had to listen to his baby-like screams. I could tell Norm was traumatized when he planted himself permanently on the sofa (video-game controller in hand), saying he needed "think time" to reconsider his career goals.

It wasn't like the rest of our time together was so peachy. So when Non-performin' Norman started hanging out late at night with all sorts of bogus excuses, I knew it was time to cut my losses. Au revoir, Norm!

It seems to me when I think about it now, I would have never gotten involved with Norm, except it was right after things fell apart with Sam.

Who's Sam? He's my childhood friend, homie, and ladder-wielding best bud. Sam had the endearing habit of throwing an extension ladder against my house and climbing in and out of my bedroom window anytime of the day or night throughout our formative years, a groundbreaking innovation in parental avoidance that made it amazingly easy for us to hang out whenever we wanted. I know that sounds pretty salacious, but it wasn't.

As you'd expect, Sam's ladder technique was a major source of controversy in the neighborhood and among my friends at school, who thought it was kind of outrageous that he could get away with it. No one believed that we were *just friends* as in "a boy who is a friend and not a 'boyfriend.' "

A friend is someone you're close to and have feelings for, but not *those* kinds of feelings. In other words, a friend is someone you haven't had sex with, and back in those days, remarkably, that wasn't on our minds.

Sam and I never fought except once—the night we went out on a test date, Sam's idea, and it was a miserable fail. It was good, it was bad, and by the end—when we kissed—it was ugly. "The Good-Night Kiss of Death," we used to call it.

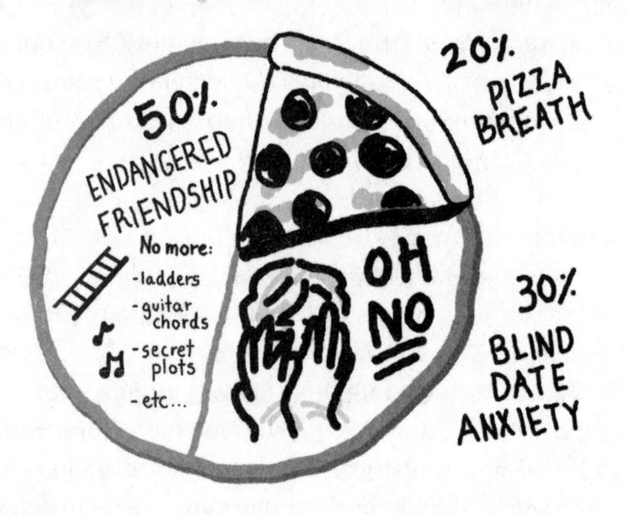

I never told Sam, but I was secretly insulted after that kiss. First of all, I was unprepared. Second, I never thought risking a good friendship for a kiss was worth it. Third, I like to think I'm a good kisser, but I didn't even have a chance to try. Post-kiss, I was totally confused, and his words stung me.

Sam didn't understand. Although he had those "more than a friend" feelings *before* he kissed me, I had those same feelings *after* we kissed, and that made me pause. If we had kissed again, who knows where it would have gone?

Who am I kidding? I know exactly where it would have gone.

"It felt like I was kissing my sister, if I had a sister," he had said, and I almost never forgave him for saying it. That was the only time I ever considered shoving that ladder off my windowsill regardless of the consequences. But I held back.

Instead, we friend-zoned each other pretty permanently.

Fortunately my parents were totally oblivious to Sam's ladder. Don't ask me how. I think it's because Marshall never did any work around the house or in the garden and he's pretty oblivious in general. I suspect Mom knew, she just didn't want to deal with it because—well, Sam and I were just friends and she could tell.

After our miscued date faded from memory, Sam once again became the human equivalent of a golden-rayed sunrise or slow-burning sunset. Total Zen. It was impossible to feel anything other than relaxed around Sam.

He was . . . my soul mate.

There, I said it. He wasn't just the person I could spend the rest of my life with. He was the person I couldn't imagine spending my life *without*. Sam Anders was the one person who knew me so well that it used to scare the crap out of me.

Everybody but me knew we'd get together eventually. It was glorious, it was beautiful, it was unforgettable, and when that summer ended, it was over. We never had one single fight or argument or even heart-to-heart about where we were going. If he walked in today I think we'd kiss and jump each other's bones, as if not a day had passed.

But as far as I can tell, he's gone, which feels so wrong. That was not how it was supposed to turn out. I can't help wondering if I screwed up.

Who knows? Is it possible that even soul mates aren't meant to be together?

If I'm being honest about Norm, I was on the rebound. I made the mistake of falling for the first gorgeous skater dude who reminded me of Sam. Clearly, I was hoping for Sam 2.0. Pretty textbook, I suppose. Maybe next time I'll go for someone in finance.

Prying Norm from his self-inflicted Gorilla Glue debacle opened my eyes to our hopeless relationship. I realized I could get stuck too, so I told Norm it was over.

His response?

"I think you're just trying to ruin our relationship." Almost instantly, I realized that breaking up with Norm was only the beginning.

I packed up and answered a roommate ad for a cozy little walk-up office conversion in FiDi. The roommate, Felice, turned out to be a real creepster of the *Single White Female* variety, but she thankfully decided to throw in the towel on making it in the Big City and moved back with her mom and dad in Scarsdale. Phew! Real-life nightmare stalker movie avoided. Not having a roommate is unbelievably awesome and hey, I'm only two months behind on my rent. Unfortunately, moving across town, not returning Norm's phone calls, and completely withholding my affection was apparently too subtle a hint for old Norm. He hasn't been able to mentally process the breakup.

Just last month I had a temp job at an office in Times Square. As I was leaving for home, walking just behind the TKTS booth beneath the big red glass stairway, Norm jumped out of nowhere and dropped to his knees in front of me and hundreds of total strangers. Everyone started cheering and I couldn't figure out why until I looked up at the massive digital screen over American Eagle. There was Norm at my knees, proposing, holding up some kind of Cracker Jack ring. We were on a screen big enough for everyone in New York City to see. I turned away, pretending I didn't know him. When the crowd started to boo, I thought they would lynch me. Like always, I found myself wondering what Sam would think.

"Well, Clarissa, do you want to give him a call?" I hear Mom say.

"Who?" I ask, wondering if she's added mind reading to her repertoire. After all, who knows where Sam is right now.

"Your boyfriend," Mom adds, snapping her fingers in front of my face, shattering my far-flung musings. "Why don't you give him a call . . . ?"

"My boyfriend?" I ask.

"We have just enough time to eat an early dinner and get to know him a little bit," Dad says, checking his watch.

Right, I remember, I'm in the midst of a surprise parental guest appearance.

"Well, see, I *would*, but . . ." I sputter. *Think fast, Clarissa, think.*

"But what?" prompts Dad. The look in his eyes is so sad. Dad seems to be spinning in some psychological hamster wheel of anticipated disappointment. I can't take it.

"But . . ."

Maybe it's the creative spirits that haunt this beloved place, or maybe it's me wanting to make my dear ol' dad happy, but I am suddenly inspired.

"But I don't have to!" Before I lose my nerve, I dash around to the opposite side of the coffee cart and throw my arms around CCG.

"Because . . . here he is. This is him. This is . . ." Time freezes as I realize I have no legitimate way to introduce him. I mean, he's the guy I refer to with a three-letter acronym because I don't know his name. My mouth is open and it feels like it's been that way for weeks, looking over to CCG in desperation and back over to my parents and back to CCG, cluelessly lost in time, sinking fast.

Fortunately, for a naturally shy and quiet person, CCG seems to have a knack for thinking on his feet. Without missing a beat (or stopping to ask why we've suddenly gone from fingers brushing to full embrace), he smiles.

"I've been wanting to meet Clarissa's parents for a while now," he says, breaking my awkward *Twilight Zone* moment. "I'm Nick," he adds and extends his hand to my father.

"Nick!" cries my mother. "It's lovely to meet you."

"I thought you told us his name was Norm," Dad whispers to me.

He's right. I did.

'Cause it was.

So I improvise . . .

"Uh, well, Norm was actually just my pet name for him," I explain feebly, "because, ya know, he was the guy I *norm*ally spent time with. And then of course, he came to represent the *norm* by which I judged all other guys and . . . *normally* I . . ."

Nick cuts me off with a wink. "I think they get it, hon," he says easily. "But, yeah, she just calls me Nick now."

"Oh, well, glad to know you, son," Marshall says, making everyone a bit uncomfortable. This "son" thing is classic Marshall Darling lingo. He called the bully who beat up Ferguson on the school bus "son." That's the guy who kinda became my first boyfriend—aka Clifford Spleenhurfer. Dad called the paperboy "son" even after the kid grew up and went to college, got married, had three kids, came back home, and sold my dad a home insurance policy. He's called guys working at the gas station "son," no matter what their ages are, even when they're older than he is. But Nick is a grown man, not to mention a perfect stranger.

Even though I'm cringing, CCG doesn't appear to be put off by it. In fact, he looks as though he finds it charming. Truth be told, I find CCG totally charming. If this were a romance novel, he'd have swept in on a white stallion instead of a coffee cart, but this is reality and the bottom line is he came to my rescue when I needed him.

And here's the best part:

His name is Nick. Now I know.

In a New York minute, my most cherished micro-relationship has massively leveled up.

CHAPTER 4

We hit the streets of the Big City, and my dad is downright giddy over my ability to hail a cab. After eight years here, it's no big deal, but my Ohio-born-and-bred father sees it as a major accomplishment. He actually snaps a picture of me with my arm up in the air to show everyone back home.

Humiliation, party of one?

Three seconds later a yellow cab minivan skids to a halt at the curb, and CCG—wait, make that Nick—opens the sliding door and allows the three Darlings to step in ahead of him. I make an invisible checkmark in an invisible box next to the word *gentleman* on an invisible list inside my head.

Dad and Nick take the far back and Mom and I settle into the middle seat. If this weren't so nerve-racking, it would actually be cute.

"Where to?" the cabbie demands.

"How about the place where you two had your first date?" Mom suggests. "It was an Indian place. I remember it sounding so great."

"Indian food?" Dad gives Nick an exaggerated elbow to ribs. "Well, now, let's not get 'curried' away!"

Dad bursts out laughing and I want to climb into the minivan's glove compartment and die. But then Mom laughs at his corny quip and my nerves about this impending dinner are momentarily overshadowed by a joyful thought: *She still thinks he's funny!* That's gotta count for something, right?

It's at this point, as I'm gleefully picturing my dad moving back into the Darling homestead, that Mom looks over her shoulder to smile at Nick in the backseat. "Oh, Nick, Clarissa's told me the name of the restaurant a million times, but I just can't think of it. It's on the tip of my tongue. I know I'll recognize it when I hear it. What's it called?"

So much for gleeful. Operation Please the Parents is about to crash and burn before it's even gotten off the ground. My brain is screaming, *Abort! Abort!* I prepare to shout out the restaurant's name before he flubs it, although I know it will seem rude and uncouple-like.

"Tamarind Tribeca, on Hudson Street," Nick answers smoothly before I can make an idiot of myself.

My jaw drops. To my utter delight and total shock, he's dead-on!

"Yes, that's it!" Mom says, with a snap of her fingers. "Tamarind. Clarissa's favorite."

The taxi pulls away as my dad, the former flower child, breaks into an off-key chorus of "*Hey, Mr. Tamarind Man*" that has Mom giggling again, and I feel myself relax. I turn to look at Nick and I'm not surprised to see that he has an enticing quiet smile on his face in sweet satisfaction of his epic save.

Maybe this evening won't be a complete kamikaze mission after all.

Nick offers to pay the cabdriver and I notice he gives him a pretty good tip for a guy who works at a coffee stand.

As I'm checking off "Class Act" on my mental checklist, and maybe "Good with Money," we follow my mom and dad toward the restaurant.

"How on earth did you know?" I whisper.

"Well, for one thing," he whispers back, "it's pretty much

everyone's favorite Indian place. And for another thing . . ." He stops short, suddenly bashful again.

"What?" I urge. 'Cause obviously I'm dying to know what this other thing is.

Nick hangs back as the door closes behind my parents. "Well, there was this one time the delivery guy from Tamarind came by my cart. He'd just come from dropping off a lunch order and he couldn't stop talking about the hot blonde at the *Daily Post* who ordered the Lucknow boti kabab and sweet potato pudding."

This floors me because:

A) Who knew the delivery guy thought I was hot? And B) in addition to my coffee preference, Nick also remembered my favorite Indian dish.

"Oh," I say, kind of stupidly. But really, I'm too stunned to say anything else.

He frowns and rolls his eyes. "Then the punk made an off-color kabob reference at your expense and I wanted to clock him."

"Clock him?" I repeat. "As in punch him?" *As in defend my honor?*

Nick shrugs. "Yeah, but I figured that would be bad for business, so I oversteamed the milk for his cappuccino instead."

Wow. Once, when Norm and I were still together, a guy grabbed my ass at Angels & Kings, a rock club downtown that went out of business a while ago. Ol' Norm couldn't seem to understand why that would upset me. I begin to thank Nick for avenging me but before I can say anything, Mom is anxiously tapping on the glass doors, waving us inside.

We're seated quickly and Dad has a silly play on words for just about every item on the menu. When he orders his full murgh angarey, he shakes his finger at the waiter and says, "And if you bring me the half, I'm going to be very 'ang-ar-ey' with you."

Yeesh, he really cracks himself up. When Nick and I exchange grins, it feels for a second like we've been doing it forever.

Mom's order includes about a billion adjustments to the preparation. She actually asks for the avocado chicken salad without chicken or avocado.

Then it's Nick's turn. Just as he opens his mouth to order, his cell phone rings. He checks the incoming number and throws me an apologetic look.

"I'm sorry, I've really got to take this." He stands up and quickly ducks into a quiet corner so as not to disturb the other diners.

"Uh, that must be work," I tell my parents.

"We understand, dear," my mother assures me, adding with a proud twinkle in her eye, "An entrepreneur's job is never done." Dad winces and I think maybe Mom's talking about herself as well. But the issue at hand is what Nick might want for dinner, because the waiter is . . . well, ya know . . . waiting, which makes all of us Darlings a bit nervous. Don't ask me why, but for some reason the Darlings fear the impatience of waiters. I mean, isn't waiting their job description?

"Clarissa, why don't you go ahead and order for Nick?" Dad suggests nervously, looking back up at the waiter as if he's worried the guy might yell at him. "You know what he wants, right?"

"Yeah, you would think," I mumble, dropping my eyes to the menu. I settle on jhinga e aatish, otherwise known as jumbo prawns, because it's a big seller and everyone raves about it. For myself, the usual: Lucknow boti kabab and sweet potato pudding, which once inspired impure thoughts in the Tamarind delivery guy. I'm hoping Nick will notice and be inspired to have impure thoughts of his own.

When Nick returns, my father asks, with an utterly straight face, "So is everything okay in the world of skateboards? Is your company still '*on a roll*'?"

Oh, dang. Dad really isn't going let that one die, is he? Problem is, this isn't Norm, this is Nick, and I have no idea if he knows a half pipe from a hookah pipe.

"Actually," I say, as Nick turns a blank face in my direction, "Nick sold his skateboard business a few months ago to pursue other things."

"The coffee industry?" Mom asks.

"Yes, and no . . ." Nick unfolds his napkin and places it in his lap. "I don't actually own the coffee cart; I just run it for a friend of mine. Denny Featherstone."

"Really?!" I blurt out. This is news to me. I always thought he owned Where Have You Bean? (shortened name trademark pending).

"Sure." Nick gives me a slow nod. "You know that, babe."

"Right!" I say quickly, feeling a little tingle in my fingertips, because no one has called me babe in such a soft, relaxed voice since . . . well, since Sam. "Of course I know that. And that reminds me, I'm going to have to give that Danny Fusterstein—"

"Denny. Featherstone," Nick corrects.

"Right . . . that *Denny Featherstone* a piece of my mind about all those extra hours he has you working. In fact, I should call him and—"

"Or," says Nick patiently, "you can wait until he gets home from his tour of duty in Afghanistan."

"Right," I say again, and slump a little in my chair. "Or I could do that."

Nick gives me a wink before turning back to my folks. "The coffee thing is just to help Denny and his wife. They've got two kids. I feel like it's kind of my civic duty. You know how that is. But my interest is, I guess you'd say, the music industry."

"You're a musician?" I ask, then shake my head fast and say in a more declarative tone, "You're a musician! Yes, you're a musician, I mean. Nick is . . . a musician." Mom, Dad, Nick—everyone is looking at me like I'm nuts. I fake a little self-satisfied chuckle. "It's actually tough dating a musician," I say, trying to recover. "I'm always tripping over the drumsticks . . ."

". . . guitar strings . . ."

"Right, that's what I meant—the *guitar strings* he leaves lying around his apartment in . . . Riverdale?"

"Bushwick."

"Did I say Riverdale? I meant the Riverdale-like part of Bushwick. Naturally I meant Bushwick because Bushwick is where you *live*. Riverdale is where you . . . get your hair cut."

I have no clue why I've added that haircut part. Fortunately my parents are from Ohio. When it comes to NYC geography, they have no way of knowing that nobody gets their hair cut in Riverdale except maybe the Riverdalians, whoever they are—maybe Archie and Veronica? Honestly, sometimes even I'm amazed at what I say.

"Oh, I love the guitar!" my mother gushes. She looks at me and asks, "Acoustic or electric?"

"Acoustic?" I guess.

Nick nods. "And electric."

"Electric and acoustic," I announce. "And he's fabulous at both."

"But I guess I'm mostly an engineer, I do a lot of mixing," Nick added.

"Very impressive," my father says. Although I'm not sure he quite understood anything Nick said. To be frank, I don't know much about it myself. "But with all that acoustic and electric guitar playing, and the coffee cart and mixing things, it must be difficult to find time to read Clarissa's writing." Dad is starting to act like he's interviewing Nick for the job of being my boyfriend. I throw Nick a look as if to say he doesn't have to answer, but he does.

"Oh, I make time," Nick assures him. "I love to read Clarissa's articles."

At this my heart absolutely swells. A guy who reads my writing? And *loves* it? This possibility is so awesome that it doesn't even appear on my invisible checklist because it would simply be too much to ask. But Nick is assuring my parents that he's a loyal reader of my work, and even though this evening is a total and utter fake, I'm actually touched.

"Which is your favorite of her most recent pieces?" Mom asks. Oh fug.

Here's another embarrassing confession: In order to throw my parents off the scent of my unemployment, I may have, on occasion, dashed off the odd article and e-mailed it to them. I've needed to write a few pieces for samples now and then anyway and I *may* have allowed them to believe that these pieces were actually being published in the, um, *Daily Post*.

For the first time Nick is looking like he's struggling, in a bit over his head. I wonder if he knows Morse code; then I could tap it out on his leg, which wouldn't be a bad idea. But I don't know Morse code.

"The one about . . . the crooked politician . . . ?" says Nick, winging it.

"They've bumped you up to politics now?" Dad says, his eyes widening. He's thrilled at the prospect of his daughter reporting on something as important as corruption in the government.

"Actually, not *that* kind of crooked," I say, tamping down expectations. "The last piece was about the politician who recently had her severe *scoliosis* treated by using a new primal back therapy and is now able to stand up straight and proud as she goes about her official duties as a leader in this great democratic land of ours." I feel like "The Star-Spangled Banner" is playing somewhere. Nick smiles and puts his arm around me.

"Clarissa really has a way with the human-interest stuff, don't you think?"

Damn, he's good. My dad is nodding like crazy and Mom's practically tearing up.

"I'll send you a copy of it," I promise. *As soon as I write it.*

Finally the food arrives. Dad gets his full order of murgh angarey. My salad looks delicious although Mom's looks like somebody has already eaten all the good stuff out of it.

The waiter places Nick's jhinga e aatish in front of him and he pulls back.

"What's this?" he asks.

Since I'm the girlfriend and I'm feeling really cozy and familiar right about now, I reach over and give the tip of his nose a playful tap. "It's your favorite, silly. Jumbo prawns."

Suddenly, Nick's face goes absolutely white.

I'm guessing I'm a little off with that "favorite dish" thing.

"What's wrong?" Janet asks. "Is something wrong with the prawns? You know, after the Gulf spill they've found eyeless shrimp in the Gulf? They don't even have eye sockets. We should just send them back." Yuck. Now you know how my mother thinks on a regular basis.

"No, no," sputters Nick. He gulps and turns to me. "It's just that . . . well, I'm a little allergic to shellfish, that's all."

"A little?" says my dad. "How much is a little?"

"Oh, ya know . . ." Nick takes his napkin and carefully pushes the plate away. "Somewhere between severely and . . . well, fatally."

Bad faux girlfriend! *Bad, bad* faux girlfriend! My parents stare at me in horror.

"Clarissa!" my mother cries. "How could you forget something like that?"

Good question.

"Well, ya see . . ." I stammer.

"It's a little game we play," he explains, giving a wave of his hand, laughing. "Clarissa knows one bite of a shrimp'll pretty much kill me, so she orders it to be funny. You know, like a joke. Such a kidder."

"I'd hate to be around for the punch line," says Dad, and gives me a disapproving look as if I just tried to murder his new son-in-law.

"It's just how we are," I say, taking my cue from Nick. "Clarissa and Nick, just a couple of pranksters in love." I quickly grab his poisonous meal and swap it with my own. "The prawns were for me all along, see? The kabab is for Nick." As I stab a plump bottom-feeder with my fork, I send up a silent prayer that he doesn't have any issues with mutton. I also take a sidelong glance at the shrimp. Thankfully, they've been pre-shelled and I presume de-eyed, if they ever had any to begin with.

The rest of the meal is mostly small talk except we get the full report on Mom's new tofu business. I kid you not. Let me explain:

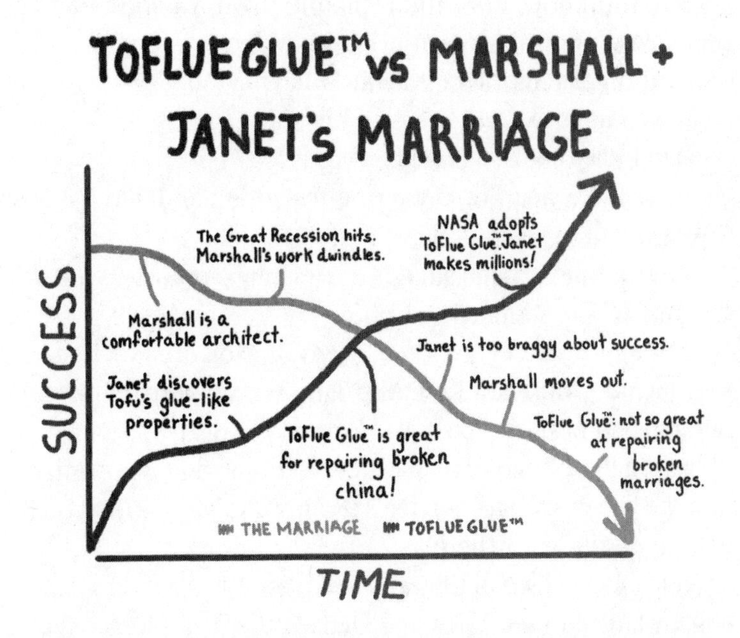

After the Ferg left home, Mom discovered that besides tofu being a healthy and tasteless source of protein, it had some serious industrial applications. Empty-nesting can be the mother of invention, at least for my mother. Using her own secret recipe, she turned tofu into eco-friendly superglue. Her "ToFlue Glue™" was great for repairing broken china, but even better for NASA. They used her glue to adhere those tricky heat panels to the space shuttle. Then as the shuttle program phased out, the

Chinese bought buckets of it for *their* space program. She made millions. Mom's financial independence also became a huge contributor to Dad's midlife depression. I can see Dad go glum as she talks about it. Thankfully, Mom keeps it to a minimum.

Throughout it all, Nick and I luckily manage to pull off a pretty believable impression of a happy long-term couple. Even luckier, no one dies of anaphylactic shock.

The only downside of the evening is when the check arrives. Dad reaches for it but balks when he glances at the total. He's been out of work even longer than I have, which means he couldn't afford to pick up the check at Papaya King, let alone Tamarind. Mom flips a credit card onto the table.

"My treat," she says. There's a big pause.

Dad forces a smile. I could cry.

Soon we're stepping out of the restaurant and into the New York twilight.

"We're going to head straight to JFK," my mother tells me. "Do you mind?"

Actually, I kind of wish they were sticking around, because then maybe Nick and I could pretend more parts of our fake relationship together, like talking about our big plans for a vacation, or my next birthday or when we're moving in together or how we like to snuggle when it's raining and . . . shit, maybe I'm getting carried away here.

The way I felt when they showed up notwithstanding, I'm really glad I got to see Mom and Dad. And let's not forget, if they hadn't waylaid me as they did, I wouldn't be standing here with Nick's arm around me.

Yep. Nick's arm is around me. How cool is that?

And he smells real good, like sea salt and beeswax, maybe the product in his hair? And coffee beans, which always warms my heart.

"It was nice meeting you both," Nick says, then gives my shoulder a squeeze. "We're going to have to cab it back to the *Daily Post*, babe."

I'm momentarily dazzled by the fact that he's just called me "babe" for a second time (which is totally fake and only for my parents' benefit but I totally dig it), so it takes me a minute to digest what he's said.

"Oh? And why is that?" I respond in a dreamy voice.

"Because," he says, waving as Janet and Marshall slide into a taxi, "that's where my Harley is."

Now I'm picturing this gorgeous guy clad head to toe in black leather, sitting astride an enormous, powerful riding machine. Believe me when I tell you, a Harley is so much better than a white stallion.

That's where my Harley is. Somebody catch me. I'm gonna swoon!

CHAPTER 5

We can't talk much in the taxi because we've found the only friendly cabbie in New York. He's an old Chinese guy who's been driving a cab forever and he wants to know where we're from and how we liked the restaurant and if the jhinga e aatish is as good as he's heard.

The old guy's such an unrelenting chatterbox that it gets me giggling. Nick smiles and shakes his head and I realize with a flutter of delight that we already have an inside joke. Norm and I didn't have an inside joke until three months into the relationship and then half the time he forgot to laugh when it came up. Mostly I just snuggle under Nick's arm, sighing to myself as his arm curves around, hanging on my shoulders.

When Chatty Cabbie says he can't understand why nice folks like us want to go to the former home of an old defunct newspaper like the *Daily Post* after business hours, Nick and I trade smiles. We pull up to the curb and Nick reaches for his wallet. But this time I pay.

"Thanks," says Nick.

"Are you kidding? This doesn't even begin to cover what I owe you."

But as the yellow cab zooms off into the night it occurs to me that I should probably still be in it. Clarissa Marie Darling doesn't have a boyfriend with a Harley parked in the alley. I'm not even on an actual date. Technically, Nick and I as boyfriend and girlfriend ceased to exist back on Hudson Street, as soon as my parents were on their way.

The fact that we didn't part company might be considered the sign of the beginning of an *actual* relationship of the true, meaningful variety.

"So you live in FiDi?" he says.

"Yeah."

"Cool. I can give you a ride home, if you want?" I nod, speechless at the prospect, as he heads for the alley, throwing a grin over his shoulder. "Wait here."

Moments later I hear what I think might be thunder or an earthquake. Then the Harley rolls out from between the buildings like some mechanical jungle cat. And there's Nick, wearing a well-beaten-up motocross jacket with a dark red stripe looking like the Bad Boy every girl dreams about.

He's holding an extra leather jacket, complete with an oversized collar and a surplus of zippers.

"Put this on," he tells me, handing over the jacket. "You'll be cold otherwise."

I slip my arms into the enormous jacket and it swallows me up. I run my hand along the tough aged surface of the leather. It's big and soft inside and makes me feel like a different kind of girl, which is cool. I'm ready to rumble. "This is the real deal, huh?"

"Circa 1959," Nick explains. "Got it at the secondhand shop on Bedford Avenue."

I zip up and throw on a helmet as Nick grabs my arm, pulling me onto the back of the bike like it's something we do every day.

"You have to hold on," he says, and he doesn't have to ask twice.

The motorcycle roars and we're off growling through the city streets, and since I'm not normally the biker-chick type, I'm a little uneasy and by that I mean my heart is beating like a hummingbird's. But maybe that's because I'm flat-out elated. My arms are wrapped around his smooth and agreeably hard abs. I'm holding on for dear life and for a lot of other good reasons, too.

As we wind our way through downtown traffic, swerving expertly through the late-night cabs and limos with the glow of taillights skidding off the bike's gas tank, I realize that he's driven right past my street. I don't actually mind, but I am a little curious.

"Where are we going?" I shout into the wind. Not that I really care. If his answer is jumping the Grand Canyon, that's fine by me.

He turns his head slightly to holler his reply. "I want to show you something first, okay?"

"Perfectly okay," I holler back as he guides the bike expertly through the neon-lit darkness. We're swerving in and around cabs and I'm kind of amazed at how dangerous riding a Harley in Lower Manhattan can be. But as I snug myself closer, our bodies in a full press, my mind gratefully lets go. I'm blissfully swept away through the city streets of Soho, dazzled by the reflections of the red, green, and white lights flashing around us.

When the purring machine slows to a halt, I find myself peering around his helmet at the East River, wondering where we've ended up. It's a deserted landing under the Brooklyn Bridge and I realize—I've been here before. Of all the movie scenes and postcards you've ever seen, I can guarantee this isn't one of them. It's just a little bit of nowhere under the Brooklyn Bridge, but to me it's Paradise, and honestly, in a city of over eight million people, I thought I was the only one who knew.

The water is shimmering and Lower Manhattan looks like some kind of hard-core fairyland—magical and edgy at the same time, all shadows and angles broken up by sparks of golden light. The bridge looms above in all its concrete and metallic majesty and I'm struck by the symbolism of it. Mr. Roebling's masterpiece is a connection, a way of bringing two totally different entities together. It's the ultimate joining. Okay, well not the "ultimate" one, but technically, I just met this guy a few hours ago. Still, as far as omens go, I'd say the Brooklyn Bridge is a good one.

He helps me off the bike and we take a few steps toward the water. "Downtown looks awesome," he whispers, but he's not looking at downtown. He's looking at me.

A shudder runs down my back and I smile. I slide closer until our hips are touching and nod toward the more humble borough on the opposite side of the water. "Well, Brooklyn's certainly holding its own."

He laughs, his fingers brushing mine as we continue toward the riverbank. "I wanted you to see this place," he says, some of the old shyness creeping into his voice. "I thought about it a bunch of times before, but we never talk about much more than coffee and . . ." He pauses, considering his next words. "I guess I've always wanted to share it with you."

It's all I can do to keep from throwing my arms around his neck and kissing him into a coma. I bet that's what a real biker chick would do. But instead, I tell him, "Actually, I've been here. A lot. It's pretty much my favorite spot in New York."

He blinks at me, surprised. "Really?"

I nod. "I found it by accident. I was lost. Well, not lost, exactly, but looking for someplace else."

"Funny how you find the coolest things when you're not even looking for them," he remarks.

Amen. This afternoon I was looking for coffee. And look where I am now. Look what I've found.

"So tell me," he says, in a voice that is both boyish and raspy. "What's your story?"

"My story?" I'm caught short, a bit overwhelmed. As an aspiring journalist I've spent so many of my last years reporting on other people's stories, and now, someone wants to know mine.

"Yeah, I mean I know you worked for the *Post* and you were like the star intern or something. Whenever I'd see you in the lobby you had so much going on and then . . ."

"Yeah, the ugly dark side of the Internet revolution."

"So how come you keep coming around?" he asks, half shy, but I can tell he really wants to know. And I can tell that he's been thinking about me all these years as much as I've been thinking about him. But I can't say what I'm really feeling because I'm dizzy. After all, I've been imagining this guy in my head forever, secretly dreaming what his espresso-scented kisses would be like and now, after introducing him to my parents as my boyfriend, I'm standing under the Brooklyn Bridge close enough to . . . well, close enough.

"The coffee?" I say after a long pause and he smiles in a way that makes me want to jump his bones.

"Yeah, the coffee's pretty good," he says, trying to keep a straight face. "After the paper closed I thought I'd never see you again. . . ." He smiles a quiet smile and I think a few more stars just lit up in the sky. I smile back and feel warm inside.

"So why haven't you moved on? I mean, are things okay for you?" he asks.

At first I think he's talking about Sam, and I pause. When will that relationship stop feeling like unfinished business? Then I realize he's just asking about life in general and next I find myself rambling on about my parents' separation, why I felt the need to lie about being out of work, and how much I miss writing about . . . anything, something, every day like I did at the *Post.*

"I feel that way about music," he says, nodding, as if he understands perfectly. "If I'm not mixing something in the studio or working a song out on the guitar, I feel like I don't exist."

"Yes!" I cry out. The reply is a bit louder than I'd meant and it bounces back under the bridge in an echo, seeming to affirm itself, and it makes me flinch. But it's so great to talk to someone who gets it. And, ya know, it doesn't hurt that he's sexy as hell, with a firm jawline and a butt like Channing Tatum's.

"What about you?" I ask.

"Me? I pretty much think about HeadSpace all the time," he says, peering out over the water. I smile but cringe inside, thinking, *Okay, he's a little groovy for me, but you can't have everything.*

"Of course some days," I say like a reflex, unable to keep myself from being a smart ass, "I think I should sublet my headspace and find one with better views."

Nick laughs and the sound is so mellow and deep that it makes my knees weak.

"I'm sure the view from your headspace is awesome," he assures me sardonically. "But I'm talking about HeadSpace, the music studio and indie label I started a while back. I took over an old mixing studio in Williamsburg."

"Oh whoa, that sounds amazing." I mentally smack my forehead like I'm such an idiot. Who knew the CCG was actually a CMG (cute music guy)? "I'd love to see your studio."

Oops.

Too much. Too soon. I wish I could swallow the words back into my throat but they're out there. I'm anxious to move past what amounts to me just asking him to take me back to his place, so I rush on.

I yammer about growing up in Ohio, about birthday parties and being the only kid in the elementary school caf-a-torium who could boast an "all tofu, all the time" lunchbox.

There is a mournful sound in the distance—a car horn? A tugboat whistle? A siren fading into the distance, I don't know, but somehow, it sounds like the soundtrack for a movie, the one I'm living. I realize I'm leaning toward Nick—and he's leaning toward me and there's nothing in between us. His hair ruffles in the breeze and I feel my chin tilting up toward him. I can smell the clean scent of his body in the balmy air and I feel a rush of warmth as he leans closer. I close my eyes and hold my breath and any second his lips will be making contact with mine. . . .

"Clarissa, wait."

What? I'm so dazed that it takes me a moment. *No kissing?* How long have my lips been hanging out here alone?

I open my eyes and finally comprehend that he's backing away.

Well, that sucks big-time.

I step backward and meet his gaze.

"What's going on?" I ask, knowing that his answer might determine whether I shove him headfirst into the East River.

"Oh man, it wasn't supposed to go like this," he says. He drags his hands through his hair and shakes his head. "I want to kiss you . . . so much."

"Okay . . . ?"

"But . . ." He closes his eyes and jams his hands into his pockets. "I've got to go. . . ."

"Go? Where?" I ask, flat-out confused.

"To the airport."

Normally, I'd make a joke here about airline fetishes and the mile-high club, but it's all too serious for that.

"Why would you do that?" I ask, already wishing I hadn't poured my heart out to him.

His head drops and he stares at his boots.

"There's someone I'm supposed to pick up."

Someone? That's a dodge if I've ever heard one. I mean, c'mon . . . if you're picking up your college roommate, or your great-uncle Timothy, or the foreign exchange student from Peru whom you've agreed to house for a semester, you come right out and say so.

You only say "someone" when you don't want someone *else* to know who *someone* actually is. But let's face it: I already know.

"Who?" I need to hear him say it.

To his credit, he looks me right in the eye. This is good because it proves he's got character. Bad because his eyes are so deep and smoky they're making my heart hurt.

"My girlfriend, I guess," he says simply.

I turn away to look at the bridge. That magical architectural gateway and its concerto of honking horns and squealing brakes disappear like fairy dust. Now it looks like a grimy old relic, just another crumbling piece of America's infrastructure.

"Oh," I say, wondering what the "I guess" part is about.

"Look, Clarissa, this happened kind of fast. One minute I was selling you a cup of coffee and actually having a conversation with you for the first time, and next I'm being introduced to your parents as your . . . guy, boyfriend, whatever. I didn't even know you were open to a relationship. And I've been waiting for the moment when . . . I don't know."

"Well, what difference does it make? You have a girlfriend," I say, annoyed.

But I suppose I was the one who catapulted us from Flirty Talk 101 to casting him in my own little improv version of *Guess Who's Coming to Dinner.* I dragged him to Tribeca, nearly murdered him with a plate of shellfish, and subjected him to an entire evening of my dad's stupid jokes.

"The thing is, I thought we would get to know each other a little, but this happened way too fast. I've thought about you for so long."

"I don't get it," I say in spite of myself, and then hear the second part of what he said in a delayed reaction like an echo. "You have?"

"*You're* amazing. And if things were . . . different . . ."

Now why couldn't he have just quit at "amazing"?

"Hey, I understand," I tell him, forcing a smile. "And really, I owe you a huge thank-you for going through with this—my dad, my mom . . . my story." I hate the hurt look in his eyes at those last words. I'm feeling really bad no matter which way this goes, so I need to just wrap it up. "I better go."

"Look, maybe we could . . ."

Could what?

"Be friends?" I ask. "Please. If you say that to me right now I'll punch you in that beautiful jaw of yours."

I reach into my bag for my phone.

"What are you doing?" he asks, looking confused.

"Calling a cab. It's silly for you to drive me home. Especially when you've got to get all the way out to LaGuardia."

"JFK, actually."

"Oh. Well. There you go." I laugh nervously, although there's nothing funny to laugh about. I'm frantically punching my touch screen and it's making me so mad I want to throw it in the river.

"No," he says firmly. "I'm driving you home."

"You don't have to . . ."

"Come on," he says and puts out his arm to lift me up onto the bike.

Maybe it's his chivalry, maybe it's guilt, maybe it's the fact that I'm still wearing his old motorcycle jacket or something else I don't understand, but in any case, I stop beating the bejeesus out of my iPhone, which seems to have frozen up anyway.

"Okay." This time when he pulls me up onto the Harley it just makes me feel miserable.

My arms automatically encircle his waist, but I catch myself and snatch them back. Those abs are for some other girl to hug.

"You have to hold on," he says, and there's something sad and knowing in his tone. It's like he's reading my mind, which makes this all the more depressing.

Reluctantly, I grasp his midsection. The geological formations that are his abdominal muscles flex beneath the fabric of his jacket. I'm still impressed, but somehow, this position is a hell of a lot less fun than it was on the ride here.

He kicks the hog to life, and when he gives it the gas it snarls in protest, as though it would have much preferred to just sit here under the Brooklyn Bridge for the rest of the night.

I know just how it feels.

We weave our way back through the city streets on the Harley in silence. The neon cityscape looks garish and phony. The ride is bumpy and I'm shaken up as we dodge and dart through the speeding clutter of angry cabdrivers. The growl of the bike, which was so powerful and exhilarating before, now just seems loud and noisy.

In front of my apartment building, Nick coasts to a stop and cuts the ignition. I slide off the bike. We're officially back in micro-mode. The boyfriend-girlfriend game is over and we are once again vendor-vendee, if we're anything at all. Although something tells me that beginning tomorrow, I'll be giving up coffee entirely and stepping up to the counter at Jamba Juice.

He called me babe. He shared his river view—our river view—and none of it felt wrong.

But he's *involved.*

I should hate him, but he did have the decency to tell me before things went too far.

"Clarissa . . ."

I look up to see that he's removed his helmet. I'm still standing on the sidewalk, like maybe I forgot which apartment was mine, fiddling with the zipper on the pocket of the vintage jacket and thinking about how this ending is almost as wrong and disappointing as the series finale of *Lost.*

He sighs. "I wish . . ."

"Me too." I nod and hand him back his jacket.

On the invisible list in my head, I put a great big checkmark in the "Not the Type Who Cheats" box. As much as I would have loved to have the memory of one kiss to take with me, it would only have made me sadder and angrier. I have to be honest—I admire his integrity.

I put out my hand and he shakes it, as if his mom were giving him medicine.

Finally, I turn and take the first step toward my apartment building. I don't look back when I hear the snap of the kickstand, or when I hear the Harley rev, or when the tires squeal as he races off into the night.

To JFK.

Then back to the wilds of Bushwick.

To his guitar and his dreams and his girl who isn't me.

CHAPTER 6

I didn't sleep well. And by that I mean I didn't sleep at all. The roar of the Harley and the lights flickering on the river kept repeating on me. Or maybe those damn jumbo prawns were eyeless after all.

At six a.m., Elvis is purring and pawing, making biscuits on my head, so I get up to feed him. It's the wide-eyed wild look he makes as he kneads my hair into knots that stupefies me. Don't get me wrong, I love my silky black cat. We get a lot from each other. I feed him and he allows me to share my silent inner dialogue out loud.

Back when I worked for Hugh, I'd set my alarm for six in the morning so I could abuse the snooze button a bit before actually getting up. It wasn't that I didn't look forward to going to the *Daily Post*, but I've never been what you'd call a morning person. Although I would linger at the kitchen window to admire the city waking up at sunrise, the stark beauty of the silent silhouetted spires reflecting the sun's ochre and pink mirrored light between the office building windows felt magical back then.

Today, it feels early. Elvis is particularly peevish this morning, so I hustle to open the little wet cylindrical pile of cat food that sustains him.

Determined not to pick over every moment of the hopeless joy and embarrassment of last night—what I call soul scratching—I pad to the kitchen, which for the last several weeks has doubled as Job Search Central. With half-opened eyes I grab the first tea bag in the canister and make myself a cup (the idea of coffee hurts too much) and settle into my desk chair. My laptop stands at the ready, with an array of cyber-career placement and "Transition to Digital Journalism" networking websites already securely lodged in my favorites bar.

Here I am in my twenties with the prerequisite encumbrance of loans that have long exceeded their nonexistent grace periods, having plunged into the dread realm of forbearance. And no, I didn't ask Mom to pay them off, though she offered. I guess I'm a bit like my dad that way.

I decided during my night of tossing and turning that Lou at the "You Don't Have a Snowball's Chance in Hell of Ever Finding Gainful Employment" Office is history. In fact, I think he should lose his job and get a real taste of what it's like, but I wouldn't wish that on anyone. A few days ago, I'd gone to the "Please for the Love of God Hire Me" section of Craigslist and found a few postings that looked promising and posted an inquiry along with my résumé, hoping to find my future employer. I would've gone to butivegotadegree.com and workforpennies .com, too, if it would help, but no one's started those websites yet. All I had to do was wait for those enthusiastic responses to roll in, right?

So far, bupkis.

Elvis tap-dances across my keyboard, distracting me, indifferent as always to my suffering. The word *pet* is foreign to Elvis. He's more like my "rub against," if you know what I mean. Or more precisely, I'm his. Which is to say that I didn't find Elvis. He found me. He showed up miraculously perched on the ledge to my sixth-floor window with no visible means of having gotten there or means of egress, a bit of witchcraft if you ask me. So I considered naming him Samantha or Sabrina until I realized his gender. Salem, the Cloven One, or just Bub, short for Beelzebub, might have worked, but I thought better of it.

Don't ask me why Elvis, my childhood pet caiman, came to mind. Elvis disappeared under mysterious circumstances. It took years to get Mom to confess that she gave away the reptilian Elvis without telling me after Ferguson tried to shove a pocket watch down his throat thinking that would win him the role of Captain Hook in the school play. Actually, I'm pretty damn superstitious about black cats crossing my path and disappearing into the night, so I invited this one in. After all, he hasn't crossed my path and moved on—yet.

I put Elvis down on the floor and wonder if I should consider hiring a headhunter. Not to be confused with a headshrinker, who is also someone I could probably benefit from, considering the spectrum of my personal obsessions. OCD, control freak, generalized anxiety disorder, not to mention my own original take on superstitions, which I'll explain at some point. I believe there's a thin line between functionality and phobias and that's a line I tend to grind, to use Norm's terminology.

"List Girl"—that's what Hugh used to call me at the *Post*. It was the way I systematized his life. As much as he complained, he loved it. I may have been guilty of working on my lists rather than listing my work, but who wouldn't want a compulsive list maker organizing their lives? Although Hugh made sure I learned that journalistically, a listicle does not a magazine article make.

It took a long time for me to realize that my list making came up just short of other more deadly disorders like hoarding, hand washing, and lock checking. Okay, I do check the locks and I still have all the hubcaps from my tweenage bedroom stacked neatly in a box somewhere. But what do you expect from a girl who by fourteen had managed to compile a list of every winning word of the Scripps National Spelling Bee for the last fifty years in order to know what word they *wouldn't* be likely to ask again? I've even made an all-important list of things I could be doing besides making another pointless list. Sometimes, it feels like I'm actually cataloging every form of life's madness, which seems a form of madness in itself.

MY LIST OF LISTS

1. Every winning spelling bee word.
2. Hottest 90s child actors.
3. Best Charlie Sheen catchphrases.
4. Places I hope to never travel.
5. Tensest WTF podcast interviews.
6. Things to do while avoiding looking for a job.
7. Places Elvis might be hiding.
8. Shoes I've loved and lost. *sniff sniff*
9. Parents' most gagworthy pet names.
10. Facial hair I've dated.
11. Things to do aside from making lists.

And the lists go on...

Elvis gives me a withering glance. His indifference to my suffering is like a Zen koan of some kind. If only I knew its meaning. Okay, he probably thinks I need the headshrinker, but let's stick with the so-called hunter of heads, because if I had a job, my obsessions would certainly get in line. One thing's for sure: If I'm getting a headhunter, it's gonna have to be on the cheap. Does that even exist? Google will know.

Shoving the slouchy sleeves of my vintage St. Anne's thrift shop blue satin bathrobe up to my elbows, I shoot the cursor to the search bar and arrange my fingers on the smooth, square keys.

H-E-A-D . . .

. . . S-P-A-C-E.

What? No!

Delete, delete, delete, delete!

I am absolutely *not* going to Google Nick's studio. That would be the cyber equivalent of riding my bike up and down his street, as if he were the cutest guy in my seventh-grade English class.

"That surly look is uncalled for," I say to Elvis, who has invaded my workspace with a condescending glare. "Scram!" I yell, shooing him away, but he doesn't budge. How unfair is it that cats are both cute and invincible? I try to refocus. "Clarissa. It's a job you're looking for, not the deets on the CCG," I say out loud, secretly hoping for Elvis's approval.

. . . H-U-N-T-E-R.

Better. Throwing myself into the task at hand, yes, sir! Can't keep a good Darling down, just ask my mom. (My brother and father might have a slightly different perspective on that, but I am not giving up!)

I hit enter and muddle through the non-applicable sites. (Wow, look at how much porn avails itself when you type the word *head* into a search engine. Really? Who knew that Cronut was a position?) But I dismiss that line of inquiry and soon I have a list of highly rated professional headhunters who will gladly pimp me out to all of Manhattan's and some of Westchester's and Long Island's journalistic endeavors.

Something about the term *headhunter* rattles my brain. What does it remind me of?

I see the skull of a tiny head with missing teeth and strawlike blond hair that looks like me in my baby pictures. The head with its frozen smile rattles like a maraca. A guy in a loincloth with some pretty radical Lion King *makeup shakes the rattle while stabbing a long pointy spear into the air. He vigorously shakes his head "no" and chants something that sounds like* "Curriculum Vitae" *but in Swahili. At the end of the spear there's a piece of paper—it's my résumé.*

Okay, let's just postpone the headhunter idea.

I sigh and take a sip of the steaming tea, not my usual java blend, and I'm immediately punished with a mouthful of Sunflower Spit or Berry Blast or whatever tea-that's-trying-too-hard variety left behind in my canister by super-slacker Norm. I'm always worried when drinking teas with hieroglyphics on the tin that I'm about to ingest something that could double as potpourri. I flash back to yesterday, remembering that businesswoman who bought an herbal tea from Nick . . . I wonder what kind she ordered. . . .

Stop!

I take a deep breath and go back to the kitchen, where I dump the horrid tea concoction into the sink and rifle through the cabinets for a more acceptable beverage. As long as I'm here, I decide to organize the contents of the cupboard, beginning with the cereal boxes. My job search awaits, but a quick alphabetical reordering should take no time and I'll feel so much more accomplished afterward: Granola . . . Kashi . . . Post . . . Quaker . . .

Lucky Charms? Must be a rogue box left over from the weekend Piper spent at my place while her apartment was bombed for roaches. Ordinarily, I wouldn't even consider introducing a single spoonful of such overprocessed garbage into my digestive system (I am Janet Darling's daughter, after all). But it occurs to me that if I don't get a paying job soon, those marshmallow clovers might turn out to be the only thing standing between me and certain starvation.

I shove Lucky, the smiling leprechaun, to the back of the cupboard and move on to alphabetizing the spices. This is sure to be less problematic. Cayenne, Celtic sea salt, chaat masala . . .

It makes me wonder if I could land a job at one of Martha Stewart's magazines. She has, like, twelve or thirteen of them, right? I wonder if Martha Living Omnimedia would go for an article like "How to Cook with Leftovers in Jail." I've heard that M. Diddy (that was her nickname in prison) made crab apple jelly and no-bake cheesecake with crumbled graham crackers, lemon juice, vanilla pudding mix, pats of margarine, and coffee creamer while spending time in the slammer. I congratulate myself on the brilliant idea, but then somewhere between the grains of paradise and the amchur powder, it dawns on my foggy brain what I'm doing.

Avoidance. Classic technique—ask any job hunter. As you wait for the phone to ring or the e-mail that will change your life, you will do *anything* to keep from facing reality. If you can't find work, busy work will do. Distraction is key! Any random act of accomplishment with a beginning, middle, and end feels better than endlessly waiting and hoping for something out of your control. Want to hear just a few things I've done while trying to forget I'm looking for a job?

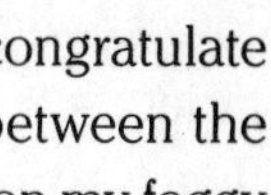

1. Painted the bathroom—twice. First Ikea yellow and then robin's-egg blue.

2. Written a novel—okay, only the first two chapters, until I found myself desperately avoiding my chosen form of avoidance.

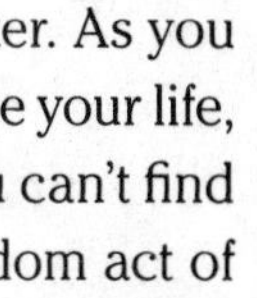

3. Researched new cellular service providers—

because clearly, the service I have is not working. If it were, the phone would be ringing nonstop, right?

4. Read every published report about millennials making up 41 percent of the unemployed, having reduced lifetime earning potential, growing up believing we're special because of Barney the Purple Dinosaur, and suffering through the dial-up age with every bad photo taken of ourselves forever on the Internet. But at least we'll never have to live without Wi-Fi short of the apocalypse, right?

NO JOBS TODAY OR EVER

Google that for a little while and see if it doesn't make you physically sick.

So enough with the spices and the cabinets already! A job! My well-ordered Kingdom of Spice for a job!

"What did I come in here for, anyway?" Elvis glances around the minuscule kitchen and I follow his gaze. Right. Coffee. Must brew coffee. I fumble through a drawer filled with tiny takeout packets of soy sauce, sweet-and-sour, ketchup, and granola bars until I find the last remaining single-serving coffee pod, and make a mental note to order more now that I'm making my coffee en casa. I take the brightly colored pod and approach the machine on the counter. It's depressing to say the least—a coffee maker that brews one cup at a time is about as lonely as it gets.

In an hour or so, Nick will be firing up Frankensteam for the morning onslaught. Those New Yorkers fortunate enough to still be working in that building will be tipping the half-and-half carafe, sharing smiles and making small talk, continuing their micro-relationship in the aura of that cool CCG now known as Nick, aka "the one who got away."

As the morning foot traffic picks up, I arrive and ask for tea. He's shocked that I haven't asked for coffee; Nick's face contorts into a mask of horror. He turns and runs. Was it something I said? Had I violated the terms of our faux relationship and very genuine breakup? Was it because I asked for tea?

"Stop!" I yell as I chase after him, but he keeps running and

when we turn the corner we're in Williamsburg somehow, darting through the gentrified streets. It looks like I'm in one of those first-person-shooter games as everything fish-eyes around me. Why am I chasing him? Why can't I just leave the poor guy alone? How many life points do I get if I catch him?

Hot on his heels, I hurdle hipsters, shove geriatric men and their walkers aside. At the edges of my vision, I see graphics that digitally ring up an ongoing tally of effective life points every time I shove someone out of my way. I dive through sidewalk racks of secondhand clothes marked EVERYTHING TEN BUCKS. *I can't help pausing to examine a pair of vintage suede Fiorucci gauchos. They're a killer deal, but Nick is getting away and now I'm losing health points fast, so I leap over the fallen sale items in hot pursuit, calling out his name (now that I know it, I might as well use it).*

If I don't catch Nick, how will I carry out my secret plan to make him drink the special cup of Lapsang souchong tea I've brought, which I may or may not have doctored with knockout drops? And how many points will that be worth?

We turn down an alley and he's cornered. I force the special cup to his face. Drink up, Nicky boy! That's what you get for being so damn cute and shy. I hold his mouth open, making him swallow it all, massaging his Adam's apple to make sure he drinks it. He awakens to find himself chained to my bed wearing his motocross jacket and nothing else. How convenient.

Hmmm . . . I pull back my chair, *let's work that fantasy for a bit . . .*

"What am I doing!?" I say, and slam my forehead on the kitchen cabinet to wake myself up. Elvis looks at me like . . . well, like I'm nuts . . . because I am. Tortured daydreams at a single-cup coffee machine.

"See what happens when I deprive myself of java?" I try to explain to Elvis, who could care less. "Just brew a cup, Clarissa, and get back to finding a job," I say, snapping the little plastic pod into the pump and clamping its jaw shut. Seconds later, the coffee beast is drooling java into my cup.

"He's gone. Opportunity missed. I just have to deal with it. Right, Elvis?"

Elvis is so fed up, he acts as if I've offended him and heads toward the window—his magic portal.

"Everyone, Elvis has left the building!" I shout, thinking I'm clever, then plop myself into the desk chair and, looking at my computer screen, I blink. How had I missed them? I blink again. There are five e-mails!

I look at the time stamps. They must have popped into my mailbox sometime last night after the heart-wrenching demise of my whirlwind sham romance.

As I click to read I can't stop thinking about my back rent, knowing I'll soon cross that shuddersome three-month limit that stands between my life as an adult and having to move back home with my parents, who aren't even together.

The first e-mail is an offer of vast quantities of cash from a former head of the Nigerian National Petroleum Corporation in return for my address and bank account number, so I'll pass on that one. The next two are in the "too good to be true" category, offering unbelievable sums to work in my pajamas at home. And the last one requires a Bitcoin account. All false hopes. Bummer. Wait. There's one more.

I click on the last one and take note that Elvis has returned. Hopefully that's a good sign. I decide not to make an announcement this time. I don't want to scare him away. This last e-mail is about a job that involves money too, but not transferring money—writing about it—as an investigative financial journalist. It actually looks like an actual job in the actual field of journalism—hallelujah. It's something called "Nuzegeek." I wonder what online name generator they used to come up with that cleverly memetic moniker.

Oh, there's one drawback. I don't really have any experience or qualifications as a financial investigative journalist, besides my blog subscription for Paul Krugman editorials and my love and admiration of Gretchen Morgenson at the *New York Times*. Admittedly I fudged and said on my résumé that I covered Wall Street. Okay, it was *Occupy* Wall Street and the piece was about the lack of Call-A-Head Porta-Potties, but a girl's gotta do what she's gotta do to get a job.

Besides, it's an interview and that is a really incredibly good thing! You never know where it will lead. I'll just have to come up with some angle that makes me at least *appear* qualified.

I squint at the computer screen. The e-mail is cyber-signed by someone named Druscilla Devereaux, assistant to "MT Wilkinson." Druscilla? That's got to be one of the vampire girls in *Twilight*, right? Or *Buffy* or one of those *Rugrats* characters? Maybe this is jobspam after all.

MT Wilkinson, huh? Never heard of him either. Or her. I hate asexual monikers because for one thing, if you ever have to e-mail this person, how do you address them? "To Whom It May Concern"? "Yo"? It's also unpunctuated, I might add, which doesn't bode well for MT's editorial prowess. But you know what? Not my problem. If MT, whoever he or she is, prefers to go sans punctuation and is transgender, what business is that of mine?

Druscilla suggests I call to schedule a pre-interview. I imagine it's so the crafty vampiritrix can decide if I'm worthy of an audience with MT. I snatch up my phone. Four digits in I realize it's only 7:47 in the morning and stop. But you can bet I will be fondling that touch screen again at nine a.m. sharp, and I will be bright, charming, and professional. I will tell Druscilla Devereaux that I would love to be pre-interviewed for an interview with MT.

I pop up from my desk chair and hustle to the kitchen for my single-serving cup of coffee, which I'm suddenly no longer thinking of as lonely. It's a symbol of my independence!

MT's assistant wants to see me!

Things are looking up!

Or at least looking somewhere.

CHAPTER 7

Since the phone is in my hand, I program the Nuzegeek number into my contacts. That way, at nine o'clock sharp I can shave a few nanoseconds off my dial time. But as I punch in the last digit, Elvis purrs and rubs up against me and my trusty index finger lingers too long on the touch screen and it's ringing! Before I can hit END, to my shock, there's a voice.

"Nuzegeek."

I'm momentarily befuddled. It's not even eight a.m. I curse Elvis under my breath.

"Hello?" the voice on the other end asks.

"Ms. Devereaux?"

"Hardly," the voice answers with that aristocratic upper-crust English accent that reminds me fondly of Benedict Cumberbatch. There's an indelicate snort on the other end of the phone. "Ms. Devereaux rarely arrives before nine forty-five," the voice continues.

"Oh." What am I supposed to say to that? Druscilla's work ethic is no concern of mine. "Um, well, to whom am I speaking?"

"This is MT Wilkinson. To whom am *I* speaking?"

Shit! *Hang up, Clarissa.* Better yet, toss the phone across the room; it's still under warranty. Whatever you do, do *not* tell MT

Wilkinson who you are, because it's 7:53 in the morning and only a desperate nincompoop would call about a job at this hour.

"I said, who is this?" MT (female, by the way) repeats in her crisp accent.

I'm tempted to murmur "cat murderer," then strangle Elvis and pretend this never happened. But I freeze—caller ID—would she know? Would the ASPCA find me? Damn you, telecommunications revolution! Curse you, PETA.

"This is Clarissa Darling, Ms. Wilkinson. I received an e-mail from your assistant—"

"Darling?" I can almost hear MT's wheels turning as she tries to place the name. "Clarissa Darling. Hmmm . . . ah, yes. You applied for the investigative journalist position. Hunter College grad. Hugh Hamilton's former intern."

Wow. What does it mean when a potential employer can quote your résumé off the top of her head? Either she's got that freaky total recall thing happening, or your CV was much more impressive than everyone else's. Or maybe it's just that nobody else applied for the job. In any case, she's spot-on.

"That's me," I confirm. "Sorry to be calling so early, but—"

"Early? Please!" MT laughs and snorts again. I hope she's not a regular snorter. "I've been at my desk since six o'clock. Apparently, you like to get an early jump on the business day, too."

Apparently I do. I suppress the urge to spout something silly about birds and worms, which is the kind of thing my dad would say in a situation like this.

"I'm calling to set up a pre-interview with Druscilla."

"So, you're interested, then? Brilliant." MT sounds genuinely pleased, which genuinely pleases me.

"I'm *very* interested," I assure her. "But since Druscilla's not in, I suppose I'll ring her up later."

Ring her up? Ugh! Why couldn't I just say "call her back" like a normal American? But having MT answer her assistant's line at this hour with her upper-crust English intonation has caught me off guard and now it's like her accent is suddenly contagious or something. I should get off the phone immediately, before I say "bloody" or "bugger."

"She'll be in around ten, I assume?"

"If we're lucky." MT laughs, so I laugh, too (hopefully not with a British accent). "Tell you what, Clarissa. Let's cut right to the chase and get you in here to meet with me directly, shall we?"

You bet your ass we shall!

"That sounds great."

"When are you available?"

I want to tell her I could probably make it there before Druscilla does, but decide to play it a little cooler than that. "I'm free later this afternoon," I say casually.

"Two o'clock, then?"

"Two it is."

"Lovely."

It's on the tip of my tongue to "lovely" her right back, but instead I go with a good ol' American, "See you then, and thank you."

The second I hang up, a shriek of pure joy escapes my lips, sending Elvis into the bedroom to escape. Seriously, what are the chances of a person inadvertently calling a place of business at sunrise and then having the executive with whom she hopes to schedule an interview actually answer an underling's phone and be good-natured about it? That's got to be a positive omen, right? And despite a conspicuous lack of vowels in her name, I have a very positive feeling about MT. She sounded really down-to-earth, approachable, like if we ever ended up in some ladies' room peeing in adjacent stalls, I wouldn't feel the least bit wonky about asking her to hand me a wad of toilet paper under the divider.

Okay, maybe that's going too far.

She just seemed nice, even with a British twang. True, Ms. Wilkinson is a bit driven, what with her office hours starting at dawn and all. But if I'm being honest, I'm drawn to high achievers (Norm notwithstanding), which is why this whole job drought has been so hard on me.

I shimmy around my apartment for a full five minutes performing a pagan dance of exultation to honor the Deity of Job Security, or at least to appease the demigod of Getting One's Foot in the Employment Door. Take that, unemployment office guy! Elvis peeks gingerly out of the bedroom to see what he's missing. I look up that total recall thing, just in case it happens to come up in conversation with MT later. Julius Caesar and Alexander the Great had it. Supposedly they knew all their soldiers by sight, all twenty-five thousand of them. For the record: It's called Highly Superior Autobiographical Memory, or H-SAM for short.

I think of Sam and suddenly I feel like calling him. I deserve it. I've got a job interview! I think he'd get quite the chuckle out of hearing I might be on the verge of doing something in the financial realm. Besides, it's been so long since I've heard from him.

Sam's not your typical millennial when it comes to social media. He has a Facebook page, but unlike Jody, who changes her profile picture at forty-three-minute intervals and has a Snapchat of every Frappuccino she's ever ordered, the last photo Sam posted was from his college graduation, and that was in 2009. He was wearing a pair of board shorts and flip-flops with nothing else under his gown.

He's not a tweeter, a texter, or fond of Instagram either, but to be fair, this is because half the time he's probably somewhere on the planet where the closest thing they have to cell phone reception is carrier pigeons. He also spends a lot of time underwater, researching stuff where the algae-to-sea-horse ratio is higher than the Wi-Fi-signal-to-noise ratio.

Sam had been a skateboarder at school in Ohio, but once he saw the ocean, he knew that was the only place he wanted to be. After only one summer in Montauk, he was cutting aerial barrel rolls across point breaks in no time. His dad, who is an accomplished sportswriter and the most laid-back parent on the planet, always said that he'd be fine if Sam became a surfer and read a few hundred books along the way. So Sam majored in marine biology and diving technology and traveled more places than I've imagined.

And get this: He writes letters. On paper! And mails them! With stamps! From exotic places. How retro. Can you imagine? I've saved every letter he's ever written, even the ones with the gloppy smudges that smell suspiciously like chum. I respond to every one but a lot of times my letter arrives at the place where he used to be and the envelope comes back to me. But I don't care. I love writing him.

I try to remember how long it's been since the last letter Sam sent me and I can't. Has it been so long that I can't even recall? Seems impossible. Well, it's time to do something about that!

I don't know if it's three a.m. in Bora Bora or on the Bazaruto Archipelago or wherever he is at this moment, but I touch the screen and tap his name. That's the nice thing about cell coverage: You can be joyfully ignorant of time zones. The phone rings once, twice, and I get hopeful, but then it skirts right to voice mail. Damn.

"Sam Anders here. Say something memorable at the sound of the tone."

Still, it's great to hear his voice, even if it is coming to me from the ether of cellular airspace and was recorded weeks or months ago. Sometimes he doesn't even have a voice message. I'm always tempted to leave something like "Can't talk long, the contractions are coming three minutes apart. Hope you get back in time." But I never do.

"Hey, Sam!" I say cheerfully after the beep. "Just wanted to catch up, say hello. It's been a while since . . . well, you know. Hope you're good. Be in touch? Anytime. Well, not exactly memorable, but you are! Miss you. Bye."

CHAPTER 8

Was it Henry David Thoreau who said, "Beware of all enterprises that require new clothes"? Maybe it was Lindsay Lohan, right after the unfortunate necklace-lifting incident. Either way, I strongly disagree. Aside from great friends, good coffee, and my First Amendment right to protect my journalistic sources, there's nothing I value more than new clothes. Especially if they're old ones. Nearly half the items in my wardrobe are two decades more mature than I am.

Elvis follows me into my closet where we breathe in the heady aroma of linen, silk, cotton, and denim. One of the things I don't hate about my apartment is the closet. By New York standards, this thing should have its own zip code. This was a huge factor when I answered the roommate ad in the Norm aftermath. Norm and I had to settle for what amounted to little more than a broom closet—fine for Norm's grungy Ziggy Marley T-shirts and worn-out Levi's 501s but not at all conducive to crinoline. So when I moved out, my real estate philosophy was simple: Keep your river views, your liveried doormen, and your on-site laundry; I'll take sweater shelves, shoe racks, and hanging space any day of the week.

Who'd have thought such storage nirvana could be found in

the Financial District? Once Felice, late of Scarsdale, bailed on NYC, my closet space doubled. I'm good for now, at least until economic necessity forces me to find another roommate (other than Elvis). Thanks to my spacious closet, vintage Jean Paul Gaultier no longer has to rub up against secondhand Alexander McQueen that I snagged at a church sale. My practically priceless Mary Quant hot pants and my very own well-worn mid-'90s Doc Martens have lots of room to breathe, and the best part is that I can continue to frequent those trunk shows of edgy, up-and-coming designers who are still broke enough to sell their samples cheap in an effort to pay off their FIT student loans.

I have a nearly boundless space to bring home all my fashion treasures and introduce them to the other clothes in my giant closet, trusting that when the overhead light goes out, they will successfully mingle, mate, and breed all sorts of new and incredible one-of-a-kind outfits. Let's face it: I've been mixing and matching since I was a toddler.

What I hate most in fashion is *coordination*, like when you wear blue shoes with a blue jacket and a blue something in your hair. I like fashion when you invent it. Not having been blessed with the sort of mother from whom I could glean any real sense of style (Janet Darling was all about the mom jeans and the polo shirts—tucked in!) left me in an open field to experiment and develop my own style.

I still rock my wardrobe enough to make some people wonder about my sanity, but as my taste evolves, I get way more compliments than ever before—especially from women asking me where and how I pulled it together.

In high school, people always wanted to know the secret of my clothes. Someone even accused me of being a postmodern Pippi Longstocking, which slightly offended me at the time. Even I didn't know how to answer them until I discovered that my secret actually had a name: Loulou.

Loulou de la Falaise.

Louise Vava Lucia Henriette le Bailly de la Falaise was her christened name. And I used to think Clarissa Marie Darling was a burden. Just imagine if one of your three middle names was "Vava"?

Loulou was radiantly beautiful with a tangle of curly hair and a laugh that crackled with delight. Best known as the charismatic muse of Yves Saint Laurent, she was much more than that to me. She was the woman who epitomized my self-made, put-together sense of who I am.

To have lived her glamorous life!

La Falaise was allegedly baptized not with holy water but with "Shocking," the scent by fashion designer Elsa Schiaparelli, her mother, Maxine de la Falaise's, employer. Loulou inspired YSL's famous women's tuxedo "Le Smoking" and his see-through blouses. She was a woman who flaunted her well-worn beauty with mermaid insouciance and a sense of amused irony and detachment.

If Hugh Hamilton was my writing mentor, then Loulou de la Falaise was my fashion muse before I even knew it.

Thanks to her shining example, I browse my quirky cache of clothing until the right ensemble avails itself. I have a sense of completeness that settles over me when I pull on a snug-fitting striped jersey skirt that clicks with a twelve-dollar pair of super-clunky secondhand platform sandals. I invite my pale peach not-too-see-through blouse into the mix, topped off with an unexpected chunky red necklace, and voilà—it's magic!

Hopefully this won't prove too challenging to my hoped-for new boss MT and my future position as financial writer. But just in case, I add my ace in the hole—cherished St. Anne's thrift shop YSL black blazer—to bring it all together.

Standing before the mirror, adjusting my blouse, I perform the usual full-bod scan as Elvis slinks between my legs. For a girl who grew up on tofu, I ended up with a pretty enviable metabolism. Not quite a yoga body, but not light-years away from it either. My physique changed a lot in my first year after high school.

Yes, I'm that snappy, lighthearted girl who mixed prints with ease and had an affinity for leggings, scarves, and Doc Martens; but now I'm a woman in my late twenties, and I have curves—mostly in the right places—and eye makeup. My once naturally blond hair requires Sun-In to stay blond, but it's grown thicker and lusher. Sometimes I tie it up in some random way just to get rid of it. Thank God the gap-toothed smile that always made me seem younger than I really was is gone—it never kept me from smiling anyway, but now I just feel better about it.

After my first year in the city, my body forecast was looking stocky with a chance of thighs. But then I had a growth spurt and put in time at SoulCycle downtown and my local Pilates joint. Since my recent budget shortfall, I've been missing in action at the gym, but thanks to my longer-than-average legs and slender ankles, I'm okay.

Do I wish I were more curvaceous up top and a little less curvaceous down on the bottom? Sure, but I can rock a tube dress when I want to and I'm not a skinny malinky, like Aunt Haddie—sister of dread Aunt Mafalda—used to say. To sum it all up, my body and I are good.

My interview isn't until two p.m., so I've planned some boning up on the financial sector or at least cramming into my head enough terms to talk my way through a half-hour interview. I slide my laptop into my bag and scan the apartment to say good-bye to Elvis, but he's already gone. Witchcraft, I tell you.

My phone buzzes just as I open the door to leave. "C! SOS JOD!!"

As cryptic as it looks, I know this is Jody's usual message when she's having a panic attack. It's the double exclamation points at the end that confirms it. I'm pretty sure she's on a shoot for some cosmetics magazine.

I hesitate. Prep for MT and high-finance summons.

Then again, Jody's always there when I need her.

If I hustle now, I might be able to see Jody, drop into Starbucks for a job cram, and still make it to meet MT on time.

"What's the haps??" I text back in Jody-speak. Can't hurt to be optimistic.

"IT HAPPENED AGAIN!!"

Oh darn. I hate to say I know what this is.

CHAPTER 9

I'm in luck. Jody's big photo shoot today is not far from the Nuzegeek office, which happens to be right near the South Street Seaport: all within walking distance from FiDi.

She's seated at a table at Jack's Stir Brew where she's already ordered us each a cup of the patented house drink—stir-brewed java. Naturally, the whole upscale barista atmosphere makes me think of Nick. I'm starting to worry I live in a coffee-centric universe. What does that say about me? That I'm serious and focused and willing to look into the future unblinkingly? That I've been awake since the '90s?

I think it's true that the coffee an individual drinks says a lot more about them than just that they're caffeinated. Here's how I see it:

YOU DRINK:	YOU ARE:
 ESPRESSO	You're a purist-especially if you prefer single origin and consider Starbucks swill. In all likelihood you hate paper cups and prefer those teeny-tiny porcelain ones.
 MOCHA	You're zany and playful or just never liked coffee that much.

And don't get me started on people who drink coffee with soy and almond milk.

Fortunately, one look at the expression on Jody's face tells me she's so totally frazzled that it'll be easy not to dwell on Nick and the myriad ways that coffee has recently led to disappointment.

Even stressed out, Jody looks gorgeous. Every woman I know would kill for Jody's lush red hair. It's practically another person she happens to carry around on her head.

"Rad threads," Jody says, taking a sip of her macchiato. Her hand is shaking. Her camera-ready lipstick leaves a magenta kiss on the rim of the cup. "Totes profesh."

Allow me to translate: Jody is telling me my wardrobe choice is "totally professional."

"Thanks," I say. "How's the shoot going?"

"Way behind skedge. 'Cause of moi," she says and tries to smile, but I can see she's about to cry, which would ruin her rather extensive eyeliner and probably drive the makeup artist crazy.

"It's okay," I say. I put my hand on hers, hoping I can:

A) stifle the tears,

B) be the best friend I need to be, and

C) get the hell out of there in time for my interview.

"Gaston is freakin', but whatevs," Jody says, as if she doesn't care. But I can tell she cares a lot. She looks over her shoulder out the window where the crew mulls around and there's a very Frenchie-looking guy with a dozen cameras hanging around his neck—Gaston, I assume. He looks like he wants to kill someone. "Needed caf in my sys asap or I'd be use. Told him, then IM'd you," she adds.

I squint at her as I mentally translate. I notice the dark circles under her eyes hidden beneath the makeup.

"Is this a big magazine?" I ask.

"Totes for me, big bucks," she says, by which I know she means yes. "*Modern Orthodontia*. I'm the cover." I guess those Invisalign braces are big biz.

I can see that *Modern Orthodontia*'s makeup artist has made a valiant effort to hide Jody's dark circles, employing what I'd estimate to be about a million dollars' worth of Clé de Peau Beauté concealer. Jody's sparkling pearly whites will dazzle them, but clearly she needs to catch up on her Zs.

"Jods, you look wiped."

"Zhausted, no winks, not one." She sighs, looking sad, chasing her coffee with a swallow of Vita Coco coconut water. "I should never go on a big one the night before a shoot. But he was leaving for Europe."

"You didn't."

"I did. It was our last chance. I wasn't going to see him for another month."

Okay, now I notice the purplish bruises on her shoulder sneaking out of her Prada. I'm hoping they can use Dermablend or even Sephora tattoo concealer on that. And I guess there's always Photoshop later. I know from Jods that models are always showing up with bruises and stuff. In this case it's not nearly as alarming as that sounds because I know she hasn't been knocked around by some guy. In fact, her BF Rupert is a pipsqueak.

Beneath all that lithe beauty, Jody Dicippio is one tough cookie. She's got four older brothers who taught her to throw a punch the minute she showed signs of becoming a serious hottie. She's also got a couple of uncles in Witness Protection, which is why any asshole stupid enough to ever lay a hand on her wouldn't live to tell the tale. Not if Lenny, Paulie Jr., and Gianni have anything to say about it. Jody could probably send the guy to the ICU herself, long before *la famiglia* even knew what happened.

Besides, Rupert is skinnier than she is. He's the kind of guy who buttons the top buttons on his shirts and wears dark-rimmed glasses even though he doesn't need them. He's a member of the hipsterati boy model world.

"You fell out of bed again, didn't you?"

"Obvi," she says, annoyed, and rubs her elbow, which I'm guessing is bruised. "Can I help it if I get excited? Aren't you supposed to get excited during sex?"

I see her point, but it's a matter of degrees.

Jody's been to a couple of therapists for this peculiar problem, which has been plaguing her since she lost her V-card to Bubba Mitchum, a boy she liked in our junior year of high school.

Bubba and Jods had planned the big moment for months, and one Friday afternoon, Bubba blew off detention and took Jody back to his house, where they did the deed in the bedroom he shared with his little brother who, needless to say, wasn't home.

The unfortunate thing was that Bubba slept in the top bunk.

Story goes that for a beginner, Jody had absolutely no trouble getting into the moment. Maybe it was because she was anxious. She goes on about how really sensitive she is down there. It sounded to me like it was great until the grand finale when Jody got a little overzealous, practically epileptic, and flipped herself right over the bunk bed's safety rail.

Bubba panicked and Jody didn't want her parents to know, so she had him call me. I was elected to drive Jody to the ER, where we told the doctor she'd injured herself running hurdles in gym. He put four stitches in her left knee, but Mitchum was so freaked, he never called her again. Now it happens every time.

"What did your therapist say?" I ask. "Isn't there anything you can do?"

"She calls it a 'reaction formation,' " she says. "I mean, I'm not supposed to just sit there like a cold fish, am I?"

"And how's Rupert doing?" I ask, afraid to hear the answer.

"Broken arm and a cut on his cheek," she says sadly. "Do you think maybe next time I should tie myself to the bedpost for safety?"

"Well, that certainly puts a kinky spin on the concept of safe sex," I say.

"Sups hilarz." Jody grins for the first time.

I try to remember I'm there to help her calm down and get back to her photo shoot. Then off to meet the punctuation-challenged MT, and time is running out.

"Maybe if you talk about what happened, you'll feel better," I say but regret it almost immediately. Jody proceeds to describe in vivid detail her amorous acrobatic achievements of the night before, leading up to her ecstatic breakdown. Phew. It sounds like what you might get if you crossed parkour with the Kama Sutra. When she finally finishes her graphic play-by-play, I feel like I need a cigarette. And I don't even smoke.

"Well, look," I say. "No one needs to know this besides you and me. Certainly not the *Modern Orthodontia* guys out there.

More important, how did Rupert feel about what happened? Are you gonna see him again?"

"Hope so, probs," she says with a shrug.

Hmm. Is that short for probably? Or problems? Or both? I swear, sometimes I need an English-to-Jody dictionary just to make sense of what she's saying.

I look at my watch and see that I have twenty-four minutes to get my butt to Nuzegeek. So much for the Starbucks job cram. There's also some PA type standing at the door ready to lay an egg.

"Jody, you already seem better. You can do this. Rupert loves you. He'll be back. I'm sure you two crazy lovebirds can work this out. But now, you've got to go out there and smile like a million dollars and dazzle everyone, okay?" I'm crossing fingers and toes.

Jody looks at me with those puppy eyes. There's a long pause and a deep breath and a determined toss of her gorgeous hair.

"Okay," she says finally.

"Don't forget we're having dinner with the girls next Thursday," I say.

"Yay! Where?"

"Dunno, some dive on the Lower East Side, I think. It's Rodgers's turn to choose the venue. I better go." I slide out of my chair, hoping to move us to the finale.

"Wait! Stop!" Jody says and grabs my hand. I sit back down and wait, watching Jody knit her eyebrows and twirl her hair, deep in contemplation. Something is whirling around in that odd mercurial mind of hers. As interested as I am, I don't have time for another session.

"There's something really important I'm supposed to tell you," she says, chewing her lower lip. The look in her eyes is both excited and confused. I count to ten, wondering how long this will take.

"Jods, I've got this interview for a job."

A painful expression crosses her face and for a moment I get really worried.

"Something about G-bomb," she says. Oh, please. G-bomb is Jody-speak for Genelle Waterman. There's nothing about Genelle I want to hear. She was definitely in that category of things I couldn't explain back in our high school days. That's why I never talked about her much. I couldn't stand the idea of her intruding on my life and I effectively eliminated her from my existence by graduating early.

"Okay, what about Genelle?" I ask, half hoping she doesn't remember.

Then, just as immediately, the pained expression vanishes.

"I forgot," she says. "Maybe I hit my head?"

"No worries, Jods," I say, "just go out there and knock 'em dead. You'll remember later. I've got to hit this interview. Wish me luck."

"Thanks, C. Gluck!"

Gluck? Jeez. I grab my case and turn toward the door.

Five minutes later, I'm standing outside the offices of Nuzegeek, right on time.

MT Wilkinson, here I come.

CHAPTER 10

On my way over I rehearse my spiel, cramming as many financial terms into my head as I can remember as the elevator door closes, but I can't help thinking about my old newspaper days.

Don't get me wrong: I'm excited to go digital, but I miss good ol' Hugh. I loved every minute at the *Daily Post*. I worked hard for every promotion I ever got there. It's not easy to go from gofer to an actual reporter.

When I arrived at the *Daily Post*, I impressed Lillian Banion, the publisher. She thought I was "spunky."

spunky (adj.) "courageous, spirited," 1786, from *spunk* + *-y* (2). Not to be confused with **moxie** (n.), 1930, from *Moxie*, brand name of a bitter, nonalcoholic drink, 1885, perhaps as far back as 1876 as the name of a patent medicine advertised to "build up your nerve"; **spunky** "having a spark," Scottish, from Gaelic *spong* "tinder, pith, sponge," from Latin *spongia* (see *sponge*). The sense of "courage, pluck, mettle" is first attested in 1773. Vulgar slang sense of "seminal fluid" is recorded from c. 1888. Not to be confused with Rocko's dog from the cartoon *Rocko's Modern Life*.

Why are girls always spunky and boys courageous? Seems like Sheryl Sandberg might want to lean in about that. I guess I've been spunky all my life. Fortunately, it's served me well.

After I started interning for Hugh, Lillian gave me my big break—covering the police scanner and interning for Hugh. Then I was promoted to writing obits and interning for Hugh, until finally I could pitch my own stories—*and*—keep interning for Hugh with pay. I couldn't shake Hugh because the big lug grew to know and love me, in addition to abusing and humiliating me, in the nicest, well-intentioned way possible, of course. Bottom line: Hugh really needed me and everyone knew it. Besides, Hugh was what they call "a brand" in the news biz.

Then Hugh, the man, God bless him, passed away, just as he would have wanted—in the middle of eating a hot dog with mustard, onions, and double sauerkraut at Billy's Fifty-seventh Street Nathan's hot dog stand. The coroner's report said something about toxic heartburn. Can you really die of heartburn? And if you die that way, is heaven just one big Prilosec?

After Hugh passed, Lillian hired me to sort through his papers and finally gave me what I'd been striving for—my own beat! At the ripe old age of twenty-two, I was making an honest living. Ah, those were the days!

All three of them.

You remember the stock market crash of '08? And remember when people actually bought newspapers? Remember when boys grew up to be men? Remember when Lindsay Lohan was a promising newcomer? Why does that seem like a long time ago in a galaxy far, far away?

"Can I help you?" a voice asks, dripping of Ivy League dining halls and championship lacrosse trophies. In my reverie I must have stepped out of the elevator and appeared lost. I gaze up at a buttoned-up Hugo Boss Corporate 1 Percenter. His teeth nearly blind me. Somewhere in Greenwich, Connecticut, or Shaker Heights, Ohio, or Munsey Park, New York, a proud orthodontist is still bragging to potential patients about these perfect teeth.

He's got a head of thick, slicked-back black hair that harkens to the matinee idols of the 1950s, and his wing tips are polished to an onyx gleam. The silk necktie (how much you wanna bet it's Charvet?) is wound into a perfect Windsor knot under his gorgeous chin. He's kind of hot in that Leonardo DiCaprio way. Is this the finance guy of my dreams?

"MT Wilkinson," I say carefully, wondering how to leave out the periods.

"Ah." One dark brow arcs upward in approval. "Let me guess. Swarthmore. Lunch date?"

"Not exactly." I return the grin. He looks me up and down, taking in my de la Falaise–inspired outfit.

"Oh, Bennington, I assume." He rolls his eyes but doesn't hesitate to check me out from top to bottom.

"No, actually I'm here for an interview."

His brows knit, the smile and interest vanish. He hesitates, and for one crazy second I'm afraid he's going to shove me back into the elevator. Or maybe down the shaft. Somehow I've shifted from eligible possibility to desperate job seeker. And how quickly did his infatuation with me disappear? Come to think of it, I don't really like Leonardo DiCaprio that much. He's kind of got a big baby face. Besides, I already know more about Mr. Baby-Faced-Buttoned-Up than I want to. I'd like to tighten that little Windsor knot until his face turns blue.

He aims his perfectly patrician nose down a corridor and walks the opposite way down the hall.

I guess that's all I'm going to get in the way of directions.

"Lovely," I mutter, and head down the hall.

The Nuzegeek offices are highly designed, sleek and industrial as expected. I stride down polished concrete hallways with various nuts and bolts embedded right into the floor as a signature design. Above, the exposed beams and metal ducts contrast vividly with the offices and their stained wooden doors. The interior design incorporates some of the elements of the ancient Seaport. There's a three-hundred-year-old winch tower in the middle of the floor that includes ancient hoists with an extra-large block and tackle suspended from the ceiling. The mix of old and new is pretty stunning for the former Fulton Fish Market warehouse, now Internet start-up.

Walking through the bustling office filled with twenty-something types who have actual *jobs*, I find the divine Druscilla Devereaux stationed at her desk outside a set of tall mahogany double doors that may or may not lead to my journalistic future.

Druscilla peers at me over a pair of tortoiseshell glasses wearing a Bailey 44 Joie de Vivre striped jacket over a white camisole. Not bad. Droozy's got her brown hair scraped upward into a severe topknot, a tight little knob that sits dead center on the pinnacle of her head. Honestly, it's a style only a Kardashian (or Tinker Bell) can get away with. Also, she's got a hickey.

"Alyssa?" Druscilla sniffs.

"Clarissa," I correct softly, feeling like it's my fault for having the wrong name. I'm not usually this vulnerable, but between my lingering joblessness and Corporate Creep's cold shoulder back at the elevator, I'm rapidly losing my swag.

She picks up the phone and announces me: "MT? Melissa is here."

"Clarissa," I murmur again, but Druscilla doesn't seem to care. Then again, maybe she's pissed that I skipped the pre-interview.

When she opens the towering doors, I see nothing but glare—MT's office window overlooks the East River, and every single wall, as well as the light fixtures, the chairs, and the very contemporary shag rug, are white. Mr. 1 Percenter's dazzling teeth seem dull by comparison. The sunlight reflecting off the river floods the white room.

So what's the symbolism here? The utter purity of Nuzegeek's journalistic integrity? Or maybe I've wandered into a Clorox commercial. Where's Mr. Clean? If this were a video game, all this gleaming white light would be a very cool effect, but in this scenario it's a little nerve-racking. I blink frantically, which probably makes me look like I'm having a seizure.

Against this dazzling backdrop, I see only the faintest outline of a woman seated behind an enormous (you guessed it) white desk. Instinctively, I shade my eyes and hope she doesn't think I'm saluting her, because that would be weird. The glowing creature before me recognizes the problem. "Druscilla, get the blinds," she commands.

Druscilla scrambles to do her bidding. In the next moment I hear a faint electronic buzz and the automated blinds unfurl and the blazing light softens to a pearly glow.

Ah, there she is: MT Wilkinson in the flesh. No throne, no spotted fur collar, no scones (too bad, because I'm actually feeling a little peckish). I stride across the room and extend my hand to hers over the tidy desktop.

My previous Google search informed me that MT was part of a wave of black Britons who came to the United States for college and put down roots. Yes, Swarthmore. She entered the start-up workforce during the "dot-com before the storm" and became a marketing exec at Zynga. She was one of the first black women tech execs and famously wrote an article in *Fast Company* about how she felt marginalized by the boys' club, but denied it was a matter of racism. She clearly got the last laugh as she sold all her stock in early 2012 before the market crashed. Savvy instincts or insider tip? I'm guessing fortuitous leak, because her Swarthmore degree was actually art history, with a minor in classical literature. Then again, maybe she's a marketing wiz and could tell which way the winds were blowing.

She started Nuzegeek with no real experience in the area of hard news, but already her news zine has pretentions to become the next HuffPo meets Uproxx, which is kind of like the last *Daily Beast*. Evidently she's a quick study.

We shake hands and the first thing I notice are her eyes.

They're silvery-gray, inordinately large in her slim face, and there's no mistaking the intelligence behind them. Her dainty features and soft ebony skin are set off by jet-black hair cut in a sleek bob. She's definitely power-dressing in a Burberry Prorsum ensemble, wearing a blazer, top, and streamlined skirt combo with a man's belt holding it all together. Her fashion sense is impeccable.

"Welcome, Clarissa." MT leans forward and smiles. "Tell me what I need to know."

The next twelve and a half minutes are me talking me: me and college, me and Hugh, me and my journalistic sensibilities. I slip in a reference to the Great Recession and the rebound, which I back up with a few money-related phrases I pilfered from SeekingAlpha.com.

"But enough about *me*," I say, finally feeling comfortable with the dazzling MT, who does in fact emit a little snort at my tiny joke. "I hope you wouldn't mind telling me about Nuzegeek and how you started this amazing new take on the news." A suck-up line if you've ever heard one, but I can't tell you how effective and important it is to suck up. A lot of people my age forget how essential it is to ask their potential employers what they aspire to and what they want. It elevates both of you.

Her answer? Honestly, I don't have a clue. But it sounds great, lots about long reads, complex topics, and immersive storytelling, entrepreneur-speak for what we know and love as "writing." Very little of what she says has anything to do with actual news as far as I can tell. But it's filled with encyclopedic details—maybe she does have H-SAM. More important, I can see that she's thrilled to lay out her vision.

"Well, Clarissa, I very much welcome your enthusiasm," MT says, reclining in her white ergonomic desk chair. I like this MT. This is going well.

"I suppose there's only one question remaining," I hear a male voice say from the doorway behind me. I know immediately it's Mr. Upper-Crust from the elevator because I catch a whiff of his astronomically pricey Creed cologne. Or perhaps that's just his disdain I smell.

Maybe it's not going so well.

"Do share with us, Clarissa, what your thoughts are on the Federal Reserve's current monetary policy of extended bond buying, and what affect you expect such a policy might have on the nation's long-term economic forecast?"

Seriously? What are my thoughts on the Federal Reserve?

"Clarissa, this is Dartmoor Millburn," MT says. "He's our financial editor."

"We met," I say dully and smile. As Dartmoor glides to the chair beside mine, I can feel the ambition radiating from him. It's ridiculously apparent how much he wishes he were the one seated before that window instead of MT. I kind of wish he were, too. Then I could push him out.

"Druscilla printed me a copy of your résumé," he explains, waving it in the air and crossing his long legs. He settles in with a piercing gaze from that baby face of his, looking ready to begin the Spanish Inquisition. "Sadly, I see nothing on this piece of paper to indicate you have an iota of financial expertise. And we aim to the highest standard for financial news on our website, Internet zine, start-up venture thing," Dartmoor says, fumbling for words, then smiles, trying to reclaim his composure. Clearly he hasn't quite adapted to his own digital transition.

"Perhaps," he suggests dismissively, "you should try Jezebel or PopSugar."

Perhaps you should try removing that big ol' cricket bat you've got stuck up your ass.

I don't say that out loud, though.

Unfortunately, the only thing I know about the Fed's monetary policy is that I don't have any. Money, that is. Judging by Dartboy's smug expression, he knows, too.

And there it is! The kernel of a notion reveals itself to me. Well, it's worth a shot.

"You know," I begin, "I can understand why you ask about

the Fed, and it *is* important for your readers, but financial reporting shouldn't be just for people who trade hedge funds and drive Lambos and Jags." I watch MT to see if this is working. "It should also be for people who have a panic attack every time they use their debit card. After all, *these people* are the demo that has the most to learn from Nuzegeek." I've got MT on the corner of her white-gold Herman Miller Aeron chair. "I think Nuzegeek shouldn't just cover the people who *have* money, but also people *without*, and in that case, I'm fully qualified, because I understand that problem quite well. That's literally my point-oh-two cents."

"Love it!" MT cries, slapping her palms on the desk and standing. "Love, love, love it. I think that's exactly what our bloody readers want and it's a prized demo that we can build brand loyalty with."

Dartmoor narrows his eyes and a little smile creeps into one corner of his mouth. Despite the fact that the guy is a total snob, I have to admit that he *is* pretty dreamy. Not devil-may-care cute like Sam, or suave and scruffy like Nick, but definitely sexy in a *GQ*-meets-*Forbes* sort of way.

He knows my idea is a great angle. He just hates that it's *my* angle.

"Dartsy dear, I didn't know a hedge fund from a hedge*hog* when I founded this company," MT reminds him. "I think Clarissa deserves a shot." I'm fascinated watching them exchange glances. Despite MT's cutesy nickname for Dartmoor and coy self-deprecating anecdote, which I am certain isn't true, I can see that Dartmoor, aka Dartsy, has just received a massive mind meld from MT. She's the boss and he knows it. He chooses another tack.

"Very well," he decrees. "I think we can all agree to a one-article tryout. I'll expect a detailed pitch by the end of the week."

Why do I feel like I was just challenged to a duel at thirty paces?

CHAPTER 11

In the hall, Dartmoor scuttles up behind me, leans close, and growls in a whisper, "Over my dead body are you getting this job."

I stop in my tracks and turn so suddenly he stumbles to avoid crashing into me.

"Guess those thousand-dollar John Lobb brogues aren't built for traction, huh, *Dartsy*?"

Druscilla looks up from the French manicure she's giving herself. I can tell by her expression that people around here don't usually talk to Sir Dartmoor like this. Somewhere in my interview skills database I know I shouldn't be standing off against the guy who holds my future in his hands. But he's just threatened me, and I won the first round in MT's office.

"Just be forewarned that I will be scrutinizing the economic underpinnings of whatever drivel you write to ascertain for a certainty that you don't besmirch this publication." He *is* kind of cute when he gets mad, and you gotta love a guy who can say "besmirch" with a straight face.

"Why do you feel this need to blackball me?" I demand. "You just met me. I can't imagine you're threatened by little ol' me?"

"Obviously you have no experience," Dartmoor counters,

trying to recover his waspy calm as he adjusts his silk Charvet. "But I have bigger concerns."

"Such as?"

"Genetics." He gives me a smug look.

It takes me a minute to figure this out. When I do, I get a little queasy. He's seen my résumé, he knows my last name. I'm betting he was late to the meeting because he Googled me, discovering I'm related to the infamous Ferguson Darling. I feel my shoulders go slack.

"My brother?"

"Yes," he hisses, "and I refuse to let your family name sully the reputation of this news . . . web . . . zine . . . thing, whatever it is."

Suddenly I'm wondering how quickly I could turn that pricey necktie into a noose.

"Ever hear of a little thing called civil rights?" I shoot back. "I'm sure you know it's against the law to refuse to hire someone based on a relative's rap sheet."

I have no idea if this qualifies as job discrimination, but it should. Since Dartmoor doesn't challenge it, I barrel on.

"Better be ready, you preppy, baby-faced elitist," I say, my voice rising to a threatening pitch. "I'm going to write such an amazing article it will be impossible for MT *not* to hire me. Not even if Michael Milken was my great-grandfather! Not even if Bernie Madoff was my favorite uncle. Not even if Jordan Belfort was my sugar daddy!" God, did I really just say that?

I stomp to the elevator, congratulating myself on such a scathing retort. Maybe I know more about this financial shit than I thought. But after the doors close, I try to cool off and realize I'm shaking. Closing my eyes, I can't believe how angry I am at that little twerp.

Not Dartboard Razorburn or whatever his name is. A different little twerp. The twerpiest twerp ever to walk the planet, who has been a major burr in my butt since the day he was born: my little brother.

Fergwad ruins my life . . . again!

CHAPTER 12

So here's the skinny on my detestable little sib: If Ferguson was precocious as a child, he became downright unstoppable as a young adult.

Fergbreath turned out to be smarter than any of us even knew. He received a full scholarship to the Sanford and Skilling College of Business and Commerce and was recruited by a Wall Street brokerage firm even before he earned his degree.

Ferguson quickly made headlines for being the youngest broker ever to rock a Bluetooth headset. He dazzled the suits down there on the tip of Manhattan Island, and for a brief moment, I was actually proud of my kid brother. He'd grown up and he was making a name for himself in the world of high finance. Despite his being a right-leaning free-market fanatic, we'd get together now and then, occasionally meeting for brunch. He'd tell me about some industry award he'd just won or the supermodel he was hooking up with named Veracruz. I would sip my mimosa and admire my baby brother in a whole new light. We were both enjoying life as young, successful, upwardly mobile New York professionals who'd been lucky enough to nail our dream jobs.

But nothing is good enough for that little twerp. He always

has to walk the crooked line. The new and improved version of Fergface didn't last long.

One morning I was at work going over the weekly column with Hugh when Tom Burkenhalter, one of the paper's financial analysts, knocked on Hugh's door and wanted to know if I had a comment.

"About what?" I asked, thinking he was pulling my leg.

"About your brother going to prison," he said.

That's when I knocked over Hugh's cherished "I AM the Liberal Media" coffee mug. And Hugh, God love him, looked up from behind those reading glasses of his, put a comforting hand on my shoulder, and kept it there while the idiot analyst persisted. Fortunately, the coffee cup was empty. As you probably know by now, I consider it bad luck to spill. One of about a half dozen other serious superstitions I regularly adhere to.

MY EVER-GROWING LIST OF SUPERSTITIONS

1. Spilling coffee = bad luck.
2. Cheese you spray from a can = bad luck.
3. When your path is crossed by a walk-around character with saucers for eyes = bad luck.
4. Buying paintings by a celebrity = bad luck.
5. Leaving hair in the tub after a bath = bad luck.

6. Not smearing your name on your birthday cake = very bad luck.
7. Anything gold = bad luck.
8. Bad taste = bad luck.

"You're sure you don't have anything to say about the fact that your one and only sibling has just been accused of losing seven hundred million dollars in a single day?"

"All right, Burkenhalter, you're not interrogating my assistant like this," Hugh said. "And I'm holding you personally responsible for my broken coffee mug. It was a present from Dick Cheney."

"Take it easy, Hugh, I just thought I'd give Clarissa a chance to comment on the fact that her brother will be the youngest person ever sent to prison for insider trading."

Good old Fergwad. Aim high, right? Go big or go home. Or, in this case, go to jail. Go directly to jail without passing Go. Coxsackie Correctional Facility, to be precise. It's a maximum-security joint usually reserved for the most violent of criminals. This place has it all—armed guards, barbed wire, electrified fence, the whole bit—and as far as I know, no Ping-Pong or croquet.

I'm sure you're asking why a white-collar criminal with no priors would be sentenced to time in the hellhole that is Coxsackie, as opposed to one of those country club prisons where they let you remove your electronic ankle bracelet so it doesn't interfere with your tennis lessons.

Well, because like all Ferguson-related catastrophes, this one had an unusual twist: The seven hundred million buckaroos he'd "mismanaged" were part of a series of trades at the recently formed hedge fund where he worked, Red City Securities. Only

Red City was a front for the Russian Mafia. As you might imagine, those comrades are not an especially forgiving bunch. They were *nyet* happy about Ferguson's sleight of hand.

When the SEC brought its case, Ferguson claimed he had no idea Red City was actually part of the Bratskaya Semyorka, or the "Brotherhood of Seven," as they were known by INTERPOL. He swore he thought the comrades were speaking Swedish and vehemently denied knowledge of the hedge fund having any nefarious Cossack connections. Then he wet his pants.

I think it was the pee stain on the front of Ferg-a-felon's Brooks Brothers khakis that ultimately earned the judge's pity. In order to sentence my brother for his crimes and protect him from the Russian Mafia, the judge sent him to Coxsackie, instead of those plush Club Fed prisons like Lompoc or Butner. It wasn't that Judge Richards was worried about Ferg breaking *out*; on the contrary, he was convinced the grudge-holding Mafiya Razboyniki would make every conceivable effort to break *in*. And, ya know . . . kill Ferg in his sleep. Something I've thought about every day of my life.

The day they sent my brother up the river was crazy. My mother assembled a little care package of tofu snacks to take, as if he were going to summer camp instead of being incarcerated for the better part of his young adult life.

Through it all, Dad was Ferguson's biggest supporter. He still believed Ferguson was innocent. Dad and I stood in the courtroom like statues, watching the bailiff cuff my brother and take him away.

"He'll be okay," Dad said, trying to convince himself.

"Sure, he's Ferguson," I told Dad, trying to cheer him up, "as in 'the devil,' 'Beelzebub,' 'force of evil.' The inmates will probably elect him class president or something."

"Hope so, Sport," Dad whispered. "He's still a redheaded little boy to me." I could see he was tearing up. I also vividly remember the aforementioned Veracruz standing behind us, sobbing her head off, crying out that she'd wait for Ferguson forever. I found that touching, until the following week when she appeared on the cover of *People* magazine cuddling the lead singer of the latest boy band, Side Street Boyz, showing off her new six-carat engagement ring.

That was the last time I'd seen my little brother. Eighteen months ago.

As I burst through the main lobby of the Nuzegeek building into the warm afternoon air, I knew exactly what I needed to do.

CHAPTER 13

After a change of clothes and a pit stop at the Korean deli for some Reese's peanut butter cups, I pick up the nearest Zipcar and head upstate. The only thing harder than getting out of the Coxsackie Correctional Facility is getting into it—for visitors, anyway.

At the gates, my chartreuse rental is thoroughly searched by uniformed guards. Once I'm through the front door, I hand over my clutch to a hefty woman who rifles through it as though it's done something to offend her. When she's finished manhandling my vintage Gucci wallet and my Apocalips lipstick (correction: Jody's lipstick), she flings the purse back at me and points to the plastic grocery bag I'm holding.

"Whatcha got in there?"

A cake with a file in it. Duh. Fortunately, I don't say that.

"Peanut butter cups. For my brother. They're his favorite."

With teeny-tiny files in them, I think, but I don't say that either. I open the bag. She pokes her nose in, then nods and motions toward the metal detector. Thankfully my cloisonné bangles don't set off any sirens. I silently vow that if anyone so much as utters the words *cavity search*, I'm leaving. There are some things I simply won't do for my brother.

Before I know it, another stern-faced guard (male this time) is leading me to the visitation room. It's a large open space, eerily reminiscent of a high school cafeteria, with tables and chairs set up at polite distances from each other. I sit at an empty table near the window (which is embedded with heavy-duty chicken wire) and wait.

This probably goes without saying, but I really don't like prison.

It smells weird, for one thing. Nobody smiles, for another. The floors squeak under my shoes and there's a nearly palpable sense that somewhere there's a guillotine about to drop. And why the hell aren't there any curtains? Curtains would totally soften this place up.

Okay, I'm rambling. But it's just because I'm nervous and I'm pretty mad at Fergwad that I even have to be here. But mostly nervous, bordering on terrified because even if I've done nothing wrong, I always feel slightly guilty when I'm in places like police stations, customs lines, even the DMV, not to mention prison.

Guillotine Ambience

Insufficient Drapes

There's no getting around the fact that there are people in this building who have committed unspeakable acts. Some judge in a black robe banged his or her gavel and declared them guilty. While I wait in this nerve-deadening place for my little brother, I wonder what he'll be like now. Weepy? Broken? Humble? Can I really be angry with him when his situation is so dire?

I try to control my nerves by thinking how transgressions, legal and moral and even my anger at Ferguson, exist on a spectrum ranging from little guilty pleasures to broken commandments.

For some reason those hair color sample charts they show you down at Sally Hershberger's salon come to mind and I calm myself by making a mental mash-up of guilt versus hair color choices.

I have the irresistible urge to cut my bangs while I'm waiting, but the sharpest thing in my pocketbook is an eyeliner brush. Then maybe I'm guilty of not taking this prison thing seriously enough.

That reminds me: My split ends could totally use a trim. I'm jonesing to dial up Bumble and Bumble, but my pocketbook won't let me. Maybe someday after I pay the Con Ed bill. For now I'll just pick at them, part of my unfortunate love affair with pulling apart my split ends when I'm stressed. Not a full-blown case of trich (short for trichotillomania) but enough for me to know I've got to stop. Piper and Jody do the same thing. Sometimes when we're together we'll all be chatting away; then we'll stop talking and silently pick at our hair.

A plaintive wail shatters my inner monologue. What the eff was that? I'm simply not prepared for this hard-knock prison life. Even as a visitor my nerves are totally on edge. Don't ask why, but it reminds me of the time Jody pierced her own belly button at my house without warning me.

Across the room, I see this enormous guy with the words DEATH SQUAD tattooed across his knuckles weeping like a baby holding what I imagine are divorce papers. I assume that's his wife, sitting on the other side of the table with her arms crossed, looking like she doesn't care. I'm riveted by this drama until I hear a familiar voice.

"Yo, C."

I turn to see my brother. At least, I *think* it's my brother. He's shackled at the wrists and ankles, being escorted by two guards, each of whom outweighs him by, like, a zillion pounds.

As much as I want to throttle him myself, I'm taken aback.

They know his crime was of the paper variety, don't they? Do they honestly think my little brother is physically dangerous?

Whoa. Wait. Is that a do-rag he's wearing?

He smiles at me and that's when I see the gold cap on his front tooth.

They sit him down in the chair across from mine. Ferguson's eyes dart sideways, determining whether the coast is clear, then he quickly slips something to one of the burly guards.

I recognize the item as one of Mom's tofu cookies. Is that what actually passes for a bribe around here? That wouldn't have even worked at home in high school. Man, this place is more depressing than I thought.

He leans across the table and smiles.

"Wuz up, my sis-tuh," he croons pretty loud considering I'm sitting twelve inches in front of him. Then he lowers his voice to a whisper. "Yo, don't mind the chains. They're my fix so I don't come across like Snow White, if you dig what I'm diggin'. Makes them homies think I'm a badass. They keeps their distance that way—well, most of the time anyway."

I grin. That's Ferg-face. Always thinking.

Now he sort of lounges back in his chair, hips forward, shoulders slanted, head tilted and bobbing as he purses and unpurses his lips.

"Ferguson, what's with the new . . . uh . . . prison demeanor?"

"Just fittin' in, aight?"

It's jarring, to say the least. As a kid, the closest Ferg ever came to joining a gang was when he signed up for Beaver Patrol at summer camp.

Across the room, the soon-to-be ex-wife stands up, snaps her fingers, and tells the Death Squad guy that he better be able to pay his damn alimony. Then she flips him off and baby-steps a getaway across the linoleum on her six-inch stilettos.

Poor Death Squad is sobbing as the guards help him up from his chair. He's shackled, too, but something tells me it's not the result of a cookie barter. As he shuffles past, he stops crying long enough to check me out.

"Ferg, man. This fine piece o' ass yo' baby mama?"

Eww.

"Nah, bro. She be my sister."

The big guy manages a nod and gives me a wink. "Yo. Nice."

For the life of me I have no idea how to respond. The only

thing that comes to mind is "Word to ya muthah," but that summons up images of white rappers in parachute pants and I really don't want to embarrass myself. Why I care about looking cool to a member of the Death Squad is beyond me, but there it is.

The guards drag him off. Ferguson and I are alone. Despite my rage, I can't help feeling bad for the annoying ginger.

"I'm sorry I didn't come sooner," I say.

"No worries."

"Are you okay? I mean, is this really as depressing as it seems? And what happened to your tooth?"

"Nah, da tooth is fo show." Ferguson pulls off the gold veneer to show it's removable. "It is what it is, yo. Besides, I got me a good hustle."

"I'm not exactly fluent in prison jive," I remind him. "You're going to have to translate."

Ferguson leans in. "I'm makin' bank in here, yo." Ferguson scans the room then adds in a whisper, "I started up a niche dating service. I help the incarcerated lovelorn find eligible mates on the outside. You'd be surprised how many gay white dudes with an Evangelical twist have trouble hooking up. Totally underserved."

"That's great," I say, trying to be positive despite the fact that I am totally appalled. Ferguson sure is a go-getter, even here.

He nods and crosses his hand over his chest in a half-wave, half-pumping motion, rapper sign language for "Word," I believe.

"So whachoo doin' here?" he asks, his voice loud again for show, I assume. "E'rething cool at home or what?"

"It's been better," I admit. "You know,

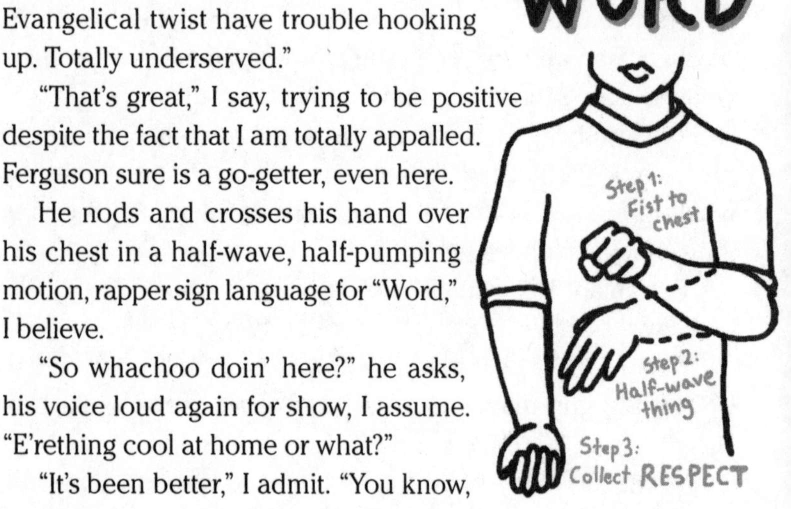

Mom and Dad are still separated, and Dad still needs a job. I saw them last week. Dad's loopy, totally depressed."

"Tell Pops it's all good," says Ferguson. "Soon as I get sprung I gawn' set him up in bid'niss."

"Bid'niss?"

"You remembers Dad's Fryfel Tower in the shape of a french fry container and all his whacked buildings?"

I shake my head, remembering the pickle-shaped pickle factory he built for Glosen's Pickles and his final and most bizarre architectural offering: an enormous round, white building for the Peoria Ping-Pong Ball Factory, which he designed to be built entirely out of Ping-Pong balls.

Let's face it, Dad's genius was unrecognized. He was the Claes Oldenburg of architecture and maybe that was his downfall—he was in the wrong business. He was so idealistic about creating "architecture for the people," instead of the people who paid him. How could he believe that companies would actually keep building those things? If he had become a conceptual artist like Jeff Koons, who knows where he'd be now. When we were growing up, Dad was the hottest industrial design architect in Ohio. That was before the Great Recession, before the entire economy went on a disastrous moneymoon and we all became financially and emotionally fragile.

The recession wiped out his client base. Commercial real estate developers could no longer afford whimsical and eccentric designs, so work became scarce, and that's why he's where he is today. Insult was added to injury when he learned that those miniature models for his crazy building designs had become collectors items and were sold in some ultra-chic design store in Soho for more than he was ever paid to make the actual buildings. Fryfel sold for one hundred grand and Dad didn't see a penny of it.

"How could I forget, Ferg?"

"Well, when I get outta here, I'm gawn' have cash to set him up. Then he can design all the crazy-ass models he want, and we gawn' sell dem motherfuckers on Q to the V to the C, for realz. I'm gawn' mass-market them online for kiddies. I'm already down with the Lego guys." I couldn't help wondering if he meant the actual little plastic figures.

As bid'ness aspirations went, this one sounded a little chancy to me. Not that I couldn't picture a Lego pickle. But I guess anything that would get Dad back on his feet was worth trying. Then again, we had all been played by Ferguson's schemes before, and that was what brought me here.

Ferguson's shenanigans had clearly caused me a problem with my only potential job prospect at the moment. As much as I wanted to make him pay, I also figured he owed me something and could help me, considering I had so little experience in writing about the financial sector.

"Look, Ferg, I'm glad you still have your little scams and fantasies, but because of your crimes you've put our whole family into an upheaval and a job prospect of mine in jeopardy."

Ferguson's goofy prison demeanor vanishes straightaway, only to be replaced by the saddest expression I've ever seen on his annoying freckled face. He heaves a heavy sigh that yields to a despair that makes me worry about him. His head droops quietly for a few moments.

"I'm sorry, sis," he finally says, looking up at me, and it's probably one of the few times I've seen the two strangers—reality and Ferguson—meet.

"It's okay. I need advice," I say.

"*Prishli mne kapustu*," he deadpans. I blink, not having a clue what he's said. "It means, 'Don't let the Mafia get your cabbage' in Russian. I did learn a few phrases. That's the best advice I got."

"Duly noted. But what I could really use is some financial background," I say, taking out a small spiral pad from my clutch. "See, I've got this new job and there's this total jerkwad Dartmoor Millburn . . . ever heard of him?"

"The name sounds familiar but it's been a while since I've been on the street or even seen a *WSJ*," Ferg says.

"Well, bottom line is I'm in a little over my head, and considering you've had some, uh, special experience . . ." I give him a sisterly grin. "And who better to get it from than the Wiz Kid of Coxsackie Prison?"

Ferguson sits up a little straighter. He tugs the do-rag off to reveal his completely bald head. I try not to stare but I totally do. I'm not sure whether he's shaved it because of prison regulations, or if the stress of incarceration has led to premature hair loss, or if it's simply a bad case of nits. In any case, it's an oddly good look for him—tough and no-nonsense, kind of like a miniature Vin Diesel, if Vin had bright orange eyebrows and a face full of freckles.

"Consider the class in session," Ferguson says in a professional tone.

For the next two hours, I grill my notoriously brilliant brother on all things financial. Ferguson had to fork over another three tofu cookies to buy extra time, and I'm surprised at what a patient and thorough teacher he is. It's amazing what you know when you've been on both sides of the law. And his analysis of Occupy Wall Street and *Too Big to Fail* would make Paul Krugman stand up and applaud. I guess you learn all the angles when you play the system.

When it's time to leave, I reach into my plastic bag and remove the pack of Reese's peanut butter cups. Ferguson's face immediately brightens and, for a moment, I see a glimpse of the dorky adolescent underneath all his streetwise bravado.

"Thanks," he says, reaching for them. "You know how much toilet paper a guy can buy with these babies?"

My heart sinks. That is *so* not why I brought them, but I guess Ferguson's world is different now. He can see the look in my eye and he leans in to whisper to me.

"Don't worry, I'm getting out of the joint soon," he says,

scanning the room. “My lawyer has an awesome plan to turn this frown upside down. Fo’shizzle.”

I give him a big awkward hug considering we can’t actually embrace with all those metal chains in the way.

“I hope so. Take care, Ferguson. I’ll see you soon, okay?” I whisper. “I’ll tell Mom and Dad you’re doing well.”

“Peace, yo. Luv to Moms and Pops,” he says with a rapper’s fist pound to his chest ending in a two-finger salute.

As I make my way back to the Zipcar, I note the violent loops of barbed wire that top the fence and decide I’m going to write this article and secretly dedicate it to Fergface. It’s going to be the best example of investigative financial journalism Nuzegeek has ever seen.

And Dartmoor Millburn, that mofo punk-ass cracker, ain’t gawn’ know what hit him, yo.

CHAPTER 14

After a week of blurry-eyed research for my Nuzegeek pitch utilizing Fergwad's impromptu "Finance for Dummies" seminar, I had vastly increased my financial awareness. Still, I knew I had to find a story that was good enough to convince MT and hold up to Dartmoor's grilling. Only something stellar and totally Nuzegeekian would suffice, and it would have to firmly identify the website with MT's hoped-for demographic. Sitting at my computer I fly through some less-than-stellar "people with no money" ideas like:

I actually researched that last one. There's this guy who raises grass-fed rabbits for meat because bunnies are cheap and nutritious. It's just that bunny burgers are kind of a downer for your preschooler when it comes to their Happy Meal.

In other words, my results at the moment: nada, zip, zero. At least nothing that I can truly stand behind as I endure Dartmoor's withering criticisms. Where am I going to find a lead?

I think of Hugh Hamilton, my late mentor, and try to channel some of Hugh's gruff advice, specifically on what to do when you get stuck for a story.

Hugh hovers over me like the Ghost of Journalism Past. "New York City is your story," he growls. "Get out on the streets. There's a story in every gutter, every bodega, and every body bag. If you're stuck, take a walk and buy a hot dog. Preferably one with lots of mustard, onions, and double kraut." Phew! These occasional visions of Hugh are scary, but they do the trick.

A change of scenery will probably do me good, and who am I to disregard the advice of a dead legend? So I stop pounding my poor, overworked laptop and head out.

Slipping on my 1977 Pappagallo flats, I stroll uptown. It's nice to be moving at a leisurely pace, because that's something that happens so rarely in New York. I meander past the St. John's campus, and make my way toward the West Village, home to the High Line and Magnolia bakery, where I treat myself to a lemon cupcake, knowing full well my mother would consider this a nutritional rebellion of the highest degree.

Wandering on, letting ideas for potential articles ferment in my brain, I pass a prosecco bar. I look up at the banner for Ciao Ragazza, a new restaurant that proudly hails itself as "the perfect place for DIY brunch." That's basically what we used to call a buffet, right?

Peering through the windows, I see fashionable New Yorkers with their toddlers crammed into CBGB T-shirts standing around a bar making fresh juices with toss-ins like berries, and a tray of mixers, acting as their own mixologists. I'm surprised it isn't Bring Your Own Prosecco. When did the term *DIY*, which used to signify a punk rock spirit of independent creativity, become so gentrified?

It dawns on me that this could be a pretty cool story. Not the prosecco place, but DIY. Not only does it exemplify all the basic principles of the free market economy that Fergface drilled into my head, but DIY is also Economy 101 that every young Nuzegeek reader might understand.

I remember Charley's Cook Your Own back in Springfield where we could cook our own steak for twenty-eight dollars. Dad loved that place. Now that was DIY before its time, and a great break from Mom's tofu. But I've always wondered: If you have to cook your own food, shouldn't it cost less? I mean, would you pay Camp Canine to let you wash your own labradoodle? Or fork over cash to Acme Car Wash and detail your own car?

I can understand picking your own strawberries and preripping your jeans. If you're homeless, a cardboard box might be what passes for DIY housing. And first-time New Yorkers know that DIY furnishings are what you find on the street.

But I'm also thinking: There's Kickstarter and Indiegogo, right? I've seen tons of blogs written by industrious millennials who've taken financial matters into their own hands by tapping into their passions and using them to turn a profit.

Clearly, the Do-It-Yourself trend is a viable business model and the people leading the charge are becoming entrepreneurs. Still, I don't want to be pitching the financial benefits of weaving your own doormats out of dog hair to Dartmoor. And I'm pretty sure a piece about a spa where you can massage yourself probably isn't going to fly. Then again, maybe if someone could find a way to distill Heineken Light backwash into automotive fuel that could power a Beemer convertible, Dartmoor would be interested.

I'm going to have to zero in on something fabulous.

Unfortunately, what I zero in on is the ultimate zero—Norm—and he's walking directly toward me.

I need to find someplace to hide, and quick.

CHAPTER 15

No joke. From where I'm standing I can see Norm, my very own ex-BF-cum-stalker, across the street reflected in the restaurant window. He's hanging out with a bunch of overage skater dudes.

With every fiber of my being, I do not want to see or be seen by Norm, so I do that stupid sitcom thing and duck into the next nearest doorway, which is some tiny Village cappuccino place.

I sit down in the far back corner and keep one eye on Norm across the street, waiting for him to move on. Slowly, I realize this is no random java station. I take a deep breath and remember that one of the most momentous moments of my life occurred here. This is Joe's Coffee. Why, you may be legitimately asking, does my entire love life revolve around coffee?

I don't know the answer to that question, but Joe's Coffee is a place I've kind of been avoiding for a while. My eyes dart across the wrought-iron tables to the very corner where it all changed between Sam and me, one autumn day almost a decade ago. Two best friends, childhood pals. Platonic to the extreme.

Across the room I see him entering now, just the way he looked that day, with his lush brown hair sticking up everywhere, his easy-to-read face with a stubble of beard and the way he smiled at me with his soft sleepy brown eyes.

That one image and it feels as though a trap door has opened beneath my feet and dropped me through time.

Sam was late and I had to get back to the paper. He was down from college, where he'd just started his sophomore year. My messenger bag was slumped beside me on the floor, filled with textbooks and notebooks for my night classes, and I'd had a draft of a small piece I was writing for the *Daily Post*—my first. It was short and I was hoping Sam would read it before I handed it in.

My internship with Hugh was in full throttle, so I'd had to jump through several fiery hoops to finagle this meager forty-five-minute furlough to meet Sam downtown. I remember that day feeling how lonely I was in the city, even with the beehive of a newsroom and Hugh being about the most demanding person I knew. There just wasn't anyone around who flat-out knew me. That's how it feels for the first few years after moving to New York.

You couldn't miss Sam coming through the door of the café. I'm surprised every girl there didn't stand up to claim him. At six foot two with broad surfer's shoulders, Sam stood out—a bright and fresh presence among all gloomy gray New Yorkers.

"Hey, Clarissa, how's it going?" he asked, folding himself into the tiny café chair.

"Awesome now that you're here," I offered and slid over the cappuccino I had waiting for him. Sam smiled graciously and shrugged off his jacket. Just seeing him sitting across from me, I could feel my breathing relax and deepen, like the missing piece of a puzzle had fallen into place.

"So how's it going?" I asked.

"School's crazy, but fun," he said, taking a long sip of his cappuccino.

"Like, a lot of work for all your classes?" I'm half envious that I didn't go to a normal college like everyone else, imagining Sam up there having a good time without all the ambitions and responsibilities I had burdened myself with.

"Yeah, that, too, but you'd think they just discovered the sexual revolution up there," Sam said, and I perked up. Kind of an odd subject to lead with, I thought. I could see he was a little uncomfortable. I guess he needed to talk about something so I figured I should dig a little further.

"Doesn't sound so bad on the face of it. What do you mean?" I don't know why, but I had to admit that Sam being up at that girls' school always bothered me ever so slightly. I hoped they appreciated him for who he was, but I put it out of my mind as none of my business.

"Well, it's a bit extreme. You can't believe how everybody is hooking up all over the place. Sometimes they barely know each other," he said.

That's my Sam, still a regular guy, the kind of guy you never see or hear about, that they never show on television in Super Bowl ads or in the movies. A red-blooded American boy, with raging hormones and all the proper working parts, but still the kind of guy who is thoughtful, soft, genuine, and put off by inappropriate stuff.

"Weird—I suppose having oodles of sex with random strangers is one of the rites of passage you forgo by choosing a job over full-time college," I said with a dollop of regret, thinking how it was pretty hard for me to relate. All things considered, I figured I could live without having to buy home pregnancy tests and whatever antibiotics work best on STDs.

"Yeah. They take the 'liberal' in liberal arts pretty seriously up there, I guess, mainly because the boy-girl ratio is so out of whack."

Sam's freshman class included the first coed admissions to his college—a small, artsy school nestled into the foothills of the Adirondack Mountains. It had been one of very few all-women's colleges left in the country up until last fall, when the administration voted unanimously to admit men into the female student body (academically and literally, it would seem). Sam was one of only about thirty testosterone-bearing individuals on the entire campus.

"I guess the administration is just new at this, probably trying to rein it in," I said, assuming we all live in some kind of rational world.

"Are you kidding? You'd be surprised how many teachers are sleeping with students. There's one—this writing teacher I have—Betty Jo Carson. She's always playing with the buttons on her blouse when we meet in her office, pulling down the shades and kicking off her high heels." I could see how this might be more stressful for Sam than a lot of other guys. Yet I can also see why he's so appealing and why a woman on the prowl would have him in her sights.

"It's kind of like every room is a bedroom up there, if you know what I mean," he said.

"That may be the definition of 'dorm,'" I added.

"I don't know if it's that way at other schools."

"They should mention that in the college brochure for recruiting," I offered, trying to lighten things up and find a way to change the subject.

"Yeah, it's kind of weird. There aren't a lot of kids up there in the mountains. It's us and the bears."

Sam laughed a little awkwardly and there was a moment of silence that made me wonder why he was telling me this. Not that we didn't talk about anything and everything. But it seemed like something was on his mind. That's when it occurred to me that I knew very few details of Sam's sexual history, and I wondered why we had never talked about this kind of stuff before. Thankfully, Sam changed the subject.

"Hey, did you hear about the reunion party?" he asked.

"What reunion party?"

"How soon the famous forget," Sam chided. "Class reunion bash the day after Thanksgiving."

"A reunion at Tupper High?" I frowned. "Already? Isn't it

customary for those things to take place at the five-year mark, or better, after fifty? We all just graduated, like, five minutes ago."

"It's been a year," Sam corrected, annoyed, as if I was being some kind of snob. "It's a chance to see everyone again, considering you weren't even there at graduation. Besides, who cares what she's calling it?"

" 'She'?"

"Yeah, that's the only glitch." Sam gave me a sheepish look. "The party is being thrown by one of your least favorite people. Genelle."

"One of?"

Genelle Waterman did the best she could to make my last year of high school, well, let's say difficult. She didn't succeed, but I didn't mind when my internship started early and I had to skip graduation. It didn't sound exactly thrilling to reunite on her turf.

"Come on, that stuff is all in the past," Sam said. "Everyone wants to see you. Including me."

"I'll be home for the holiday," I reasoned aloud. "So I guess I could go."

"Yeah, what's the worst that can happen?" he said, more as a statement than a question.

Sam shoved his hair out of his eyes and when his hand came down to the table, it inadvertently landed on top of mine. It's a sensation I've felt a zillion times—Sam brushing against me in some accidental way, just part of how we communicate. We've always been easy with each other—his hand on my arm, my hand on his hand, casual touches here and there. It always happened when we talked. But this time it felt different. Kind of annoying, actually. Maybe it had to do with being far from home. I dismissed it at the time.

Our conversation slipped easily to my internship, and when he asked how I was doing at the paper, I reached into my bag and pulled out the article. He jumped right in and I watched him read, nodding, grinning, and knitting his brow at all the right places.

"Wow," he said. "This is amazing. You're, like, a real journalist. I like how you manage to lay out the facts, but still embed your own personal spin on the subject. That's so you."

I was about to thank him, but at that precise moment, his legs shifted under the table and brushed up against my knees. What were his knees doing here all the way on my side of the table? It was a stupid little bit of bodily contact, but something was unsettling about it in a way I hadn't expected. When did Sam get so tall and lanky?

"Sorry," I said, reflexively touching his knee again with my hand and moving to the side. But that touch felt like an even bigger deal and I knew in that second that something more was going on. Sam was surprised, too. This was definitely more than just me and Sam bumping knees . . . as friends.

"Hey, pal, put those knobby knees of yours back where they belong," I joked, trying to restore my equilibrium.

Sam's cool and careful, so he didn't say anything.

He's your best friend, I reminded myself. And then a thought exploded in my mind, like a piano being dropped on my head from a second-story window: *Can men and women be friends? I mean, can they really be just friends? Okay, yeah, Sam and I are a shining example . . . and yet . . .*

"You must have gotten taller," I observed, laughing.

"Yeah, that never happened back in the lunchroom at Tupper," he said, a little embarrassed.

"No," I awkwardly agreed.

Sam went to the counter for another cappuccino, and returned moments later with a paper cup emblazoned with the Joe's logo. I was a bit surprised that he ordered his beverage to go, but I guess he was playing it safe. I had to get back to Hugh anyway.

On the sidewalk, we said our good-byes.

I remember heading back to the paper thinking how Sam and I were the perfect team. Friends in the most complete sense. Still, I was trying to mentally decode the meaning of what had just happened. We're such perfect friends and we're perfect together—why aren't we . . . *together*? How many times had someone asked me that question? I must have touched his knee dozens of times before—but this time that act wasn't so much a matter of crossing the boundary between friendship and romance as erasing it. Two weekends later, at the Tupper High School reunion, everything changed.

"Yo, Clarissa!"

Who in this place knows my name? I wonder. Blinking out of my memory, I look up and blink again.

Shit.

Norm.

He's standing right in front of me, sucking up way too much of my personal space. I grimace.

"I never heard from you. Did you get the flowers I sent?" he asks. "You're not just letting ol' Norm hang out there to dry again, are you?"

I could scream. Not only am I *not* happy to see Norm, but I'm instantly reminded that one of Norm's most pathetic habits is that Norm insists on referring to himself in the pitiable third person. You'd think a copywriter trained by Hugh Hamilton would have known better than to get involved with someone who talks about himself in the third. Hugh would have eviscerated him. Yet another reason why Norm was such a colossal mistake.

"I did receive the flowers," I snarl at him and stand. "*And* the balloon-o-gram, *and* the Legume of the Month Club membership, *and* the official certificate notifying me that an endangered baby Sri Lankan elephant has been sponsored in my name."

Norm gives me a lazy, self-satisfied grin. "Thought thirty-two cents a day was a small price to pay to make you happy. Not to mention how comforting it must be for the baby elephant."

"Yes, and I gave them to the Kute Kritters Day Care on my street," I say, although I've never been sure if Kute Kritters is day care for kids or pets, but that doesn't matter right now.

"Norm, what is there about 'over' you can't understand?" I demand. I've said this to him more times than I can count, but, as usual, it doesn't seem to register. What did I ever see in this idiot? Oh, right . . . he's got abs you can grate cheese on.

He takes my hand and tugs me toward the door. "Come on, Clarissa. I want to show you something."

I pull my hand away, but follow him because it's the only way out and that's where I want to go. The old skater dudes are still hanging around outside. They're crossing the street heading toward us.

"See those guys? I just sold three of them five brand-new custom skate decks. Aging hipsters love 'em. You've got to see the new boards—they're awesome. I'm officially a business now, and ol' Norm is about to make some serious bank. I've got a major backer and my peeps doin' the gluin'. No more Gorilla Glue for me. Honest. I've sworn off it."

"Congratulations," I say dully, ignoring Norm's plea for redemption from our early skateboard-making debacle. I look for the best direction to dash. "Let's just be clear, we're still broken up—you have to get that through your head, okay?"

The aging hipsters join our little tête-à-tête and Norm makes his big play in front of them. "Aw, come on, Clarissa, give good ol' Norm another chance," he pleads. "You're the snappiest, most rad dudette I've ever met. How about you and ol' Norm take my new newfound cash and celebrate with a chow down? You're my queen, Clarissa, you know that."

I grind my teeth as they all turn to look at me. I postulate that if the rejection is spoken in Norm's native tongue, in front of his peer dude group, it might sink in, probably the one thing I haven't tried.

"No, Clarissa does not want to go out to dinner with poor ol' Norm. Clarissa and Norm are broken up, kaput, finished, and will never be getting back together, ever. Clarissa has a big job interview at the Seaport tomorrow, so Clarissa has a lot of work to do, which is why Clarissa is walking away from ol' Norm right now. Again. Forever."

I turn and make a fast exit, before any more pronoun-free conversation ensues.

"Whoa, dude, she just threw your heart on the ground and stomped all over it," I overhear one of the bearded *Big Lebowski*–ish hipsters say.

"Yeah, just shows she's pretty hung up on me," Norm responds.

Wonders never cease. I keep walking.

"See ya soon, babe," he calls after me.

Turning the corner, I hope it's just a figure of speech.

CHAPTER 16

On Thursday morning I'm back at Nuzegeek. I've chosen an outfit that will likely render Mr. Millburn apoplectic: a '70s-era cotton candy–pink jacket nipped in at the waist and a pair of jet-black, raw-silk, high-waisted, wide-legged trousers à la '70s YSL. I've secured my hair back from my face and wear a pair of round, wire-rimmed sunglasses, John Lennon–style. I'm pretty sure MT will approve. She may dress like a super-chic professional, but I'm betting she's a gal who appreciates fashion verve when she sees it. Dartmoor, that vulture, is waiting for me in front of MT's double doors. We exchange sneers and allow Druscilla to escort us in without comment.

Again, the white glare of MT's office flares before me, but this time, I'm ready for it. I smoothly lower the sunglasses to the bridge of my nose while Dartmoor stands there blinking manically until Druscilla works her magic with the push-button electric blinds. You'd think, after working here all this time, he'd be better prepared. It's a moment before his pupils return to normal size, and this gives me time to select the better chair closer to MT's white desk.

Point: Clarissa.

"Love the shades," says MT, her nude-glossed lips spreading into a smile.

"Thanks."

"Shall we get to the pitches?" Dartsy suggests in a snippy tone. "Finance for the trailer park crowd, was it?"

"My favorite auntie lives in a trailer park," says MT coolly. "Lovely double-wide just outside of Surrey."

Dartmoor shrivels a bit in his seat.

Point two: Clarissa.

I take a deep breath, decide not to give him time to recover and go into my song and dance.

"So, from Martha Stewart to the post-hipster demographic, the DIY economy is taking America by storm."

"Oh God, save us, DIY is so boring, tell me you're not going to write about making macramé suitcases?" Dartmoor snorts derisively, but I notice MT seems interested. Confidently I continue, describing my plan to bring a bit of this trendy DIY culture to Nuzegeek's readership by examining how a new breed of entrepreneurs will be impacting every sector of the economy. I provide the applicable statistics and trot out a slew of expert testimony documenting the influence of DIY on traditional modes of commerce and schools of thought in retail, thereby reinvigorating American capitalism.

Damn, I sound smart! And what's even better, I actually have stats and quotes from some of the most successful DIYers waiting in my briefcase, including their sales figures and projected earnings and all kinds of fancy, finance-y crap to fling in Dartsy's face. And speaking of which—I can see from his expression that he's recalibrating, aware now that he's underestimated me. Clearly, he's regrouping.

"Please, Clarissa, if you wouldn't mind, let us hear the specific sectors of the economy you're talking about?" Dartmoor challenges.

I give him a big, serpentine smile. There's nothing like overly polite hostility. I have to admit I kind of enjoy sparring with him.

"Well, let's start with the lodging sector and the thirty-six-room hotel being built from heavy-gauge steel cargo shipping containers on the east side of Detroit as part of the riverside reconstruction."

"Sounds uncomfortable," Dartmoor says, wincing. "Not sure we can run that anytime soon. We've just commissioned a series on new hotels. I'm sure our guys are covering that."

My ass, I think. *He's just trying to shoot me down.* But I smile sweetly and stifle the urge to scream, *Moron*!

MT gives me a patient smile; my cue to move on to the next pitch. She knows.

"Okay . . . well . . ." I muster my aplomb and sally forth. "Mason jars. Americans love 'em."

"I've never heard of him," Dartmoor sniffs. "Who is Mason Jars?" MT and I share a glance. Now we're both trying not to laugh.

"It's not a who, it's a what," I explain with exaggerated patience. "Old-fashioned glass jars that are used for making preserves and pickling food are appearing throughout every sector, repurposed in all kinds of clever ways at restaurants and bars, as storage containers, consumer packaging. It's environmentally conscious, recyclable, good old Americana, and more. Entrepreneurs behind the trend are cleaning up."

"Oh, goody," Dartmoor exclaims sarcastically, "we're going to do a story about jars. That's sexy."

MT throws me a glance that tells me this isn't worth fighting over.

"Anything else, Ms. Darling?" Dartmoor asks. "Or are you done wasting our time?" Dartmoor smiles, self-satisfied, like the Cheshire Cat in *Alice in Wonderland*, but I know it's all for show and he's just trying to bully me into giving in.

The problem is, I *am* kinda done—with one exception.

"You've got to understand," I say, more to MT than Dartsy, "I think Nuzegeek could be the webzine for a new generation of entrepreneurs. Even if every one of their products isn't scintillating, their ingenuity, creativity, and impact will be. These people and their followers could be a major part of your demographic."

MT perks up. I'm speaking her language and Dartmoor knows it. He realizes he's got to do something fast to shut me down and he senses a weakness.

"Well, that's a very nice idea, actually," he begins, "only that's not what you've shown us. I think perhaps we've heard all there is to hear."

"For today," MT amends. "I don't see any harm in giving Clarissa an extension to absorb our concerns."

"What? I hardly see why. She's had her shot. Besides interesting generalities, there's nothing here to discuss. We need reporters with real financial insight and *experience*. We have to put Nuzegeek first; we don't have time to babysit novice writers. Launch is in two months and our readers, viewers, Internet people, whoever they are will judge us instantly with their clicks and their mouses. We simply can't . . ."

But MT and I have stopped listening because even though Dartmoor is swooping down on me for the kill, there's some other kind of fierce commotion outside the towering mahogany doors and it sounds really weird.

Dartmoor finally notices that no one is paying attention to his coup de grâce performance and stops blathering. He stands to open the doors, and I believe if my entire career weren't on the line, I would collapse in shock.

Norm.

Standing right there before us is effin' stalker boy restrained in an eye-popping deadly-force chokehold at the capable hands of Druscilla. Is she MT's bodyguard as well? Does she have a degree in martial arts?

"Nobody gets in to see Miss Wilkinson without an appointment!" Druscilla yells as Norm struggles to break free.

This isn't happening, I tell myself. But it is. Norm has crashed my pitch meeting as if it were a college keg party. He's even *dressed* like it's a keg party, in cargo shorts, a brand-new T-shirt featuring his company's "All Decked Out" logo, and a pair of Vans.

I pull myself together. My job possibilities are likely hopeless. Not only have I failed to turn back Dartmoor's onslaught of objections, but at the moment where I was about to receive a reprieve, the most obnoxious male on the planet, the most baneful association I have ever made, has intruded and looks like he's choking on a hairball. There's nowhere to run and nowhere to hide. I'm so furious I feel like my head will explode, so I drop all pretense that a job is a possibility.

"What are you doing here?" I demand. "And how did you even know where I was?"

Druscilla loosens her grip enough to allow him to form words.

"Ol' Norm isn't as dumb as he looks," Norm says, gasping for air. Definitely a debatable assertion. "You told me."

I did?

"Excuse me," Dartmoor intrudes, utterly pleased by the turn of events. "Who is Norm?"

I'm tempted to say, "He's a friend of Mason Jars," but I resist and stay focused on the idiot who is being physically restrained by MT's able administrative assistant. I still can't figure out how he could have possibly known to show up at Nuzegeek.

"I only told you I had an interview," I say. "I never said *where*." I stop for a minute and rewind to our fleeting encounter at Joe's.

"You said the Seaport!" Norm proudly reports. "Which is why I've been to every office in every building on every block down here. Good thing I had my board, otherwise it would have taken me forever. I might have missed you." I notice his intricately designed custom deck, leaning against the file cabinet. Wow. It's pretty cool. No wonder people are buying them. He's come a long way since our permanent-Twister days.

The phone rings and Druscilla is flummoxed. She doesn't seem to know what to do. MT nods and like a bull terrier following her master, she releases Norm from the headlock to answer the phone.

That's when I notice something strange: MT's eyes are locked on Norm, looking hungrily at his shaggy hair, movie-hero facial features, and skater's physique. Hmmm. I wonder . . . and begin to formulate a plan, but before I can say a word, the situation gets worse.

Norm, free from Drusy's chokehold, with oxygen unfortunately restored to his poor, challenged brain cells and blood rushing to his vocal cords, drops to his knees in front of me, his eyes filled with a psychosis that passes for "love" and that Norm would pathetically call "hope."

"Clarissa Marie Darling . . . will you marry me?"

"Oh my," MT gasps, moved by pure emotion. She clasps her hands to her heart and I think she might do something ridiculously British, like swoon.

"This is too good," Dartmoor says with a satisfied smile, excited beyond belief by my humiliation. He looks like he's on the verge of having a spontaneous orgasm.

"MT, as entertaining as this is, please, do we really want someone who associates with this kind of nut job working here at Nuzegeek?" he says, but MT isn't listening. She can't seem to see beyond the kneeling nut job's handsome cheekbones.

"Norm, you're embarrassing me," I say evenly, managing to recover my cool. "You shouldn't have come here. We're not together. We're not a couple. I'm not going to marry you no matter how many times you ask."

He looks at me in genuine shock. How he seems truly surprised each and every time, even though I've turned him down over and over again, is absolutely a wonder of denial that neuroscientists should explore.

"It's because you think ol' Norm's broke, isn't it? You think ol' Norm will never amount to anything, admit it!" he pleads.

I shake my head, wondering how many times I've had to explain. I'm about to answer, but ol' Norm is on a roll.

"Do you realize how many aging hipsters are out there willing to put out big bucks for my decks?" Norm says and makes a "hang loose" hand sign. "I'm rolling. Babe, I'm ready to level up big-time."

"Norm, it's not about money or your career possibilities. Really, we had our chance, it's over," I answer as quietly and compassionately as possible, thoroughly embarrassed and saddened that all of this is playing out in front of my only current job prospect. I really had a chance here, even if I was desperately fighting for a foothold. I prepare to apologize to MT for even thinking I might have a job at Nuzegeek and hope to go home and cry into my pillow as soon as possible.

"Okay, okay, as exquisitely entertaining as this is, it's time for *some* of us to get back to work," Dartmoor intercedes like he's everyone's father.

"Hey, suit dude," Norm calls out to Sir Dartmoor, "you should cool out and get down with my biz-i-ness. You might want to buy one of my boards. Even straight stiffies like yourself are getting into it." I stifle a laugh. I hate to say it, but I don't think Norm is right about Dartmoor. He probably sleeps with his tie on.

"Look, Norm, I'm sure your little skateboard company will sell a few boards in Astoria, Queens, or wherever the rock you live under is, but we have a website to run and . . ."

"You guys have a website? Whoa! Clarissa didn't say anything about that. I've got to tell Bezos about you folks, maybe he'd throw some money your way. Those Amazon suits are putting down real bucks for me," Norm says and honestly, I figure he's out of his mind, but I have to find out.

"Bezos as in Amazon?" I ask.

"Yeah, just got the confirmation this week," Norm says and pulls out a piece of paper. "It's some DIY support thing they're doing. That Bezos baldie is opening an online store for my decks and droppin' down serious cash investing in ol' Norm here. Considering they're a company of nerdheads in suits, those dudes are pretty cool. Hey, did you know they publish books and make

TV shows now? I hear he's even bought a newspaper." Whoa, I forgot about that.

I grab his piece of paper and I'm reading it, totally floored that it is, in fact, signed by none other than Jeff Bezos. You'd think he'd have someone else to do the actual signing for him. Without warning, a voice comes whispering into my head. It's Sam's voice, speaking to me from the past, from Joe's Coffee, years earlier: *"I like how you lay out the facts, but still put your own personal spin on the subject."*

I stare at Norm with his ab-hugging new logo T-shirt and his letter from Jeff Bezos at Amazon and I know in an instant exactly how to score this gig. Lucky for me, Norm is an irrefutable example that the DIY approach can be profitable. And he is the profile that makes it a story. A story I know personally.

"Actually," I say, turning to MT, "I don't need an extension. *This* is my pitch."

Dartmoor and MT look a tad baffled. And why not? My "pitch" is still on his knees in front of MT's office.

"But what about the marriage proposal?" MT asks, genuinely disappointed at this sudden shift back to business. "That was so romantic." She still has her eyes locked on my former BF, so I figure I'd better act fast.

"All Decked Out is Norm's DIY venture, and, as you can see by this handsome logo tee, Norm's DIY has become quite a big deal despite these unforgiving and trying economic times. Therefore, as the first in my *series* of DIY articles, I would like to profile Norm and his company."

The words trip off my tongue eloquently as I explain to the dreamy-eyed MT and the scowling Dartmoor my plan to present a "trials and tribulations" account of Norm's rise to skateboard notoriety and success. I finish by indicating the still-kneeling Norm with an exaggerated *Wheel of Fortune* spokesmodel arm flourish.

"So what do you think?"

MT is still gazing at Norm, who has remained steadfastly in proposal mode.

"Oh, I do," she answers on a sigh. "I do." Then she catches herself, realizing what everyone else is thinking, and stammers, "Um . . . what I mean is, yes, I do *like it.* Quite a lot, in fact. It's brilliant. You're hired."

"Thank you!" I say, grabbing clueless Norm under his arms and hoisting him to his feet.

"Wait!" Dartmoor says. "Don't I have anything to say about this?"

"Of course you do," says MT, "as long as it's 'Welcome to the staff, Clarissa.' "

Dartmoor seethes, but I couldn't care less. I'm hired.

And weirdly enough, I owe it all to Norm, his skateboard obsession, and his Kutcher-esque cheekbones. Still, I don't want to risk him doing anything weirder than he already has, so I'm ready to wrap this up.

"Well," I say, "Norm and I had better get going."

"Must you?" MT says, clearly only giving a damn as to whether Norm must. I smile and nod yes. "Oh, I understand—I assume you must," she adds wistfully, her upper-crust training kicking back in. You never know, she might even think there's still some kind of spark between Norm and me.

"Yep, ol' Norm has to go back to work," I say, trying to put some distance between Norm and the idea that we're together.

"Norm does?" he asks bewildered, finally realizing that MT's eyes are fixated on him, and he's looking back at her realizing for the first time certain other possibilities.

"Actually, I'm sure Norm would be free for lunch some time," I mention offhandedly. "Right, Norm?"

Norm nods, in that charming empty-headed way of his.

MT does what any self-respecting CEO would do in this situation: She conservatively bats her eyelashes.

"Perfect," I say, grabbing one of MT's cards off Druscilla's desk and shoving it in Norm's shirt pocket. I shoulder my briefcase, pick up Norm's deck, and head for the elevator. Norm reluctantly follows.

"I'm out of here," I say, smiling at Dartsy, "because, ya know . . . I'm just really anxious to get home and start working on my *assignment*." Oh, that feels good. I have barely enough time to catch Dartmoor's desultory sneer as the elevator closes.

As soon as the elevator opens in the lobby I drop Norm's deck on the designer inlaid floor, watch him walk out, and press the elevator up button, giving him a little wave good-bye as the doors close again.

I get out on the mezzanine balcony and wait until I see the confused half dude, half boy make his way home. Months of being pursued by my very own stalker have taught me a few diversionary tactics.

Minutes later on the street I'm ready to leap in the air like Marlo Thomas in the opening of *That Girl*. You know, the one that used to play on Nick at Nite? I want to run and spin. I even contemplate flying a kite in Central Park.

Jumping for joy, I feel my phone vibrate.

It's a text message from G-bomb, Genelle Waterman, the ultimate buzzkill, the last person I'd ever want to hear from.

Oh, sugar—whatever it is can't be good.

CHAPTER 17

Some say that Vladimir Lenin coined the phrase, "Two steps forward, one step back," or was it "One step forward, two steps back"? I swear it had something to do with dialectics or Hegel and materialism, but I can't remember. Either way, I know he wasn't talking about an episode of *Dancing with the Stars*. I do know that every time I think I'm getting a few paces ahead on my own personal curve, I wind up being jerked backward by my past. Take the darling Fergwad appearing on Dartmoor's radar, for example.

It's as if you go through life tied to one enormous bungee cord—you try leaping into thrilling new territory, but you can only go so far before karmic elasticity yanks you back. Sometimes I think all of humanity is in serious danger of getting whiplash.

Once in a while the nostalgic pull is positive, like hearing a They Might Be Giants song and remembering it was the first tune you ever downloaded on your MP3 player. But mostly, it's the not-so-great stuff that sucks you back.

Life is like that stupid board game, Sorry!, where you try to progress your pawn (how's that for symbolic?) around the board, but other players are always waiting to force you off the path. According to the rules, they have to say, "Sorry!" But you know they don't mean it. Funny how the space on the board you get sent back to is called "Home." Well, why not? That's where you find the heartsick parents, the self-destructive brothers, the lost loves, and the high school enemies.

I wonder if everyone my age feels this way. I wonder if we all have to make a superhuman effort to keep moving forward toward all those things we're supposed to achieve in life.

It was Friedrich Nietzsche who rattled off that inspirational little tidbit: "That which doesn't kill us makes us stronger." Personally, I think what doesn't kill you *almost* does. So I don't see the upside. I'm sort of half empty on that *what doesn't kill you* thing. Go ask someone with PTSD, I'm sure they'll agree.

What Friedrich forgot to mention is the corollary: That which we don't kill can come back around to haunt us and make us miserable. Which is why I should have buried Genelle Waterman the night of her reunion party.

Genelle Fucking Waterman. I don't know if that's her real middle name, but I like to think it is. She is definitely one of those high school–specific memories you hope you never have to deal with again, like rainbow meat, cliques, lockdown, drama bitches, and bullies.

For four years, Genelle and I quietly (and sometimes not so quietly) loathed each other. Oddly enough, this animosity was not inspired by any single cataclysmic event—she didn't pelt me with maxi pads in the locker room shower or dump pig blood on me at prom, so it certainly could have been worse. She did plenty of bitchy things, mind you, and I confess, once in a while I succumbed to my darker instincts and gave as good as I got. But mostly we just tormented each other at a PG-13 level by saying nasty things about each other. Why girls endlessly torture each other in high school, I don't know. When exactly does sisterhood kick in? As I get older, I wonder why, truthfully, girl-on-girl social abuse never seems to stop no matter how old you are. I've always tried to find my peeps, my safe pocket.

Thank God Facefuck, I mean Facebook, wasn't big in those

days or the war between Genelle and I would have been way worse. Sure, the occasional term paper or hair scrunchie mysteriously went missing, but mostly it was just annoying, harmless bullshit that took place on school premises, not online. Outside of Thomas Tupper, our Venn diagram of life very rarely overlapped.

But on the night of Genelle's lame one-year reunion party, she totally crossed a line. Actually, that night I crossed a line, too—one just for me—and Sam did, as well—but it was a very different kind of line.

I wore this cool flowered yellow-and-blue dress over my jeans and my nicely weathered Doc Martens (for good luck and old times' sake). The party was a streamer-and-balloon-bedecked bash with more kegs than I could count and nobody was twenty-one, so I had no idea how Genelle got around her dad. The honorable Councilman Louis Waterman had a strict no-booze policy. Hell, I thought her mom was in the Temperance Union (yes, it still exists).

Clifford Spleenhurfer was DJing and I have to admit, he had become pretty good at dropping the beats. He certainly had a shedful of turntables, crossfaders, and ginormous speakers.

I don't know why, but it felt like every guy there had a condom tucked into his wallet. I know that every girl had shaved her legs, armpits, and certain other nether reaches of her female anatomy. And there was the sudden appearance of multiple tattoos and piercings. Not to mention a plethora of weed.

I had tried marijuana like everyone else, but didn't personally partake, maybe because there wasn't as much floating around the newsroom as, say, a college dormitory. The predominant self-medication of choice at the *Daily Post* was alcohol, and old boozers were not an attractive enticement to drink.

Then there was the traumatic childhood New Year's Eve incident where Ferguson and I had secretly stayed awake until midnight. When Ferg and I ran into Marshall and Janet's bedroom yelling "Happy New Year!" at the top of our lungs and found them buck naked tugging on a joint, it was vastly too weird an experience to assimilate. I still shudder at the thought. So does Dad. It kind of cured me of the desire to smoke pot. I mean, I know my parents used to be hippies and all, but it wasn't an image I wanted in my brain.

That night people came to Genelle's party full of agendas as if they wanted to reset the record on high school. Everybody (with the notable exception of me) had recently finished his or her first year of college and were two months into their sophomore year. I guess they were over their freshman jitters and at "peak recklessness," all ready to show the old gang that although we may have been innocents when we left Springfield, higher education had changed that forever.

Genelle's agenda was simpler: Get Sam back.

Yes, once upon a time in high school, Genelle and Sam were an item. They had dated for two months, three weeks, four days, and thirty-five minutes back in our junior year. Unfortunately, I remember every minute of it. Sam and I talked about it on a play-by-play basis. She was cuckoo for his Cocoa Puffs, although sometimes I wondered if she was just trying to piss me off by forcing him to divide his time between us. She definitely decided within the first week that as much as she loved Sam, the one thing she needed to change about him was me.

I took great satisfaction in knowing that he never climbed a ladder into *her* bedroom window. But still, they held hands in the lunchroom, made out in her car, talked on the phone, and did that whole ridiculous "you-hang-up-first-no-you-hang-up-first" thing for almost the entire time they were together. I can't tell you how many times I had to listen to that one. I'd pull my tongue out with fire tongs before I'd tell Sam or anyone to hang up first. It's just too stupid.

Anyway, after that disturbing knee bump under the table in New York, I felt awkward when I saw Sam at the reunion. For the whole party, I couldn't stop looking at his mouth when he talked. Don't ask me why, it was totally sexing me out. Like I was noticing for the first time how his lips formed words and it made my knees weak.

Our bone marrow–deep friendship had morphed. I knew it, he knew it, and as soon as we ran into Genelle, she knew it.

She threw herself at him as if they were long-lost lovers, and Sam looked so uncomfortable I felt sorry for him. Genelle escalated her efforts while getting plastered out of her gourd. All she got out of Sam was a polite, "Good thing this is your party, because you're way too wasted to drive home."

Then Sam startled me by grabbing my hand and giving me a look with those warm brown eyes of his and said, "Let's get out of here. . . ."

The heat from his hand made my whole body warm. Why hadn't we ever held hands like that before? He certainly didn't have to ask me twice and the confidence in his voice put any doubts out of my mind. After all, he's the cautious one between us.

I felt Genelle's death squint boring into the back of my head as Sam and I left the party together. His dad's red pickup truck was parked outside. I've always loved that truck and I always will. As we drove away, I glanced back and saw Genelle standing on her front steps still watching us, the party behind her shifting from rowdy to raucous.

A few blocks later Sam pulled over into the parking lot behind Reveille Church, and the sexual buzz was so thick it seemed like the composition of the air around us had changed. I was trembling, shivering. His hands drew my hips toward him, sliding me closer across the red pickup's comfortable bench seat. We grabbed each other, gasping and hungry for each kiss, his fingers pulsating, pulling at the edge of my jeans. Every smell and taste overwhelmed the next.

Tearing one more kiss from my lips, Sam paused, pulling back to look at me. Our eyes met unflinchingly, raw and unfiltered. Was there any question? Any doubt? It felt like he was looking into my soul. Slowly, he began again. His little kisses to my neck turned into bites, a whimper of pain escaping me. More kisses behind my ear and in the corners of my mouth became long, searching slow ones. He had his answer. There was no hurry anymore, just certainty about what we were going to do.

Soon his fingers were tightening in my hair, drawing my open mouth toward his, sucking on my tongue, nearly biting it. As his hand made its way down my spine to my waist, he leaned back, pulling me down with him, still kissing, and bringing me farther on top. I dug my hands through his hair, biting his lips. I pulled off my dress and threw it in the back of the cab as he unbuttoned my jeans and I unbuttoned his.

With one thrust he was inside me, consuming me. I gave myself up to his arms, to his body, driving deeper, smooth and hard, shuddering uncontrollably as he let go. There was something amazing about us coming together so simply, so naturally, and so completely without talking or saying anything.

Afterward, we lay naked on the seat and our bodies fit together, two halves of a whole, our breathing long and slow.

To find Sam in my arms was heaven, momentous, earthshaking. It sounds too simple to say everything in our lives had led up to that moment, but it felt that way. Neither of us knew what to say, even though I'm sure all kinds of thoughts were clouding our minds. I lay there in silence, drifting in and out of a delicious sleep.

"I've never done that before," he said, his soft voice waking me. I opened my eyes and leaned up on one elbow.

"You mean with me?"

"No. Never at all."

"What? Really?" I didn't believe him at first.

"Yeah."

I had to lift my head up farther to look at him to see if he was kidding. He responded with that low-key Sam kind of shrug and smiled.

"Coulda fooled me," I said, lowering my head to his chest. "Never?"

"Nope."

"Why not?" I asked, still breathing him in.

"Came close, did lots of other stuff, but didn't want to until now," he said.

"Don't go saying you saved yourself for—"

"I'm not. Just didn't," he said. I could tell he was a little defensive. "You?"

"Not . . . like this. Suffice it to say I've never done it . . . before . . . in a red pickup . . . with you," I said, snuggling closer, but suddenly wondering if that was okay with him. I wanted to say more about everything I felt, how being with him eased my rumbling mind and soothed my tired body, my soul, but I didn't.

"You never said anything about it," he said.

"Yeah, I know. It wasn't so great." I immediately worried if that made me sound like someone who slept around a lot, but I decided to let it rest.

We fell softly asleep, easily intertwined in each other, his arm around my waist, mine curled across his chest, his breathing warm on my neck until we were stirred by fire engine sirens in the distance that seemed to be growing closer. But even then we didn't give it a thought. The windows were fogged up with condensation and we were cut off from the world in our own cozy sphere of tenderness and warmth that I never wanted to leave.

It wasn't until the knock on the window that we jumped, scrambling for our clothes before the door opened. The fireman was pointing a flashlight in our eyes.

Sam was mortified. I was worried, too. At least the fireman had the courtesy to knock.

"Sam Anders?" he asked and Sam nodded. "Clarissa Darling?" I nodded dutifully. "We've been looking for you."

It took a while to piece together what had happened. Our first clue came later the next day when we were walking downtown. Every classmate we encountered gave us a wink or some kind of snickering smile. Nothing like your entire high school knowing that you had unambiguously hooked up with your closest best friend. Fortunately, most everyone thought it was pretty rad except you-know-who—Genelle Fucking Waterman.

Jody filled me in later on what occurred after Sam and I left the party. Genelle did three more Jell-O shots, muttered something about "not letting that Clarissa bi-otch have what was rightfully hers," then triggered the fire alert on her parents' house alarm system pad—a direct line to the Springfield Fire Department. Considering Mr. Waterman is a councilman, every division in Springfield responded.

Former high school classmates in various degrees of intoxication scattered. Kegs were rolled to safety, bongs were hidden in oversized purses. Most people panicked and tried to get out of there as fast as they could. Poor Clifford was struggling to get his DJ gear out of the joint as the fire department arrived. Jody tried to help Genelle hide the last few kegs in the garden shed when the G-Bomb passed out on the lawn. No one in the history of Springfield, Ohio, had ever heard of someone calling the authorities on their own party, but Genelle is a pioneer in her own way.

Our stalwart defenders of public safety saw pretty quickly that there was no fire, but when they tried to revive Genelle she kept mysteriously muttering about—guess who?—Sam and me. So with nothing else to do but solve the mystery, the erstwhile firemen of Engine Company No. 5 of the Fire and Rescue Division set out on a search for us that ended with a polite knock on the cab of Sam's dad's red Ford pickup.

News of me kissing Sam for the first time (I mean *really* kissing Sam for the first time, not the other first kiss that I don't count) spread through Springfield like the house fire that never actually happened. But everyone was mostly unsurprised. The number one response was, "Weren't they doing it all through high school?"

Talk about an epic fail. Genelle was humiliated. If she didn't hate me before that moment, she sure as hell hated me after. Even though she was the one who called in the first responders, I felt sorry for her. Almost.

My phone buzzes again and there's another text from Genelle.

"I really want to meet up for a girl chat!!"

Oh God, a girl chat with my least-favorite girl.

"I've got big news!!"

Okay, really. What is wrong with her? Why she would want to share big, medium, or even small news with me is impossible to imagine. Why she thinks I care is unfathomable. . . . You know, on a level of trying to understand one of those *Doctor Who* episodes.

I text back a very polite generic brush-off, something about being busy with work, and "Thanks for getting in touch."

I guess I'm a little curious, but this time, I'm using all my energy to make a concerted effort to move forward and ignore the great big bungee cord of life.

High school had its wonderful moments, but I'm not going to let it pull me back. I've got bigger things ahead. And even though it takes major willpower not to remember things like Sam's amazingly soft lips and my fingers running through the soft brown curls of his hair that night in his dad's red pickup, I need to stick to the path.

If only I can find it!

CHAPTER 18

For the next few days, I hunker down at the computer and work on my article. But what the piece really needs is "legwork," as Hugh used to say—not of the Wikipedia or Google variety, but firsthand and in person.

So here's the bad news: I have to hang out with Norm and schlep to South Williamsburg where his manufacturing operation is headquartered. Let me rephrase that: Where Norm and three baggy-pants slacker dudes doodle on rolling toys for grown-up boys whose favorite movies are of the *Jackass* kind, and who consider wise-ass MTV reality stars Rob and Big their role models.

Okay, so maybe Norm's setup is a little more sophisticated than that. I have to admit that Norm is really giving it a go and there is money actually changing hands, going in and out of the company in what looks like an actual flow of supply and demand. He's gotten some serious business and accounting advice—I guess from "that Bezos dude." I interview Belinda, his accountant, who is a no-shit numbers lady, and I'm impressed that she has the purse strings firmly in hand. This is validating for me, considering I took a total leap into the unknown pitching the story to Dartmoor and MT. I get a wee bit of credit for good instincts. Lots of credit for thinking on my feet and surviving.

Norm has also cooled out on the stalker tendency because of MT and their mutual fascination, opening up a potential new line of business for me: "Matchmaking for Stalkers." Think about it—how many stalkers and stalkees would live better lives if you could hook them up with someone who really wanted them and likes that kind of attention? Actually sounds like a line of business for Ferguson more than me. The good news is that despite Norm's pronoun problem, he seems to be able to actually talk about the business.

I spend a few hours asking questions, jotting down notes, and taking some photos. Surprisingly, Norm is all business. Somebody has talked some sense into this guy. I also notice MT's business card pinned with a nail to the plywood board that passes for his desk. Luckily he's got this frizzy-haired geeky kid in charge of "manufacturing," i.e., the Gorilla Glue part of it all. I consider mentioning Janet's ToFlue Glue but think better of it.

I take all kinds of pictures for the piece—some are pretty cool and make ol' Norm look like a movie star. Central casting, anyone? Around four o'clock I leave the industrial All Decked Out warehouse. Despite the short deadline Dartmoor managed to throttle me with, I opt to catch my breath, take a break, and look for a bite to eat. It's nice to get lost in Williamsburg for a while.

I stop by Grumpy's for a coffee (okay, are you detecting a pattern here?) and look over my notes. It's pretty deserted except for a few production assistants with clipboards and stopwatches and even one of those movie clapboards from a television studio nearby shooting some HBO show.

Then I head south down Kent Street past Brooklyn Brewery, stopping by the El Diablo Taco Truck for a carnitas, finding a very cool storefront exhibition space filled with shelves and shelves of sketchbooks crowdsourced by every crazy kind of artist, writer, and performer, and finally stopping at Mast Brothers Chocolate next door. I'm pretty happy. Coffee, tacos, and chocolate. My kind of diet.

On the way to the subway I saunter by a cool-looking building with a funky arch over the door fashioned out of rusting bicycles welded together. Then I see the sign:

HeadSpace.

Shit. This is Nick's music studio. Every uncomfortable memory and longing comes slamming in even though I figured I'd forgotten about him.

Frozen in my steps staring at his front door, I'm simultaneously dreading and praying that he might come walking out from under that funky arch made of bikes. Was I inevitably drawn here by some unseen force set in motion by my parents arriving that morning and my coffee spilling? If only I had used the spilling antidote to that omen of bad luck, as I had known I should.

The words "*I have a girlfriend*" keep echoing in my brain. What if he came out with said girlfriend? And what if they were all lovey-dovey and kissing each other? Shit.

I've got to pull myself away and move on.

Then again, what if he came out alone? What if he appeared, all excited about some new group he just signed, and when he spotted me, his face lit up?

"Nick! What a surprise," I'd say. "Is this your place? Who knew? What a small world. I was just down the street interviewing the next great skateboard mogul—my former BF, by the way—for my super-prestigious new job."

"Undoubtedly," Nick would say, with a bit of jealousy in his eyes. "All because you're a journalistic genius. I know. I've read all of your stuff—or at least charmingly pretended to your parents to have read the stuff you admit you haven't even written. But I know you're brilliant anyway, and I can't wait to throw my arms around you and kiss you a thousand times in all the wrong places. . . ."

Okay, there are a few things about this standing fantasy racing through my head that suck—number one: Nick still has this mysterious girlfriend. And number two: It's not going to happen. It's a daydream, as in fantasy, as in self-inflicted torture.

I'm so frozen up in my own headspace in front of HeadSpace, picturing Nick, telling myself to move on, literally and figuratively, I haven't noticed that out of the entrance beneath the welded bicycles a girl has walked out and is standing in front of me.

From her low-riding, hip-hugging, red plaid pants to her massive black platform lace-up boots that make her eight inches taller than she is in real life, she looks like a total badass.

As she stops to light a cigarette, I read her black T-shirt. It says, "EAT LSD, PRAY to Satan, LOVE no one." She wears gobs of eye shadow, dark glistening red lipstick, and tattooed on her chest is something that looks like a demonic gummy bear.

Her hair is so woven up it looks like crocheted dreadlocks, but underneath it all, I can see that she's actually kind of pretty. She turns in my direction and I freak. I look down at my feet. When I gaze up again she's walking around the corner. Could this be *the* girlfriend? Whoever she is, she's imposing.

I pick my jaw up off the sidewalk, breathe for the first time since seeing her, and head the opposite way for the Bedford L.

When I get home to FiDi, I can't stop myself from Googling HeadSpace. Nick's studio website is dazzling: all energy, mood, and alluring music. It includes a variety of photos of alt-rockers of every ilk—trap, folk, dreamy Lana Del Rey pop divas, banger rock, and then one rocker chick in particular—Roxie Buggles. Her smirk says she plans to inflict herself on the world in a very big way, whether the world is ready or not. There's no mistaking it: She's the girl I saw standing outside of Nick's studio. Scanning his website with dread, I look for photos that might show Roxie and Nick together, but I don't see any. My jealous research is inconclusive. But there is a YouTube video of a live concert where she throws herself around the stage and exposes her boobs. Pure Courtney Love and kind of old hat if you ask me.

I shudder, then realize it's just my phone vibrating.

"Let's grab a cuppa coffee pretty please? Now? ☺ ☺ ☺ ☺ !!"

Another text from Genelle? What is *with* her? I note the excessive use of emojis and exclamation points.

Okay, my curiosity has now officially transcended my good judgment. I text back.

"Ok. Downtown Manon Café?"

G-Bomb texts back.

"On my way !! So excited to see you !! XOXOXXO"

Oh, fug. The XOXs totally gross me out.

Here's hoping I don't totally regret this.

CHAPTER 19

Everyone knows that scene in *The Godfather* where the Corleones choose Louie's joint because it's a nice safe place that isn't on Sollozzo's turf. That's the place where they've hidden a revolver above the toilet in the bathroom and Al Pacino comes out of the loo and pumps his enemies with three bullets to the head, starting an all-out gang war. Well, hyperbole aside, that's exactly why I suggest meeting Genelle at Manon Café in the Financial District. It's my turf. I know all the exits and I can make a quick dash if things get ugly.

I realize that by now you probably think I'm a shill for the coffee bean industry or I'm volunteering for the Fair Trade Movement or that I have some misplaced addiction issues—like I should be taking meth and contemplating a career breaking bad. Well, maybe there's truth in all of that or maybe I have caffeinated karma hopefully good to the last drop, but mostly it's Hugh's fault.

Thankfully, Hugh gave up the booze twenty-five years before I appeared on the scene, otherwise I'd already be in rehab. But coffee? It was coursing like a muddy river through his veins. Morning coffee, afternoon coffee, evening coffee. And let's face it, when you're drinking decaf coffee with dinner so you can "sleep" and you're drinking coffee to cure your morning coffee headache, you've got a problem. Needless to say, I wanted to keep up with him and stay in his head as per my job description, so I found myself drinking more and more of the brown stuff. At least I found the good brew. Hugh didn't care how good it was because he sadly never stopped to actually smell the coffee beans, buds, pods, or whatever. I'm sure it was a replacement for other issues, like his mother's milk or something. I've stopped cold turkey and dealt with those pesky morning headaches several times to keep it under control. I certainly don't drink the stuff after three p.m. and I plan to stop again sometime soon to do the "Two-Day Look Better Naked Cleanse," just not right now. Not as I'm about to meet G-Bomb. I need to be alert, my reflexes instant, and prepared to look this girl straight in the eyes.

Genelle's already there.

Don't you hate people who are always on time? Isn't it a sign of civility to be a few minutes tardy—just to allow everyone else a minute or two of leeway? I'm sure the French have a rule about this. But there she is, waving excitedly in her fully coordinated powder-blue dress with a big light blue bow and a little blue barrette in her auburn hair. Yuck. Perky as ever.

"Clarissa! Over here!" she says, which is kind of obvious, since she's the only one sitting in the place and the café is tiny anyway. Pulling up a chair I notice there's something different about her, which takes me a few moments to figure out.

"Hi, I'm so happy to see you," she gushes. I immediately begin to wonder if the real Genelle Waterman has been abducted by aliens, probed, and—whoa, has she had major breast augmentation? Good work, actually. Who knew aliens were good at breast implants? But it doesn't stop there. Something about her face has changed. Is it because she's smiling at me? I've never seen her do anything but scowl. This has to be some extraterrestrial life-form inhabiting her much bustier shell.

"Hey." I smile warily. "What's up?"

"So much, actually." She gives me a big grin and sits posture erect. "How do you like my new look?"

"You look . . . good," I say, not knowing the exact etiquette when it comes to breast implants.

"I got my boobs done!" she says proudly, as if it's not utterly obvious.

"Well, wow. They're cute, I mean, they look . . . awesome." This conversation is already weirder than I ever expected.

"And I don't wear glasses anymore, remember?"

"Yeah, that's right. I knew there was something different about your face," I say, wondering if this is why she brought me here.

"Mommy got me that laser process," she adds. "But you know, that's not all."

"Oh, really?"

"I got a new nose!" she says and turns profile. Her nose does seem thin and delicate, but I don't remember her nose being that big or odd before.

"What was wrong with your old nose?" I can't help asking. This is too weird and I have to know more.

"Well, you see, this is what the doctor showed me." She takes a napkin and a pen from her pocketbook and draws a nose on it. "Okay, this was my old nose, and you're right, there wasn't anything really wrong with it. But look at this. . . ." Genelle takes her pen and draws another nose within the first one. This one is smaller and perkier.

"And what is that?" I ask, settling into this very strange, intimate conversation with a person I can't stand. I figure everything is an experience and you have to live life to the fullest, so I might as well find out.

"That's the nose *within* my nose," she says with total satisfaction, "and it's perfect, don't you think?"

"Wow," I say, and mean it in many more ways than one,

hoping that my utter astonishment at her plastic surgeon's manipulative chicanery translates into something positive for her sake.

"Gee, Genelle, this is all great and I'm really glad you invited me to get together," I say. "I take it that all this—the new you—is the big news you wanted to tell me?"

"Oh, no! I'm sorry, I have no idea why I went on about all that." She giggles, suddenly silly. "Look, I know you probably didn't want to see me, but I'm so glad you did."

"Well . . ." I begin, but she jumps right back in.

"That's okay," she says. "Believe me. I get it. Therapy works wonders, doesn't it?"

"Then so, what *is* the big news?" I ask.

"Well, the last time I saw you—"

"Genelle, let's not talk about that, really. It's okay."

"No, it's not okay," Genelle says, adamantly reaching out to touch my hand. I try not to run out of the coffee shop screaming, but if she doesn't take her hand away soon I will freak. "I apologize for everything I did. Everyone knows Sam loves you."

Then why did he disappear? Why did it all fall apart? I wonder painfully.

"Clarissa, I was just so jealous and angry. . . ." She closes her eyes and I worry she might have some kind of fit, so I brace myself in case she starts speaking in tongues or spewing forth devil puke. "I behaved so badly, but—it was a turning point! It was. Because of you, I pulled myself together to take that long, arduous path up the gravelly road of life to be a better person!"

"Wow," I say again, calculating that my enthusiastic non sequitur will be misconstrued as an expression of support. "The gravelly road of life, huh?" Covertly, I use my peripheral vision to confirm where the exits are.

"Yes, it's true. I hoped you would be impressed," she says, self-satisfied. "In fact, I wrote a book about it! It's coming out next month."

"Really? A book? You're a writer?" I hope that doesn't sound competitive or threatened because that is *absolutely* what it is.

"Oh! Don't worry. I didn't mention you or Sam by name," she says. "It's a self-help book!"

Genelle slides an advance reader's copy of her tour de force across the table that she had ready sitting under her pocketbook.

I quickly glance at the title: *A Mean Girl's Guide to Change, Love, and Enlightenment.*

"It's based on my love life," she explains. So if Genelle is a love doctor, maybe fucking *is* her middle name?

"Oh, really? Amazing," I say as totally laid-back and blasé as I can, even though I am not. Maybe *Shifty Shades of Gray* or *Just One Shade of Gray* would have been better titles. I don't say that, though. Knowing Genelle, she'd go home, write that as a follow-up, and make a million bucks. For the record, I never ever really considered her formidable enough to be called a "mean girl" because she was so ineffectual, but I guess everyone likes to remember high school his or her own way.

"Yes, and it's all because of you, and I wanted you to know," she says, teary-eyed.

"Well, thanks." I have no idea what else to say.

"And, like I said in my text message, I have *big* news."

"Wait a second," I say, truly amazed. "There's more news?" Bigger than the fact that she has new eyes, a new nose, a new bod, and a book deal? I'm starting to feel like I'm a sluggard. I better get out and get a facial at least.

"There is . . . this!" She flings her left hand toward me, wrist dipped, fingers splayed.

Um . . . you have carpal tunnel syndrome from all that writing? I want to say, but then I see it. Genelle Waterman is wearing the Rock of Gibraltar (but much shinier) on her left ring finger.

"Wow," I say. "You're engaged to a . . . jeweler?"

She laughs so loud that the barista looks alarmed.

"You are a *stitch*, Clarissa! You've always been funny!" she says and gives me a punch in the shoulder. It takes everything I have not to haul off and sock her in the jaw.

"No, my fiancé is Wendell Fleckerstein, he's a corporate lawyer. Of the Fleckersteins of Westchester County, which is why we're getting married out here. I've been shopping all week. It's going to be incredibly posh and exclusive. His parents are friends with the Kennedys; several of the Kennedy cousins will be there." She turns up her new nose and bats the eyelashes over her newly shaped corneas, stiffening her posture, stretching, and accentuating her new boobs. "But not any of the scandalous ones."

"I didn't know there were any other kind," I say half under my breath. She cackles again as if I'm Louis CK.

"You're so funny." She laughs. Reminder to self: Stop making jokes, even bad ones, until I've exited the premises.

Meanwhile, the point of this exercise has finally soaked in. Under the guise of a sugary fake apology, G-Bomb wanted me to know about her various surgical improvements, her new career, and her fabulous husband-to-be. Machiavelli would be proud (not to mention Mrs. Machiavelli, who I'm sure had a few tricks up her sleeve to keep the prince under control). There's nothing more cunning than making sure your old enemy knows how well you're doing and even giving you credit for their success. Genius. I've got to hand it to her: She's one twisted sister. Message received, and now it's time for me to say good-bye. I knew this would be a waste of time. I get ready to wish her luck, but before I can say another word . . .

"I invited your parents," Genelle blurts out of nowhere. "I'm sure their separation has been stressful for you." Okay, now I *am* going to punch her.

"Really? That's great. Well, look, I have to go. . . ."

"Jody's parents, too," she says. Right, I think the councilman and Jody's dad are fishing buddies or something. "And Jody, of course."

"That's nice," I say and then can't help adding, "I guess the more witnesses who can say they actually saw you become Mrs. Wendell Peckerstein, the less trouble you'll have enforcing the terms of the prenup when the time comes." *Bad Clarissa. Bad.* Don't drag this out or try to get even. Get up. Get out. *Run away! Run away!* I pull out my chair to leave.

"It's Fleckerstein," she says, taken aback. I admit I take a tiny bit of satisfaction seeing her annoyed at my snide comment. Oddly enough, she leaves the prenup comment alone. I've got to get out of here before I say or do worse.

"Well, Genelle, this has been an amazing experience." I stand. "I can't tell you how pleased I am that you have done . . . so much . . . with . . . what you have. Really. But I have to go."

"Wait!" She stops me, grabbing my arm. God, I want to kill her.

"I want you and Rick to come, too." I look at her quizzically. I don't know anybody named Rick.

"Rick? Rick who?" I ask. She notices my confusion.

"Your boyfriend."

My what? I don't have a boyfriend, and even if I did, how would she know?

Oh no.

Damn it!

Could she mean Nick?

"First of all, it would be a privilege to have you both there," she continues, "and I have to admit that when I heard you guys were having a little trouble I thought it might be good for you both to come. It might help. You know, Wendell proposed to me after we went to his sister's wedding. Weddings can be so romantic for unmarried couples. I write about that in my book."

Whoa, where the hell would Genelle find out that I have a hypothetical love interest, let alone that we were having hypothetical problems? And are we? I mean, I guess we are, since we're not even a hypothetical couple anymore or ever really were, hypothetically speaking, and that's about as hypothetical as it gets. I'm getting a headache just thinking about it.

"Genelle, I don't understand. We've been enemies since middle school."

"I always thought we were more like frenemies."

"Nope. Enemies. No prefix."

She sighs. "Okay, fine. But we're adults now, right?"

I wonder: *Are we? Are any of us? Ever?* But I allow it. "Yes, we are."

"Well, I really want to put the past behind me. Start my new life with a clean slate, and you've done so much for me, showing me what I mess I was," Genelle offers, and I really, really, really want to kill her.

"That's all fine and well," I say, "but I don't know what you're talking about. I'm gonna need a little more info." I begrudgingly sit back down.

"Well." Genelle takes a moment to exhale, knowing she's captured my attention. "You know how the Mommy grapevine works back in Springfield. My mom told Janet all about the wedding and your mom told her all about how things were going south with you and Rick, right?"

Okay. Let's just freeze everything right here for a moment and think about this before Genelle says another word.

It was unforeseen by me, but understandable that my parents might have alerted the Springfield Mommy Network that they had met my "boyfriend." That would indeed pass for news back home. But why would my mom think that Nick and I were having trouble? Our fake dinner date went exceedingly well once we worked the kinks out. If anything, Janet should have been bragging to Mrs. Waterman that I was in a fabulous relationship with a gorgeous coffee-brewing musician who's allergic to shrimp and gets his hair cut in Riverdale!

I need to nip this in the bud and put this whole thing away.

"There's nothing to repair," I say, standing again. "Nick, not Rick, and I are terrific. We're madly in love. And the sex is incredible." Don't ask me why I say that. It's just that I'm furious now and damn if I'm letting this artificially enhanced person get the upper hand with me.

"Oh! Well, that's great," Genelle says, almost blushing. "But . . . really?" she says, giving me a sad clown, lower-lip-protruding look of sympathy.

"Really," I say defiantly.

"Awesome. I'm so glad things are going so well for you and Dick."

"Nick."

"Right. Nick. Sorry. Well then, all the more reason for you two lovebirds to be my guests of honor at the wedding. I can't wait to meet him. He sounds wonderful. I'm sure he's a total hottie."

He most certainly is. Most fictional characters are and, as far as being my boyfriend goes, Nick is about as real as Edward Cullen.

"That's nice of you," I say calmly. "I'll check to see if he's available, but he's usually very busy. Runs his own music studio. In fact, I think he's got a brunch date with Jay Z and the Queen Bey that day."

"I didn't tell you what day."

"Oh. Right. What day is it?"

"A week from this Saturday. I mean, if you two are able to drag yourselves away from that cozy love nest of yours. Unless you have a problem with that?"

"No problem. None at all," I state emphatically. Why did I say that? I meant I have no problem. As in: I don't care, get lost. Not *We—Nick and I—have no problem.* But as soon as the words escape my lips I know it's come across the wrong way. I sigh. I have to get out of here before I dig an even deeper hole and crawl into it. "Wouldn't miss it. Gotta go." I head for the exit I should have headed for a full half hour ago. Right after she asked me about her new boobs.

"See you at the wedding," she calls after me. "By the way, I'm registered at Neiman Marcus!"

I push out the door and wonder if Neiman Marcus sells Molotov cocktails.

Tonight is girls' night with Jody, et al., and I need to go home and get ready. I can't even begin to describe how badly I need to confer with my posse right now.

Jody, Rodgers, Piper . . . *help*!

CHAPTER 20

Pianos, a club on the Lower East Side, is Rodgers's venue of choice for our monthly night out.

Over the heads of people in the packed bar, Rodgers is standing on her chair, wearing a leather top, faded jeans, and knee-high lace-ups, waving at me, her tangle of curly dark hair bouncing.

"C! Over here."

Being that Rodgers is a drummer, she picks places with music. This one is seriously Lower East Side—probably the last refuge that hasn't been gentrified. An added plus is that tonight there's no yellow police tape, chalk outlines, or abandoned needles on the sidewalk out front.

The place is thumping loud. It's the people who make NYC fascinating, and the crowd in Pianos tonight is as eclectic and interesting as it gets: Everyone drinks out of jam jars (take that, Dartsy), there's a guy at the bar who seems to have gotten his fashion sense from the last three Batman movies, and I notice lots of animal tattoos along with some finely trimmed facial hair, and quite a few people taking pictures of what they eat with their phones.

At the opposite end of the restaurant on a slightly raised stage is a band called the Fernandos that includes an accordion, banjo, cello, and chanteuse. You don't see that in Springfield. I think, sadly, that Nick probably knows this joint. I look around, hoping for a brief moment that he might be here.

I shoulder my way through the crowd to the table in the corner where my most trusted advisors seem like they are each about three martinis in. I have some catching up to do.

"Hi!" I throw my arms around Piper, who is all cleaned up for a change. She usually wears some paint-splattered boy-shirt and jeans caked with the palette of her current work, but tonight, she's wearing a black-and-white striped top and whiskered black denim shorts. I look around to see if she's brought her girlfriend along but apparently not. Phew. The girlfriend doesn't totally mix well with the old gang. Rodgers jumps down from her perch and gives me a big 360 hug.

"Love the place," I say.

"Yeah. There's this lounge upstairs called 'Upstairs,' naturally; kind of a showcase for up-and-coming bands. The Hefties are playing there next month."

We bump fists.

Rodgers is the drummer in an alt girl band called the Dead Hefties, but not because any of the band members are particularly chunky. They named themselves after the trash bag. Go figure. She and her family emigrated from Trinidad and she has a degree in economics from the Sorbonne, no less.

Jody and I opt for an air kiss. She looks beautiful; her hair is so lush it almost takes up the whole seat next to her. She's all Brandy Melville in a dainty floral sundress that's mostly backless. Actually, it's mostly fabric-less. I think how amazing it is that we pay so much money for a wisp of cloth. It's less than one square yard. And then that whole OS thing is BS for everyone besides Jody. But I have to admit it looks great on her and there are no apparent bruises as far as I can see, which is either a good sign or just means Rupert's still out of town.

I order a drink and the girls fill me in on the dish. Jody's got another big shoot next week for some haute couture designer who scraped her way out of a backwater town in Alabama and won some reality fashion show contest.

"All her Ds look like overalls, which is adorbz but totes side-boob and cheeks, tad inappro-pro," Jody says, leaving a few of us wondering what she's talking about.

Piper has been painting nonstop; she's the artist in our group. I notice a little bit of ochre paint behind her ear, but decide not to say anything. Usually it's in her hair, too. She makes these massive painted sculptures that after years seem to be finally catching on, and she's preparing for her first gallery show in Chelsea.

And Rodgers has the Upstairs gig to look forward to.

"'Sup with you, C?" Jody asks, sipping her dirty martini. "Did you jam on that J-O-B?"

"Natch!" I can't help saying in Jody-speak. My Nuzegeek news is met with a chorus of war whoops and the demand for another drink and more fist bumps all around.

I fill them in on MT and Dartmoor, the Norm-on-his-knees episode in front of MT's office, and my subsequent profile of his business venture.

"Totes amaze," Jody remarks. "Norm is supz sexy, but I think he's bi."

"Sexual?" Piper asks.

"P," Jody replies.

"As in polar?" Rodgers asks on behalf of us all. Jody nods and looks a little embarrassed that we have so much trouble following her. I know she has other friends, or betches, as she says, who totally abbrevspeak. It must be nice for her to have those peeps or tweeps or whatever she calls them who always understand her.

"Speaking of mental disorders," I say, "I had coffee with someone from Springfield today. You'll never guess who."

Jody launches in, obsessively. "Clifford? Paulie? Olivia? Don't tell me!" I shake my head repeatedly as she lists absolutely everyone we know from home. ". . . Hillary? Elise? Elsie?" Piper and Rodgers look at us like we're talking about a lost tribe in Papua New Guinea.

"Genelle Waterman," I say, finally figuring it's gone on long enough.

Jody almost shoots gin out of her nose.

"G-Bomb? Why the effin' eff would you do that?"

I give them the Cliffs Notes version of Genelle's superboobs, her faux apology, her wedding invite, and my misunderstood, ill-considered acceptance.

"Somebody's marrying that trampage?" Rodgers snorts. She's never met Genelle but she's heard enough about her.

"She's planning to invite you, too, Jody." Jody makes a disgusted face as if she's stepped in a sidewalk dog pile while wearing sky-high Louboutins. "I could kick myself for saying yes," I add.

"Why did you?" Rodgers asks.

"I just couldn't let her have the upper hand. High-schooling, I know," I answer.

Everyone quietly absorbs that remark. We've all been there at one point or another—reacting to people, especially childhood friends, as if we're still in tenth grade.

"Well, you're not actually going, are you?" Piper asks.

"I kind of backed myself into a corner over the whole Nick thing," I say.

"Did I miss something?" Piper asks. "Who's Nick?"

"That's CCG's real name."

"Whoa! You know his real name?" Rodgers asks.

"Micro-relationship violation!" Piper scolds, wagging her finger at me.

"Tell me about it." I sigh and drop my chin in my hands.

"Rewind," Rodgers demands. "When and how did you score his real name?"

I'd forgotten how long it has been since I've seen my peeps.

That's the problem with being a freelance writer: You're stuck in your head so much of the time that you forget there are other people in the world who don't know every tiny thing that has happened to you.

I recount the story of my faux double date with CCG and my parents. The near poisoning at the Indian restaurant and the Harley are the big hits of the story.

"Supz hilars," Jody declares and everyone agrees. "CCG sounds yummers."

Then I get to the uncomfortable part where we're millimeters from each other's lips and we don't kiss. Everyone moans in disappointment. Me, too, all over again. It feels like all the air has gone out of the room.

"I hate to admit it, but I can't stop thinking about him. I was practically stalking him this morning. Not on purpose, but somehow I ended up in front of his music studio, this really cool place in Williamsburg called HeadSpace."

"Whoa!" Rodgers throws her hands in the air like she's on the wrong end of a stickup. "Are you telling me that the CCG you've been obsessing over all this time is actually Nick from HeadSpace?"

Piper frowns. "You know him?"

"Well, yeah! I've played drums on some of his tracks." She sips her drink and gives me a grin over the rim of the glass. "Guy's got the cutest ass in indie music, I'll tell you that much."

"No argument there," I say. "I don't know what to do."

"Okay, let's get this straight," Rodgers begins. I know what's coming next. It doesn't matter how many tamarind martinis Rodgers might drink, she's still the one who minored in algorithmic design at the Sorbonne, the second-oldest academic institution in the world. Her logic is impeccable. We frequently stop to ponder her delineation of an issue we're obsessed with figuring out. I'd give anything to triangulate the Nick-Genelle-wedding dilemma, so I'm a very attentive student.

"So you lied to your parents about Nick and ended up falling for the boy." I nod.

"Then G-Bomb shows up out of the blue and says she knows you're not getting along with the boyfriend you don't really have? There's something I'm missing here."

I nod again.

A high-pitched scream pierces the air. We all turn to look at Jody in shock at the eardrum-popping noise that only certain breeds of dogs can tolerate.

"OMG. WTF. ICB!" Jody seems to be speaking in tongues. Or letters, anyway.

"Jesus, Jody! What did you have to pierce my eardrums for?" Rodgers asks.

"I just remembered what I was supposed to tell C last week!" She takes a fortifying slug of her martini and looks me in the eye.

"My 'rents ran into your 'rents at the VS buying the CCC on the PM," Jody says. We all look at her blankly.

Then each other. Then back at Jody.

"Okay, Jody, you'll have to explain," I ask.

Jody takes a deep breath and excruciatingly translates to normal-speak, as if we're from a foreign country. We can all see this is very taxing for her.

"My pa-*rents* ran into your pa-*rents* at the C-*VS* buying Coricidin PM," she says, painfully articulating every word as if English was our second language.

"Wow, she even abbreviates her abbreviations," Rodgers comments. "That's impressive."

"But where does Genelle come in?" I ask.

"Genelle's mom was there, too," Jody says. "Jan told them that she and Marsh met your BF, but later, at JFK, saw some betch snogging him at arrivals and they were like WTF."

"My mom said 'WTF'?" I ask, astonished.

"IDK. Maybz. I think."

"Well, the icing on the cake is that Genelle Fucking Waterman has invited my parents to the wedding, too," I add, pouring salt on my own wounds.

Honestly, I haven't a clue what to think about it all when I notice Rodgers giving me a knowing nod. That means that the algorithmic formulas she's been calculating all this time in her highly advanced frontal lobe have all fallen into place.

"Pretty sure we're talking about Roxie."

"Roxie?" The name sets off a little warning bell in my brain. "Roxie . . . *Buggles*?"

"Yep, you've heard of her?" Rodgers nods gravely. "The chick makes Courtney Love look like a pet gerbil."

As I suspected, Nick's girlfriend is the rocker from the website that I saw in the red plaid pants in all her glory outside HeadSpace the other day.

"She doesn't seem like his type," I say in what may be the understatement of the century. "Look, is this her?" I tap the screen on my phone and pull up the photo of Roxie I was looking at earlier.

"Okay, that's cray-cray," says Jody, "we're just going to pretend it's not at all creepy that you have this girl's picture on your phone." I can tell she's alarmed—she's talking normal.

"Don't worry, C, you're way prettier than she is," says Piper. "And I bet you have a much shorter rap sheet."

"Listen, Nick is always complaining about Roxie," Rodgers says. "They have that on-again, off-again thing. I know for a fact that he's tried to get out of it altogether but keeps getting sucked back in somehow. She has a knack for throwing scenes and for some reason, he falls for it. It's like his fatal flaw or something."

"Maybe they were in an off-again when he almost kissed you," Piper adds hopefully, "or maybe they're in an off-again right now?"

I feel like my face is an open book when she says that. I know they can all see what I'm feeling.

Jody puts her hand on mine and turns solemnly to address the others.

"I say C goes back to that coffee cart ASAP and spills the wedding sitch to CCG all cajj." It only takes the rest of the girls a second first to translate what she's said and then to consider.

"Right, then if he's still with Roxie, he'll say no," Piper reasons. "If they're over, he'll say yes."

"That solves everything," Rodgers adds.

"Ya think?" I ask, cringing as my heart perks up.

The advisory board nods in agreement.

CHAPTER 21

Relieved to be alone with my thoughts, I walk back toward FiDi down Bowery, which is surprisingly well lit and still busy this time of night.

So Dad and Mom saw Nick kissing Roxie at the airport. That amazes me not only for the obvious reasons, but also because I know how hard it is to find someone at JFK when you're actually looking for them. By sheer coincidence, my parents just happen to stumble across my pretend boyfriend without even trying. It's an occurrence that's so damn unlikely, I have to make up a new word just to describe it:

> **serendumpity** (n.) the inevitable discovery of what we would rather not know. Coined in the present by Clarissa Marie Darling. *seren + dump + -ity* the antithesis of **serendipity**, 1754: coined by Horace Walpole, which was based on the Persian fairy tale "The Three Princes of Serendip," whose heroes "were always making discoveries, by accidents and sagacity, of things they were not in quest of." See related synonym **zemblanity** William Boyd, 1998.

My folks must be devastated knowing that the guy I was supposedly mad for is cheating on me with a rocker girl who looks like Alice in Wonderland on acid. It kind of begs the question, why the hell didn't they call me the minute they disembarked in Ohio and warn me that my guy had gone astray? But then again, Janet and Marshall Darling have a lot on their plates right now.

It's still early enough for me to call home. So as I throw my keys on the table by the door, I decide to "grim up," as Aunt Mafalda used to say, give Mom a ring and just come out with it. All of it. Everything—from the demise of the *Daily Post* to the lie about Nick being anything more than my former caffeine dealer. Then if there's an actual chance for Nick and me to be together, it won't be based on this circuitous nightmare.

"Hello, Darling residence." I can't believe she still answers the phone that way. It's so old-fashioned.

"Hey, Mom."

"Clarissa!"

"Listen, Mom, I want to—"

But that's the last word I manage to get out of my mouth. Mom starts talking a blue streak about how worried she is. Marshall's so completely down on himself that she can't take it anymore.

"Do you have any idea how hard it has been to live with someone who is *always* depressed?" she says. It makes me depressed just thinking about it.

Apparently they've been going to therapy with some new doctor, an Austrian woman named Dr. Leisl Lyman, which is helping a little.

"He's finally admitted he can't get past the fact that his wife is earning three times the money he ever made," she vents with some relief. "I love your father, and I know how proud he is, but he and I didn't exactly sleep through the entire women's liberation movement."

"But Mom, isn't Dad—?" I begin again, but she talks right over me.

"Don't defend him, Clarissa. I understand you and your dad are close and that's fine. I love him deeply. But Marshall and I marched for the Equal Rights Amendment in Washington when we were still in college. We watched the 'Gloria Discovers Women's Lib' episode on *All in the Family* and even the *Maude* abortion episode together. I remember Marshall crying when he saw that. And this is the man who gave me an official U.S. Treasury mint condition Susan B. Anthony coin for Christmas!"

I can see and hear that this has been building up for quite some time between them. I guess it's good that the issue is on the table.

"Well, I can see how you feel," I say, "but I don't think you should give up hope. . . . I mean, it's probably tough for Dad not to have a—"

"I do have hope, Clarissa," Mom interrupts again. "In fact, the good news is that we've been invited to Genelle Waterman's wedding, and Marshall wants to go!"

"I know," I say glumly. "So have I."

"Wonderful," Mom says. "Weddings are such happy occasions. They have a way of helping people rekindle their romantic feelings, don't you think? It's the 'wedding effect.' People can't help believing in love when they see a blushing bride."

I try to picture Genelle's cheeks turning pink. Considering her new physiognomy, I'm guessing her bashful blushing days are long gone.

"Weddings are about hopes and dreams and promises," Mom tells me, channeling her inner Hallmark. "It's just what our relationship needs." She pauses.

I wonder if I might be able to change the subject. I wait a fraction of a second to see if this is a real opening for me to speak.

"Speaking of relationships . . ." I begin timidly.

"Yes, speaking of relationships, I think it will be good for you and Nick, too," she says firmly. "I hope to see you both there."

This is my opening, my chance to tell her the truth: that what they saw in the airport doesn't really qualify as cheating because Nick and I were a scam from the start. This is my opportunity to admit that I made the whole relationship up on the spot, out of the blue.

I hesitate.

And why, you might ask?

Which is worse: Letting my parents think my boyfriend is a two-timer, or telling them the truth about me? I lied straight to their faces not only about my love life, but also my employment situation. Mom's already worried about Dad and his struggle to reinvent himself in the job market; I don't want to add to her burden. And then there's Genelle F. Waterman to consider. Genelle would be more than delighted to hear that I'm a bigger fake than she is, and the thought makes me want to scream.

Finally, where would that leave me with Nick? I mean, if he's *on-again, off-again*, isn't there still some hope? This wedding might represent a chance for that little spark that was ignited down by the Brooklyn Bridge to be rekindled.

I sigh. "I can't wait to see you, too."

Let's admit it: I'm a wimp.

"Listen, honey," Mom says abruptly, "I've got a batch of brownies in the oven. I've got to dash."

We say good night and I head straight for the bedroom and face-plant into my pillows.

I can't help wondering where Roxie is tonight. Is she with Nick?

"*Off-again, or on-again*," I whisper into the darkness. "*Off-again, or on-again. Please let it be off-again.*"

CHAPTER 22

He's a bit startled when he looks up from Frankensteam and sees me standing there. I'm a little shocked, too. It took me three times hiking around the block to gather enough courage to walk through the revolving door. Before I dashed inside, I was seized with the thought that this whole plan was hatched three martinis south of common sense. Rodgers's elegant algorithmic formulas from the night before seem a distant memory. I can't remember a single reason this was a good idea, but I've come this far, and there's Nick, the scent of Colombia brewing, and my favorite old haunt, the *Daily Post* building, so I take the plunge.

"Hey, Clarissa."

"Hey, Nick."

Okay, so we have now officially ritualized our departure from the micro-zone. Names have been spoken aloud and cannot be retracted. It's super early and there're only a few other people milling around the lobby. Clearly, I'm not here on a whim.

"Great to see you," he says, a little surprised. "How've you been?"

"Good," I say. "I got a job."

"Wow, awesome! Then this is on the house," he says, preparing my usual. He looks a little shy, but genuinely happy for me.

I take the cup and his hand lingers, our fingers touching.

"I didn't think I'd see you again," he says, getting to the crux of it.

"Neither did I," I admit. "I mean, think . . . I'd see *you* again . . . either. But then I realized that the other night was all kind of weird and wacky and you were honest with me."

"Yeah, about that . . ."

I flinch, fearful of what he's going to say, but he's interrupted by a customer who orders a grande dirty soy chai, no water, extra foam. I notice the trust-fund hipster in his dark-frame glasses and pomade hair is carrying a bag from the Anarchist Bookstore on First Avenue. When the guy and his overly complex drinking beverages are gone, I take the opportunity to change the subject.

"Have you ever been to that place?" I ask. "The Anarchist Bookstore?"

"Been there?" Nick laughs. "I used to practically live there. The Gotham Book Mart in Midtown, too, before it closed."

"Oh yeah, I remember the old Gotham," I say, sipping my coffee. "It was the second thing I fell in love with when I moved to New York."

"What was the first thing?" he asks.

"You'll laugh."

"No, I won't."

"You'll think I'm silly."

"Nothing wrong with silly." He gives me a half grin.

"Okay, I am a die-hard devotee of the Mermaid Parade in Coney Island. It was one of the first things I ever went to when I moved here. Aunt Haddie took me every year, she loved it."

I see the smile of recognition percolate up from inside him and I have to admit, it totally turns me on how his face comes to life and his eyes brighten when he's thinking about something.

"That's hilarious," he says. "Me, too."

"Okay, you're just saying that."

"Clarissa, really, what guy would say that if it weren't actually true? I'm sure I've already compromised myself by admitting it. I used to play drums for the fun of it in a band that marched in the parade behind the Singing Crustaceans—you know, the girls with the blue lobster bikinis? The guys had to paint our chests blue and wear blue wigs as we marched playing 'Rock Lobster.' I think they called us the Blubbery Mermen of the Deep."

We both laugh. God, he's adorable. And there's a total lack of weirdness happening. I've been sulking about the missed kiss, the airport thing, and all the disappointment, but now that I'm standing in front of him, I'm not feeling anything but good. I decide that before I lose my nerve, I better get on with it. I take a deep breath.

"Look, I've got to go to this wedding."

"Friends getting married?"

"Actually, my archenemy." He crooks a grin waiting for the punch line.

"No joke. For reasons I'd rather not discuss, I have to go and I really, really don't want to go solo. And on top of that, my parents are going to be there, and . . ."

"Your parents? The ones who think you and I are madly in love?"

Shit. Why did he have to say it that way? I know he's being ironic, but he's looking at me with the softest eyes and it gives me a kick in my stomach—or is it my heart? It makes me want to kiss him or run away or maybe both. I don't know what to say.

"Yep," I say, "only parents I have." I take another breath and continue. "So. I wanted to know . . ."

"You want me to go to a wedding as your date?"

"Well, when you put it like that, it sounds terrible. Doesn't it? I mean, it could be completely platonic, right? We don't have to be lovey-dovey or kiss or touch or dance. No yucky stuff." I stop talking, feeling like a six-year-old at a Barbie party. "I'm sorry, I guess you didn't like your role as my significant other."

"Not true. I did like it," Nick says, "but I figured the reviews weren't so great for obvious reasons."

"No, they were excellent," I assure him. "Raves, actually, except . . . up until . . . well, you know, except you have a girlfriend, right?"

Nick takes a pause. Even though I worry that someone will slip in and ask him for a doppio macchiato soy extra foam and ruin our moment of truth, I'm thankful. His pause gives me a respite to feel like a normal person again after putting myself out there. I can breathe in and out and prepare for the response.

"Are your parents doing okay?" he asks. I wonder if this is his roundabout way of saying no, or if he's giving himself time to take stock of his relationship with Roxie and make a decision. I want to give him room because I figure the next thing he says is going to predict whether or not there's any future between us. *On-again or off-again?*

"They're not great," I say honestly. "Dad's still bummed and Mom's hoping that therapy and handfuls of rice at a wedding will turn things around."

For the first time, I realize: Standing this close to him, I don't really care about Genelle or my parents or saving face after all. I just really like Nick and I hope he says yes because I hope he feels the same way about me.

"You know, this girl I was going out with, the one at the airport?" Nick begins, not really asking a question but rather identifying the obvious person we're not talking about. He doesn't even know that I know they were kissing at the airport between the luggage racks. "It's always been screwed up as far as I was concerned. I produced this totally kick-ass album for her and it almost leveled us up to a record label and a deal that would have been pretty big career-wise. We hooked up in the middle of it all and then it crashed. Ages ago, really. But it was like we had a baby together or something. I can't explain."

"You don't have to talk about it."

"No, I want to get it out," he says. "I don't know why, but when the deal fell apart, I felt like I had let her down. It wasn't my fault. But there were all of these hopes and ambitions, and this girl, well, she's pretty crazy, and she knows how I feel and kind of uses it against me when it's in her interest. It's pretty messed up. I financed the production with my studio so I've had a lot invested and I've been trying to disentangle myself. With the financial obligation, it hasn't been easy. It makes something simple like selling coffee for a living appealing. Just add that to my list of lifelong regrets, right next to getting a Luke Perry haircut in middle school."

Wow. That's more of an answer than I ever expected. He didn't once say "love," "girlfriend," or "Roxie."

"So, where are things with you two?" I inquire . . . okay, kind of demand, deciding it's one of those "ask now or forever hold your peace" moments. Maybe Mom was right about that wedding thing. Weddings do make you think about life in different terms. More important, I want to know the facts: *on-again or off-again?*

"What I'm saying is that it was a mistake. That I was trying to live up to something that I felt obliged to and that I can't keep putting myself out there like that . . . and that I'd love to come to the wedding of, well, your archenemy. It would be great to hang out again."

"Really?" I almost squeal. I want to kick myself, I sound so stupid. "I mean. Really. That's good," I say with as much maturity as I can muster. I can't help smiling at him, though I'd prefer to be kissing him until he can't breathe.

Shit. This actually worked. At least for the moment.

"But there's one thing," Nick begins, and I cringe—*off-again, on-again?* "About this no-kissing, no-touching, no-dancing clause . . . I'd like to leave that open to negotiation, okay?"

Nick crooks that grin again.

"Sure, I'll consider that," I say. Am I blushing?

"You know, I'm glad you came by, because Denny finished his tour of duty. He's coming back from Afghanistan," he says. "My barista days are finished and I was worried I wouldn't be able to tell you."

Whoa. Things are changing quickly. Life is moving on. Our micro-relationship would have been finished anyway. I flash on walking into the *Daily Post* building and finding Nick and Frankensteam gone without a trace and it makes me sad. I can tell that we're both reflecting on our last coffee cart moment. We'll probably never visit this old building again.

"So, what time should I pick you up?" he asks, breaking our contemplation.

I finish giving him the details as some fuzzy-headed intern comes down with a long coffee order including five lattes, three black, one with extra cream and sugar, and four iced mochas with whipped cream. The morning rush has kicked in. I silently nod good-bye and leave him to his work.

The minute I hit the sidewalk, my thumbs fly into a texting frenzy. Our group thread is abuzz delivering Jody, Piper, and Rodgers the fabulous news. The first two responses come like lighting:

"Woohoo!!" Piper texts.

"My blk lace demi cup bra wl b perf," Jody shoots back.

Rodgers, though, is a little slower off the block. Finally, her message pops up.

"HAVE FUN," she writes. "JUST WATCH OUT FOR ROXIE."

It's good advice, even if it's in all caps, but I decide not to dwell on it. Feeling lighter than air, I practically skip to Nuzegeek.

Off-again for Roxie. On-again for me.

Here's hoping it sticks this time.

CHAPTER 23

Pulling at least one quote out of Norm that doesn't include the word *dude* was quite a challenge. That's why I've been sitting in a nondescript cubicle in Nuzegeek's sleek offices in an area known as "the bullpen," combing my notes and QuikVoice files for the last two hours. I have a lot of work to do if I'm going to make Dartmoor's deadline.

The bullpen is filled with modular, gray-upholstered half walls and reserved for freelancers in need of a place to work. I'm told no one ever comes here. Most writers have a more comfortable workspace, are juggling eight or ten jobs, or prefer to avoid face time with nosy editors and decide to write at home. But me, I like digging in and being rooted somewhere, so I've decided this is going to be my base of operations. Naturally the Wi-Fi is massively great for research.

There's one downside to all this, and he's hovering right above me.

"I hear you'll be attending the Fleckerstein-Waterman nuptials," Dartmoor is saying.

I look up, startled.

"Say what?"

I had hoped to avoid running into Dartsy right away and I'm

kind of astonished by what he's saying. For the life of me I can't believe that he's talking about the Fleckerstein-Waterman nuptials I'm attending, but then how many other Fleckerstein-Waterman nuptials could there be?

The fact that he's gone out of his way to find me can't be good.

"I said, I've been informed that you will be attending the wedding of my good friends Wendell Fleckerstein and Genelle Waterman?"

"And how would you know that?" I say, more bluntly than intended. I force myself to remain calm, wondering in what universe Dartmoor and I coexist in overlapping social circles.

"I'm the best man—how could I *not* know?" he responds with indignation. "I have to say, Clarissa, I was a tad dumbfounded as well when I discovered that you're friends with Wendell's beautiful bride-to-be."

"That makes two of us," I mutter—on both the "friends" and "beautiful" score. I'm dying to tell him that her boobs are fake and she had her nose pinned—is that petty of me? Yes. I restrain my inner sixteen-year-old. Besides, do I detect a softening in Dartsy's tone? I wonder.

I'm also at least a teeny bit interested in how this tidbit of information rose to the attention of the two people at this very moment I hate most in the world. It raises a terrible possibility that the people I dislike might actually get together to talk about me. Every paranoid's nightmare.

"I'm curious," I say, "it must have been a tad odd that I came up in your conversation?" Tad? Why would I say tad? That's what Dartsy just said. I've got to stop this mimicking thing I do. Someday someone's going to punch me in the face for making fun of the way they speak.

"Well, Aubrey and I were dining with my old college chum Wendell and Genelle at the Arlington Club the other night when I mentioned your appearance and all the brouhaha with the skater boy on his knees," he rattles off, "then Wendie's beautiful Genelle went totally bonkers when I mentioned your name."

Whoa. I hope you don't mind if I stop everything here to diagram Dartmoor's last sentence? Even though sentence diagramming went out in the Stone Age shortly after Misters Reed and Kellogg (yes, I'm obsessed with diagramming sentences enough that I actually know who invented them) made a fortune off their literary invention, my crotchety old English teacher Mrs. Walker was a throwback. She insisted we all know how to diagram sentences even though it had ceased being part of the Tupper High School curriculum back in the '60s, when my parents were in school. Heaven forbid you were dyslexic like poor Chubs Wolenski.

Hugh was also known to pull out his bloodred editing pencil and make wayward apprentice writers diagram pernicious sentences as a punishment when he became frustrated with their writing. Thankfully, he never had to do that with me.

If it isn't obvious by now, I'm an unrepentant meanderer when it comes to ideas and understanding everything going on around me (aka "explaining"). I've never met a tangent I haven't liked. That's why diagramming has been good for me. When I really float off into the never-never land of thoughts and ideas, diagramming anchors me.

I know that makes me a total writing geek, but constructing, deconstructing, and reconstructing sentences helps me figure out what I wanted to say to begin with. I honestly think a good sentence diagram is a work of art. Hey, I'm as vernacular as the next girl, but I still think unscrewing a sentence can be revealing—maybe it's even a hedge against early-onset Alzheimer's.

So when I hear a fine specimen, like Dartmoor's last utterance, sometimes I just have to stop and mentally picture what it would look like diagrammed. It also helps me highlight what is truly weird about what has been said. Case in point:

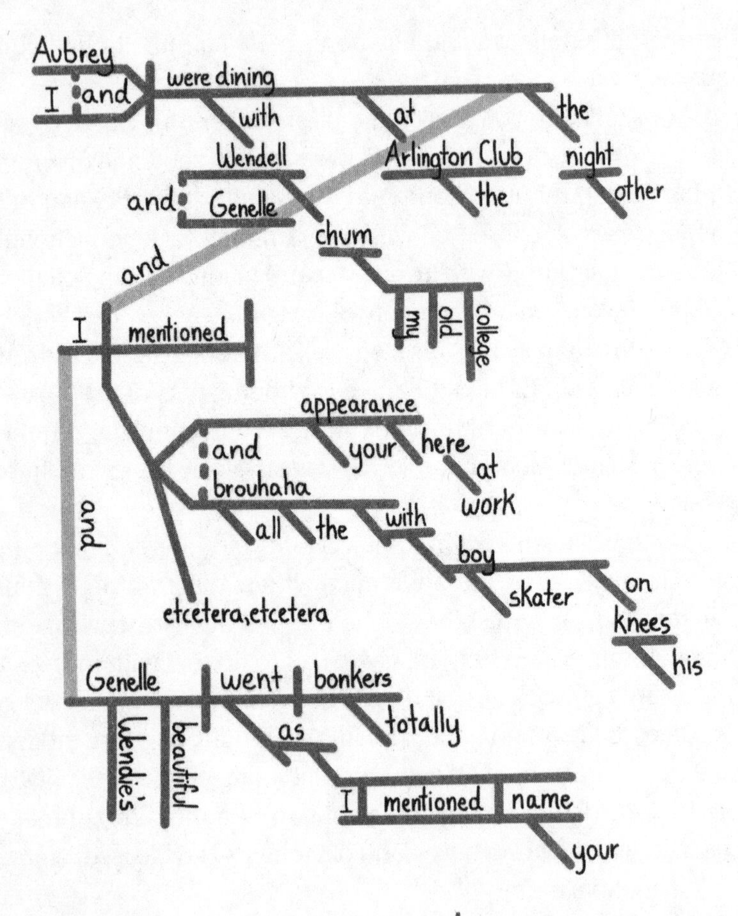

Here we have Dartmoor Millburn, an economic genius who's supposedly a member of some crazy Delta Gamma Epsilon Honor Society at Wesleyan School of Economics (I did my Internet homework), and he's managed to cram into one run-on, compounded sentence such a jumble of prepositions, indirect objects, linking verbs, and predicate nouns that it takes three lines of diagrams to make sense of it.

As every stalwart sentence diagrammer knows, the more a diagram wanders around the page and folds back on itself, the more you can assess whether the genius behind the sentence is Joycean in his understanding of the English language or just plain full of BS.

What do all of those wandering clauses reveal in Dartmoor's case? Well, pretty much that his mind is a convoluted mess and that he's probably lying, if not in fact, then by inference.

I also find the term *bonkers* a curious one for Genelle. Is that how she refers to her new superboobs? Or how Dartmoor the Great thinks of them? Perhaps a Freudian slip (which you can't diagram, by the way).

And where did the parents of these kids get their names—from *Game of Thrones* or Monty Python? I know Clarissa isn't exactly typical, but Aubrey and Wendie née Wendell? I'm more than thrown by the potential gender-bending implications. What name could be more ambiguous than Aubrey? Isn't that just a dyslexic version of Audrey? Unless it's a guy's name, but that's too much to process in the moment.

"I know we've gotten off on the wrong foot," he says, "but I'm looking forward to some non-work time to get to know you better." This makes me shudder. "I'm sure you'll like Wendie, Genelle's beau, he's my closest college chum. We worked on Wall Street together and rowed double sculls at the Henley Regatta."

I'm really suspicious now. Not one nasty personal inference about my brother, my lack of experience, or a mention of my impending deadline and doom. Not an insult in sight. The softer tone, the sharing of pretentious intimate details, and was that an apology? Why does this sound familiar? G-Bomb's insidious convoluted mea culpa rattles in my mind. Some time ago it dawned on me that her maneuver was more twisted than I initially thought. She knew that my parents saw Nick kissing another girl. Her "everyone loves weddings" line was most likely designed to expose that rift further rather than fix it. Now enter the evil Mr. Dartmoor Milburn fugue-ing the same theme.

Coincidence? Collusion?

Potato? Patahto?

"I understand *you've* found yourself a real catch. Music producer, is it? Genelle says that your mother raves about him. Is he another one of your DIY entrepreneurs? You certainly have a knack for these boys."

Fortunately, Nick and I are good . . . right? *Off-again, on-again* no more? But doubt lingers now that Dartmoor will be there. Too many malevolent forces are gathering in a confluence of events that is making my head spin. What exactly have I gotten myself into? A storm is brewing and I can feel it. *My stomach lurches.*

The good ship Nuzegeek *pitches and tosses, buffeted by heavy gales. The gray cubicles slide down the deck and over the railing into the deep churning seas. On-again and off-again waves flooding across the ship and back out into the ocean. Where's Nick when I need him? Oh no! There he is, bobbing up and down in the black water! Up and back down again. Will he disappear among the waves? Block and tackle lines swing dangerously, pendulum-like across the deck as sheets of rain fall slant-wise. Drenched again, it feels as though I could be thrown overboard at any moment, dropping into the turbulent depths. Grabbing a nearby backstay to lash myself to the mast, I hear a loud snap. The line breaks free from the cleat and I am flying, swinging out over the dark churning waters, out of control. . . .*

"In any case," Dartmoor says as I transition back to reality and try to wring out my brain, "this Mr. Wonderful of yours has *got* to be better than that lovesick skate freak. Speaking of which"—he leans down and adds in a conspiratorial whisper—"seems like MT is getting in touch with her inner Avril Lavigne."

He looks up and I follow his glance to see MT skateboarding down the Nuzegeek office hallway with Norm running by her side to steady her.

"That—I'll never forgive you for," Dartmoor says.

CHAPTER 24

I decide to take a breather on my Nuzegeek article. Between the momentary lessening of tensions with Dartsy and all my diligent work, I'm feeling almost comfortable about meeting my delivery date. A quick stop at Amarcord Vintage to see what they've got in the way of dresses I might wear to a wedding is on my agenda. Amacord is a mecca for "pre-loved" clothing. It's upscale without being snooty, and even though it might be the teensiest bit out of my usual price range, I think it's going to be worth it.

No matter your economic condition, you have to at least try to dress for success at work and socially. Considering what a big deal this wedding is shaping up to be, I figure it's worth dressing the part. I refuse to consider the psycho-sociological implications of shopping as a sedative or nerve calmer. Besides, as long as it's secondhand or on sale—it's a bargain, right?

I head for Lafayette Street.

Inside the tidy shop, I let my fingers trickle along the rows of hanging garments. I have to smile, contemplating what the soon-to-be Mrs. Wendell Fleckerstein would think if she knew I'd be wearing a "used" garment to her wedding. She'd consider it gross, like maybe I'd catch a disease from the residual microscopic flakes of skin that might be clinging to the fibers. She'd also assume my decision was money-based and that I couldn't afford a brand-spanking-new frock from Bergdorf's—which is true. So on that score, she's right. But I have far better reasons than thrift and a love of classic couture for preferring vintage clothing.

For me, every dress tells a story. Every pair of hand-sewn trousers and every satin-lined skirt tells a tale. When I see a mid-'60s Pucci mini sheath, I know there's history deep within the fabric. Somebody fell in love in that dress, or kissed a stranger on New Year's Eve, or learned to dance the Watusi. History lives in every cuff, every hemline. I get to imagine all kinds of past adventures my clothes enjoyed.

Bungee jumping into your own past has its drawbacks, but time travel is another, and it's way more satisfying. Diving through the vintage racks, it feels as though the further I go back in time to another world of glamour, the smaller the sizes are. Lots of black dresses that say they're my size aren't.

I've always felt that trying to understand how clothes are sized requires advanced trigonometry and higher calculus. Something that Rodgers is way better at than I am. Curiously, I've never seen Rodgers in a dress. There must be a connection there.

She's probably insulted by the concept of vanity, as in "Vanity Sizing." A brilliant marketing idea, but really, shouldn't it be called "Feel Better Sizing"? Women don't like to think that they're bigger, so that's where the vanity part comes in. Just to give you an idea: Marilyn Monroe was a size 14 in her day, and today she would be a size 8. Would that have made Norma Jeane feel better? Who knows. No matter, you have to ignore the silly numbers and go by sight and feel. Not that I expect anything to be actually ready to wear. I always have to pull out my trusty Singer to snug up the fit.

As I meander through hanger after hanger, everything seems too expensive or too stodgy. I run the names of the other vintage stores nearby in my mind, prepared to jump ship for an alternative. I'm about to give in to disappointment, when I see a shimmer of black hanging across the store two rows down. It's the sexiest little wisp of an LBD.

I hustle over and stake my claim. The smart little dress has a structured corset-shaped bodice while the bottom half is an embellished small skirt above the knee. Not exactly tea length, but let people like Genelle worry about that. It takes me a moment to realize that this simple little scene-stealer is a Reiss Saskia and more contemporary than everything else in the rack. I wonder what society darling sold this one. I cringe, afraid to look at the price tag. Dare I hope? I sneak a peek. No *way.* A little pricey, but not too bad. The vintage gods have been kind today.

In the dressing room I slip it on and when I come out to look in the mirror, the girl at the register has envy in her eyes. She's almost exactly my age and size. I see her brow knit ever so slightly and I know what she's thinking: *How did that little gem escape my scrutiny?* I figure I better hurry up and buy it before she makes up some excuse as to why it costs more or grabs it for herself.

I snap a photo with my phone and text it to Jody for her approval. She responds almost instantaneously with a winky smiley face fashioned from punctuation marks. As a writer, I'm always pleased to see the general public embracing the semicolon, regardless of how they choose to employ it. I'm amazed that she hasn't made the transition to emojis. Hard to believe there's a history of making faces with punctuation marks and Jody is old-school.

I slap my cash on the counter and while I wait for the clerk to bag my treasure, I begin to picture Nick and I together. *He smiles when he sees me in the dress and puts his arms around me, his hand running down my spine. I turn and put my fingers through the curls of hair at the nape of his neck and . . .* I have to stop myself.

See, this has always been one of my personal issues—my alt fantasy life. By definition, it has almost nothing to do with what is actually going on. I'm good at imagining whole futuristic scenarios, ambitious possibilities, and in many ways, that's been a plus. It's helped me find my goals and go for them. But there's a downside. I tend to imagine relationships before they happen, every phase of them, including how they might end. And most of the time, they don't turn out the way I imagine. Or worse: I'm so tied up in what I imagine that I don't know what is actually happening. Sometimes I'm so worried that the relationship might end, looking for all of those negative signs, that I think it's over before it's over. *No predicted endings*, I tell myself, and try to listen this time.

I wonder if that's why I'm so confused about Sam. See, after our notorious high school reunion . . . ahem, union in the red pickup, Sam and I fell in love. Even though there was a female-to-male ratio of almost 18 to 1 at his college, he spent every spare weekend he could in the city with me. He had this awesome dog named Pie, a mixed border collie and shepherd, and the three of us would go everywhere together. Pie was like our guardian angel. We'd go out to Montauk on weekends and while Sam taught me to surf, Pie would wait on the shore watching us until we came in. If we got separated on the beach or in the street, she'd go back and forth between us until we were together again.

Meanwhile, Sam's marine biology professor Miquelo Archipenko selected him for a prestigious summer internship in Italy at Istituto Superiore per la Conservazione ed il Restauro, the Underwater Archaeological Operation Unit in Naples.

It turns out there are more sunken, "drowned" cities in the world than you could ever imagine. Although they haven't found Atlantis (yet . . .), there are the ruins of ancient submerged sites in Yonaguni, Japan; Pavlopetri, Greece; Heraklion, Egypt; Atlit-Yam, Israel; and many others. If you believe that's all fantasy, think about what almost happened to New Orleans after Katrina or NYC after Hurricane Sandy. Cities get submerged. That's the way of the world.

Near Naples, there's an underwater city that is an archaeological park and where they have been undertaking the preservation and restoration of buildings over the years—all beneath the water. It's called the Underwater Archaeological Park of Baiae, and "going to work" there means slipping into a diving suit and strapping on an oxygen tank. The town is called Baia, named after Odysseus's navigator. It was the Hamptons of the ancient world, the place where Caligula built a pleasure villa and where Nero murdered his mother, Agrippina. Lots of scandal and excess, just like any good resort community. That's where Sam and I spent our summer of bliss.

Sam's dad offered to take care of Pie and staked Sam some living expenses. Sam flew ahead a month in advance and found a little apartment on Via Laura that was pretty cool—all stucco and tile with a tiny kitchen. He began his total-immersion Italian lessons and his brotherhood of diving comrades opened every door for us.

Normally, I'm not much for cramming my butt into a wet suit, breathing like Darth Vader, and strapping sixteen pounds of weight around my waist in order to sink to the bottom of the ocean. But having Sam for a guide and the chance to see the wonders he had told me about made even that claustrophobic nightmare tolerable.

After a beginners course in the Parco Piscini, aka the public swimming pool, I had the basics covered for a short dive. But the first time I jumped in I sank like a stone and immediately freaked out. Fortunately, Sam was there for me with a safety rope. He grabbed my mask and made reassuring eye contact while I continued to breathe, slowly calming myself down.

As we dived beneath the translucent Mediterranean through the entrances of underwater villas, the sea horses scurried between the marble nyphaeum (fancy talk for nymphs) and the statues of Polyphemus (the one-eyed son of Poseidon) and Dionysus (famous Greek party boy). It was exquisite and otherworldly.

Every morning at work, Sam explored the wonders of ancient drowned atriums and colonnades with seaweed and fish swimming through them. I've never seen him happier.

Every evening on dry land, we were joined at the hip, learning how to eat and cook—way more than I ever learned from Mom. In Italy, we ate the most extraordinary meals in tiny ordinary *trattorias* and *rosticcerias*.

The next day we'd try to figure out how to prepare what we had eaten the night before. Italian food is great that way—you taste every ingredient and you can find those same ingredients in the nearby open-air market, the same markets where the restaurant chefs shopped. We only had to follow our taste buds to learn how to prepare the most delectable food. We bought wedges from wheels of Parmigiano rather than shaking those cardboard containers of Kraft cheese, we made our own spaghetti and pizza dough. Sam would buy homemade sausage and pancetta and every week we'd take our five-litre bottle to the local wine store and fill it up from a pump like at a gas station. It was a lot more exciting than shopping at the SuperSaver in Springfield.

Sam and I were the charming young American couple everywhere we went. To cries of "*Ciao bella!*" and "*Ciao ragazzi!*" we made our way through a sweltering, heavenly Naples summer.

During Sam's underwater mornings, I sat on our tiny sunny terrace writing my senior thesis for school. I chose as my topic "Gaming Education: An Investigation of Game-Based Social Emotional Learning (SEL)," something near and dear to my heart. Despite my early video-game passions, I hadn't turned out to be a gamer girl myself, but I still found it interesting. So I figured it would be a good topic for my thesis, considering I had navigated my childhood issues by making goofy video games of one sort or another. Social-emotional learning and video-game play has become a big deal in the edu-gamer biz. Fortunately, I had a title with a colon for my thesis—the most crucial requirement.

As the summer came to a close, we had one last balmy night of rapture in our little *appartamento al mare* and made our plans for the future. We were so in love, there didn't seem to be any question whether we'd continue our Naples adventure back in New York City. We discussed every detail and it seemed like Sam was totally on board. He seemed fine with moving back to NYC from the time-frozen depths of the sea. I'd go back to Hugh, and the *Daily Post*, and Sam would join me after checking out one more underwater site in Greece with his team and then . . . well, we had even bigger plans for the future.

Every moment after I returned to New York that September, I felt like Sam and I were still together. Everything I bought was for us. I checked out restaurants where we might go. I walked wistfully through the Union Square farmers' market compiling possible menus we might cook. When he sent word that he was flying to Egypt to work on another site and he would be delayed for six more weeks, I never worried. I was busy with my own job and I still imagined Sam showing up in the weeks to come—we had agreed, right? Besides, waiting for Sam was still better than being alone, on my own again, in New York, even if I really was actually alone, on my own again, waiting for Sam.

His team went from Greece to Egypt and from Egypt to Japan and it was pretty hard to complain because they were all really prestigious short-term gigs. It's funny when you're in love: You assume it's all good and it will be okay, until you realize it's not.

Now I see that the whole time back in New York, I was

pretending and I didn't even know it. Even when I first met Norm, I figured I was still with Sam and it was okay to hang out with someone to pass the time. I didn't know if Sam was with anyone. But if I'm honest about it, he probably was—at least some of the time.

If only we still had Pie, our guardian angel, herding us back together.

So if it ended at all, that's how it ended. There wasn't an argument, a problem, or a discussion. Sam just literally and figuratively dropped out of sight somewhere beneath the seas of the ancient world. Pretty weird considering what we had agreed we were going to do that last balmy night in Baia.

We were going to run off together somewhere and elope. Yep, it would be just for us—all seclusion and romance. We weren't even going to tell anyone right away. We planned to fill people in later and have a big party. It was so secret that I've never said a word about it to anyone, until this day, not even to Jody. It's pretty hard to tell someone about a disappointment so crushingly personal that even now it seems totally unreal.

What happened to Sam, the most dependable person in the world? Why was he a no-show? Didn't we talk it out and both decide it was what we wanted to do more than anything? I tried to ask his dad about it but I never got an answer and I could see it made him nervous. Did Sam change his mind? Was he carried away on some secret mission? Will I ever know?

"Here's your change," the shop girl says cheerfully. I look at her, wondering what she means and shake myself back to reality. Her face has turned from envy to admiration. "Love that dress—I would have bought it if you hadn't!" She smiles.

"I know," I say, and manage a smile in return.

"I hope you wear it someplace wonderful," she adds as I take my bag and leave.

"Me, too," I say.

CHAPTER 25

Anxious and excited, I manage to survive until Saturday afternoon. It's not clear which part I'm most excited and anxious about: my dress, Nick, or this weird wedding stacked with people I dread. Nick and I communicated once in the span of time that has elapsed between our final Where Have You Bean? visit and this very moment. It's so strange how often communication seems to go dark right before a big relationship event. There was only one eight-word text confirming the time he would be at my place of residence. Just eight words.

I made the mistake of getting ready on the early side, which leaves Elvis and me alone to entertain ourselves. I challenge him to a staring contest, but he yawns and refuses to look me in the eye. When I persist he runs away. I give chase into the kitchen but he isn't there. How he can disappear in a tiny apartment this size is beyond me. Sorcery, I tell you!

My brain obsesses less if I'm rushed or a few minutes late so usually I avoid being ready early. The kitchen clock ticks off the seconds—yes, I'm fixated on the long black hand that makes its abrupt little thrust second by second, emitting the tiniest tap, like the sound of Elvis smacking on food, or gum snapping, or the clack of high heels when you walk.

The longer I wait, the more anxiety outweighs excitement, and the more I think about Nick and his boomerang girlfriend Roxie. Roxie is practically the definition of a bad penny. The way Rodgers and Nick have talked about her makes Roxie sound capable of almost anything, including feigning death and then *slowly rising out of the grave, her tattooed arm thrusting sharply from the dirt to drag Nick back into her Crypto Goth Netherworld.* Shit. Please, Clarissa, stop? Get a grip. No need to go paranoid schizo on me. Me being Clarissa, naturally. Sometimes even I get lost in my inner dialogue. But there's just one thing that I absolutely need to know . . . *Where is Nick?*

Elvis has returned and he's giving me the stink-eye. What does he know that I don't?

I can't help thinking that maybe Roxie's gotten word of our impending rendezvous *and handcuffed Nick to the radiator in the basement dungeon of her apartment.*

"Calm down," I say so loud that Elvis scurries away again. He doesn't like it when I yell out loud to myself and pace like a madwoman. But then who would?

"Do something worthwhile," I say. "Check your hair."

But my hair is perfect. Yes, I double-check in the mirror. It should be. I spent hours on it.

Usually I just clean the kitchen, the bathroom, the corners of the cabinets. That keeps me in check and has the added advantage of establishing order and good hygiene. It's not full-blown severe OCD. Besides, I object to the *DSM-V.* That's the *Diagnostic and Statistical Manual of Mental Disorders, Fifth Edition*, where psychiatrists catalog diagnoses for everything from post-caffeine intoxication disorder, trichotillomania, sibling relational problems, post-traumatic embitterment disorder, as well as good old-fashioned penis envy.

I mean, I'll admit to some serious caffeine intoxication and a little trich now and then, and Lord knows I have difficulty dealing with my little brother, but I don't remotely envy anyone else's anatomy.

I prefer to think of my behavior as eccentric and colorful. Like my superstitions.

It's been speculated by behavioral scientists that superstitiousness and obsessive-compulsive disorder actually exist on a continuum. I've read the reports. That's how OCD I am! But after poring over the symptomatology on all the neurocognitive data, I feel as if in my case, I've taken superstitions to a whole new level of creativity and understanding with a very healthy twist.

Take, for instance, "spilling"—the frequently overlooked omen of bad luck. Admit it, you probably didn't even know that spilling is bad luck, did you? People simply don't understand how an unfortunate spill can lead like a chain reaction to an even more unfortunate series of interconnected events that are almost impossible to know about or even predict. Similar to the butterfly effect.

When you look at this whole chain of events with my parents and Nick, it all began with an ominous spill. I couldn't help worrying about it at the time. But you may wonder, what is there to do if something *accidentally* spills? Are you simply a victim of fate, unable to change the outcome? Will events keep cascading out of your control? No. I say no! Not if you have the *antidote*! That is my innovation. See, I believe that for every superstition, there is an antidote—a counterbalancing ritual that creates a restart and reestablishment of order and progress. Fight magic with magic, I say. Or is that something that Gandalf said on his way to Isengard in the film version of the first installment of *Lord of the Rings*? I forget.

All I know is that bad and unlucky things happen, you can't change that. But you can adjust how you react and take preventative measures. So, for instance, if you spill, then you must spill again from the remainder of the glass or cup or whatever. This antidote, or "re-spilling" as it's called (okay, I'm the only one who calls it that), stops the onrushing possibilities of fate and resets the path of your life in a take-charge, positive direction.

Think about it: Where would I be now if I had just stopped when Mom and Dad surprised me in the *Daily Post* building and spilled again? How would things have turned out differently? Maybe I would have decided to come clean with the truth then and there and all these events of the last week would have been unnecessary and I would be on an entirely altered path.

I believe there are these serendipitous or serendumpitous moments in life's journey where, like switches on train tracks, our lives shift direction for a split second or forever and we can find ourselves for better or worse on a separate and distinctive parallel journey.

That's why I "keep" Elvis, I guess. I couldn't bear to have another black cat cross my path and disappear, and it's nice to have another Elvis in my life, so I opted for him to stay.

There is a famous Chinese legend where the gods tie an invisible red cord around the ankles of those who are destined to meet. Two people connected by the red thread become lovers, regardless of time, place, or circumstances. The magical cord may tangle and stretch, but it never breaks. Kind of like a cosmic pinkie swear. Sam and I seemed to be connected that way, but did our red string snap?

Or was Sam simply my "first love," a concept I'm not fond of because it implies that we have a second love, and a third, and so forth. If we all have "first loves" and subsequent loves, how do we really know when we have experienced "true love"?

And what about Nick and me? We seem to be connected somehow. Didn't Albert Einstein say, "God doesn't play dice"?

I have read that scientists who study string theory insist that we live in a multiverse filled with universes that encompass all possible outcomes. In some separate universe, Sam and I eloped and are happily hitched, Nick and I never spoke to each other, and Elvis and I are hurtling through space in a rocket ship. Or not.

What is fate and destiny in a multiverse world? Are we all fated to multi-exist simultaneously alive and dead just like poor old Schrödinger's cat? At least I gave my cat an actual name. And how does the multiverse apply to love and fidelity?

Let's face it, as far as we have reason to know and believe, in this universe I didn't spill again. Like it or lump it, this is the universe I'm stuck in, and events have hurtled forward out of my control until this very moment. Thankfully, Nick and I have reconnected as though nothing ever happened before.

The second hand continues to drive unrelentingly forward as I watch and listen to it click.

It's not quite time yet but—*where is that boy?* Shouldn't he be sending me a "getting close" text? Elvis reappears from around the corner. I'm sure the little devil thinks this is all one big game of hide-and-seek. In fact I'm convinced he actually thinks I'm just a big cat, only dumber and more clumsy because of my size. Cats are so self-centered.

Okay, Clarissa, get it together. Breathe in. Breathe out.

I take another breath to calm myself and seriously consider something more important—changing my shoes.

See, the first pair I put on is always the most gorgeous, but usually the most painful. So I slide a different possible shoe selection on each foot and do this flamingo thing where I stand on one leg, comparing different shoe options by standing sideways in front of the mirror. Kitten heel on the left foot (switch), strappy stiletto on the right. Platform pump on left foot (switch), ankle bootie on right. That went on this morning for, like, fifteen minutes, testing shoe after shoe until I ended up going with the ones I had on first because, as I could have predicted, those were the best choice all along. Anyone could have predicted they were the best choice all along. The danger, as you can probably guess, is that I could have gotten carried away, trying on every pair, and the buzzer might have rung mid-flamingo.

Fragrance was another thing I dilly-dallied with. I put a little bit on the inner wrists and behind the ears, just like Mom taught me. Then I had to be careful not to get carried away. Feeling frisky, I put a little behind my knees. I thought about doing that movie thing where I spray a cloud of perfume into the air and walk through it, but I stopped. I didn't want to smell like the perfume girl at Bloomingdale's, and who knows? It might be allergy-inducing for Nick.

There's not much left to do so I settle on the purse check. Altoids: check. Lipstick: check. Feminine hygiene apparatus: check. Condom: check. I take out the condom, worrying about what that says about my expectations. House keys, cell phone, travel tissue: check, check, check. Then I go back and add the condom, just in case. Check! Then I take it out. Sometimes I get totally stuck on this one.

Shouldn't he be here by *now*? This is where things get dangerous. I have been known to step outside my building to test if the downstairs buzzer is working. I've even managed to lock myself out on occasion doing this. I decide not to go down today because I'm terrified Nick might pull up just as I'm ringing my own buzzer, which would look particularly dorky.

Okay, he's still not here and now I'm heading into that nightmare territory of thinking that I gave him the wrong address, wrong time, or the wrong day.

WHERE THE FUCK IS HE?!

Bzzzt!

The sound makes me jump, but it's music to my ears. He didn't forget, get lost, change his mind, get chained to the radiator, or drop dead from a rare and undetectable allergy. *He showed up!*

I'm so excited that when I open the door I can't keep Elvis from slipping out. Damn. No time to chase him now. He always comes back in ways I never understand anyway. He wouldn't just leave, right?

I take another deep breath and head out the door.

CHAPTER 26

"Wow."

"Wow yourself," I say.

We're standing on the sidewalk in front of my building. Somehow we're both astonished. I love what he's wearing beneath his motocross leathers—super-skinny black pants and a narrow-cut long-lined dark charcoal jacket, navy-checked patterned vest, and a pocket square with a complementary white linen shirt. Simple, but all tailored within an inch of its life.

"You look amazing," he says.

I hadn't realized I was holding my breath waiting for him to say something.

"That dress is dangerous . . . for a bike. Walking around, too," Nick says, smiling.

He hands me the same all-encompassing leather jacket I wore the first time and I slip into the luxury of it, feeling as though I have truly rejoined my first pre-spill reality. Somehow fate, the multiverse, or whatever you prefer to call it has pulled that train track switch the other way and events have totally realigned to where they should have been in the first place. Maybe the effects of that tragic unaddressed spill have worn off.

Short dress, high heels, and all, Nick pulls me up on the

Harley. The hog practically purrs, happy to welcome me back. Maybe it even missed me.

I am not stupid enough to forgo safety for style, so despite the hours of careful coiffing, I put the helmet on without question.

Nick revs it up a notch and the bike rumbles like a jungle cat, making me feel rebellious and cool.

"Ready?" he asks.

"You have no idea."

As Nick revs the bike into gear, we glide away from the curb. I snuggle up against him, holding tight around his waist. I've come full circle—holding Nick and riding down the road where I belong.

I don't know why, but as Nick's Harley screams onto the highway, I think about how far I've come. It's one of those leaps of time that make me feel older in a good way, like I've grown up a notch or two. As the Harley accelerates, the city landscape blurs into countryside and I wistfully reflect on the assorted stages of my brief existence:

MY SWEETHEART AGE

When I still snuggled up to Mom and gave her kisses and Dad chucked me on the shoulder and called me "Sport." Those were the years when everything came down to that old *Sesame Street* song: "One of These Things Is Not Like the Other." Life was as simple as telling apples from oranges.

MY EINSTEIN YEARS

Those days were followed by My Einstein Years when I explained it all and knew everything. Boys (particularly brothers) seemed oblivious and naive in those

e=mc²

days. I remember Mr. Sapperstein, our neighbor and local pharmacist, standing in the kitchen and going on and on to my dad about the differences between boys and girls he saw in the pharmacy.

"If a fourteen-year-old girl comes into my store, she's got money in her pocket and she knows what she wants and what it costs. She knows all the makeup brands and their relative merits," he'd say. "But if a fourteen-year-old boy comes into my store, he doesn't have a penny on him. He doesn't know what a pharmacy is and he's probably lost or up to no good."

Now I realize my Einstein period was easy-peasy because I coasted so smoothly through those tween years. I was better than the game. My goal in life was to be the star of my own reality as opposed to being a reality star. These days, everyone is so obsessed with being famous that they've created new categories of fame to accommodate as many people as possible. You can be Tumblr Famous and YouTube Famous. You can be Reality Famous or become a Bravolebrity. Was it Countess LuAnn de Lesseps from *The Real Housewives of New York City* renunion special with Andy Cohen who posed the ontological question, "If you're not famous for something, do you even exist?" Or maybe that was just another quip from Andy Warhol. Warhol managed to say it all about fame and begin the inevitable devaluation of style, fame, fashion, and art for generations to come.

DRAMA QUEEN TEENS

Lucky for me, I lightly skimmed above this stage. Being BFB (Before Facebook) made it a little easier than it is today. Somehow I skirted the sex, drugs, and drama years partly because we were in tiny Springfield and partly because my mom and dad were so different from everyone else's, so I was pretty focused and directed. Some escape the sex and drugs, few escape the drama. By drama I mean all the girls at school holding grudges, throwing fits, bullying, and the shifting love-hate alliances that dominate high school life. The High School Valley of Death, I call it. Girls can be so tough on each other, criticizing each other's bodies way more harshly than any boy.

PREMATURE MATURITY

I hit this phase when I moved to New York. Sort of Einstein Years Lite Redux. As I matured in those first few years in New York City, I thought I was incredibly smart and independent until I got my butt kicked at the newspaper by everyone else—people who were actually experienced.

THE AGE OF INDECISION

That's when I hit my mid-twenties, post-Norm, and found myself unemployed. Every day I'd hope and pray for clarity. All those things that were crystal clear when I was fourteen seemed foggy and confusing. The Great Recession didn't help.

The truth is that it's always a bad time to be a twenty-something. Just think, in the Middle Ages, being twenty-something was peaking and everything after was old age. Charlemagne won his first campaign at twenty-seven, and Alexander the Great was only twenty-two when he conquered Greece. It makes my mind spin.

But right now I don't have to think about all that. I just have to snug up and hold on to Nick while the rising whine of the motorcycle catapults us down the highway. Which brings me to my big decision, arrived at over the course of the week: Today is the day I'm going to come clean with my parents, no matter how much my mother yammers on. Regardless of the obstacles, I'm going to tell them about the *Daily Post* going belly-up (especially now that I have a new job). And most important, I'm going to tell them the truth about the night they met Nick and saw him with Roxie at the airport, especially because he'll be right there standing close to me.

As far as I'm concerned, holding on to Nick and flying down the highway could last forever. Here's hoping that G-Bomb's wedding doesn't ruin this.

CHAPTER 27

I'm staring at Botticelli's *Birth of Venus*, aka Venus on the Half Shell—in ice. Genelle wasn't kidding when she said her wedding was going to be posh. I'm captivated by the glacier's worth of ice sculpture and what it says about mankind's inability to come to grips with global warming. There might be more ice here than all that's left on the polar shelf. I notice that even the carver has felt compelled to enhance Venus's proportions significantly. Venus—the goddess of beauty, sex, and fertility—seems to have undergone a breast enhancement and augmentation to the degree that her hand, which never covered much to begin with, now barely covers anything at all. Botticelli might have been appalled at the corruption of his feminine ideal, but after all, it's Genelle's wedding and it's clearly indicative of her revisionist bent, so to speak.

And speaking of things that are bigger than natural, I marvel at the architecture of the country club itself.

When I received the vanilla-scented invitation I couldn't help Googling the venue where Genelle's nups were taking place. Formerly christened Woodlea, "The Sleepy Hollow Country Club" was a Stanford White manse built by a Vanderbilt and incorporated as a club by a Rockefeller. Its members have ranged from J. J. Astor to Bill Murray.

Moments ago we were roaring up the endless driveway until we reached the towering gates.

"Park your Harley?" one beefy attendant asked. Decked out in Armani, the valet staff seemed a bit overdressed. Makes you wonder how much to tip them. Luckily, that wasn't a problem for us, because Nick just roared past and found a safe place to park the self-serve way. He'd never let one of those guys lay a finger on his bike.

We locked up the helmets and jackets and walked toward the massive main building. There's only one word to describe the place.

immensitude (n.) the impression of being bigger than big, 2013; comb. form of ***immense*** (adj.) (mid-14c.) from Latin *immensus*, meaning boundless, immeasurable, and ***attitude*** (n.), 1660s, via French *attitude* (17c.), from Italian *attitudine* "disposition, posture." ***immensi*** + ***tude***, as in "too big to fail," 1984, first used to describe bank size by Stewart Brett McKinney, or "enough already" based on the original Yiddish "genug shoyn." Citations include: surfer term of astonishment ref: Maverick Waves, 1974; portions of pastrami at Katz's Deli, cited in Yelp, 2007. Also see related citation from adult entertainment industry, "Frankenstein Zone," in reference to penis size.

Beyond the main entrance we encounter a sweeping view of the Hudson and the expansive velvety green lawns that slope to the river. Little boys from the age of three and up flock around us with upturned collars like miniature Tucker Carlsons in their tiny sweaters draped over their shoulders dressed in red, green, and yellow Ralph Lauren pants. Little girls scream and play tag in floral sundresses, some pearls, and even a few mini tiaras. Most of the male attendees are dressed in khaki pants and navy jackets and not a few bow ties. The groomsmen, who seem to move everywhere together en masse like a swarm of colorful auklets, are wearing coral pants, navy blazers, and matching coral ties with what look like little whales on them. I assume they don't realize that they're wearing an endangered species.

The women wear Carolina Herrera, Kate Spade, and a surplus of Lilly Pulitzer dresses. This reminds me of how shocked Hugh was when he found out that Pulitzer had come out with a line of brightly colored dresses. I had to stop him from throwing his prized framed gold Pulitzer medallions out the window of the *Post* building.

Everything at the country club is fratty, semi-nautical, and totally coordinated in a way that makes me twitch uncontrollably. Louise Vava Lucia Henriette le Bailly de la Falaise would have screamed. Nick and I stick out like downtown clubbers in a sea of purple and green Country Club Prep. Nick is speechless as he takes it all in. I assume in Bushwick, New York, he doesn't often see colors like teal, daffodil, mayonnaise, and ecru.

"Come on," I say, "let's find an out-of-the-way, discreet place to sit."

"Whatever you say," Nick says. "I feel like we've just entered an alien universe."

There are waves of white chairs spread across the lawn and it seems as though we've arrived just before the ceremony as everyone is settling down. I spy Jody waving at me enthusiastically, arm in arm with Rupert who, I notice, has a black eye. Despite the injury, they are obviously in love. As they slide through the rows of chairs to take their seats, I can practically see wedding bells ringing above their heads. I guess the wedding effect is working for them.

Nick nudges me. "Your parents are waving," he says.

I glance around, find Mom and Dad near the front, and give them a tiny Queen Elizabeth wave of my hand. The wedding effect seems to be working on them, too. I wonder who will catch the bouquet. I hope Marshall does, for his sake.

And there up front, surrounded in the aforementioned swarm of coral and navy blue, is the dread Dartmoor—the lead groomsman distinguished by his coral bow tie. Next to him, I assume, is the lucky groom Wendell Fleckerstein, who appears pretty normal in a solid anchor blue suit, dark tie, and dark-framed glasses. G-Bomb's hubbie-to-be is a bit on the nerdy prep side, but that's cool. I steer Nick toward two empty chairs in the back—better to have easy access to egress, I always say.

Nick's regular shyness seems to have returned, but as he puts his arm around my chair I slide closer and his arm falls over my shoulder. Everything feels as it should and I'm quite comfy in the back row, experiencing my own mild version of the wedding effect. I still haven't quite gotten over the fact that I'm sitting at my archenemy's wedding with the guy I thought got away. It's not lost on me that this might never have happened if it weren't for Genelle.

In the far-off distance, the pinging of golf balls on the golf course and the rattle of dishes and wineglasses being placed on a table somewhere echo across the lawn.

Club members claim online that the Headless Horseman threw his jack-o'-lantern at Ichabod Crane—the naive, gangly Tappan Zee schoolmaster who dared desire a girl above his station—at the exact location where we're sitting. But then again everyone in the hamlet of Sleepy Hollow probably says that. I bet there are "The Headless Horseman Slept Here" signs at the bed-and-breakfast places in town.

The bride's and groom's families face off from either side of the aisle. I'm sure Bridezilla Genelle put them through a protracted, emotionally fraught, multilateral negotiation leading up to this day. They look exhausted. But I must admit, it's all excruciatingly well planned.

As we await the bride, I examine the bridesmaids. They are wearing truly ghastly purple dresses with foofy sleeves, way too much crinoline, and some kind of doily thing in the front that make them look fat and flabby. I detect Genelle's handiwork in their embarrassment, calculated to make her shine all the more. There's probably a "how-to" chapter in her book about it.

As the band—the Westchester Swingadelic Funksters, according to their alphabet-crowded bass drum—strikes up a jazzy medley of "Hava Nagila" and "Jesu, Joy of Man's Desiring," it dawns on me for the first time that Genelle is marrying out of her Protestant tribe. I wonder who's converting. Apparently, the answer is no one.

A rabbi and a minister walk into a wedding . . . I know it sounds like the beginning of a joke, but that's *actually* what's happening. Two very round and jolly men, one wearing a tallith over his suit and tie and the other wearing a purple stole and white robe, have arrived to co-officiate the wedding in tandem, and they're walking down the aisle toward the flowered chuppah where Wendell, Dartmoor, and company are waiting.

As they settle in, the band strikes up the wedding march, and there is Councilman Waterman—wearing what looks like a very Ichabod Crane top hat—walking the lovely bride down the aisle.

A moment here to comment on G-Bomb's wedding dress: The dress is extravagant and exquisite. It starts at the bottom with its six-foot train and taffeta bodice that includes cascading floral appliqués, but when you get up top things get a little crazy. The busty bride has gone strapless and she's definitely intent on letting her unnatural assets shine with no form of restraint, except maybe body adhesive. Somehow the corset beneath is even more figure-boosting and you can tell that Genelle's struggling to keep her cleavage under control in the emotion of the moment. She really needs to cover those puppies before they start barking.

Then again, I'm not here to criticize. I'm here to make an appearance, say hello, and leave so that Nick and I can finally spend some uninterrupted quality time together.

As the ceremony begins in earnest, the rabbi-minister team

begins to alternate opening remarks and blessings. It's apparent that the couple loves each other very much, and by that I mean the rabbi and minister. Oy vey, they're practically finishing each other's sentences. I'm expecting them to break into the ol' soft-shoe any moment or tag-team wrestling.

When the minister recites the Lord's Prayer, the bride's side of the aisle joins in, and when the rabbi says a blessing over the wine in Hebrew, the groom's side follows along, separate but equal. The rabbi-minister team makes a big deal of passing the rings around. I thought they might even juggle or do a few magic tricks like pulling the ring out from behind the bride's ear, but no such luck. Soon it's over and everybody puts their eight hands together—that's the bride, the groom, and the two religious leaders. I wonder if they'll all be going on the honeymoon.

Finally, Wendell kisses the bride. Her new boobs do not pop out, and all is well. Now it's time for the glass-breaking ceremony. The rabbi gives a long explanation about the meaning of this colorful ritual. He says something about how the glass's permanently broken state symbolizes the marriage bond. Supposedly it's a representation of the fragility of human relationships.

"And it's the last time Wendell will get to put his foot down!" some old bubby cracks nearby and I resist laughing. But come on, people, about this glass-breaking ritual, aren't we really talking about symbolically losing your V-card here? I'm far from a Talmudic scholar—I'm not even Jewish. In fact, I thought we were Buddhists when I was growing up, but that doesn't keep me from having my own deeply held opinions. I mean, what else is supposed to get broken on a wedding night?

Intent on definitely putting an end to whatever the glass underneath the towel symbolizes, Wendell stomps decisively but his feet fly up, sending him tumbling to the ground. Everyone gasps. Dartmoor picks him up and brushes him off immediately. I guess that's his duty as groomsman. Wendell recovers his composure and then to avoid utter humiliation hurriedly stomps again—but there's no distinctive, lightbulb-popping, shattering glass sound. We all cling to the edges of our white wooden folding chairs, watching in suspense as he stomps again and again until he slips a second time. The wedding crowd collectively inhales, astounded.

The rabbi shakes his head and restrains Wendell before he tries another time. Wendell is visibly shaken as the rabbi whispers some secret advice in Wendell's ear and makes a minor adjustment to the towel. You can tell the rabbi is an old pro at this. After two more vigorous stomps, we have a breakthrough—the familiar popping sound resounds across the lawns of Sleepy Hollow. Everyone yells "Mazel tov" on our side and "Thank God" on the other. Although I wonder how this bodes for Genelle and Wendie's marriage, I'm standing and applauding as happily as anyone else. I'm crossing my fingers, wishing the best for the bride and groom and secretly praying that Nick and I survive the reception.

CHAPTER 28

We make our way through a tunnel of ivory roses, green hydrangeas, and calla lilies to the reception area. I'm thinking: Let's say hi to Mom and Dad, offer my little mea culpa, run the required reception gauntlet wishing Genelle, Wendell, and Dartmoor (if we have to) our best, and get the hell out of here.

"So, besides the boob job, the nose work, and her poor taste in wedding dresses, what do you hate about her?" Nick asks. That's what I like about Nick. He's quiet, even shy at times, but he sees everything.

"Decide for yourself," I say, nodding to his left, because Genelle has spotted us and she's jiggling her way over. She manages to keep together what little there is of the upper part of her wedding dress and drag her train and Wendell across the lawn all at the same time.

"Clarissa! It's so great to see you!" she exclaims loud enough that the entire wedding party can hear and gives me what must go down as one of the most uncomfortable hugs I've ever experienced. I notice in the process that she's sweating profusely. "And this must be Rick! Are you guys okay?" She gives us her practiced, lower-lip-protruding expression of sadness, making me think she must have a degree in mime from Juilliard.

Nick looks nonplussed. Me, I'm gobsmacked. Yes, I use that word because it's the only one big enough and weird enough to describe how I feel. Wendell and Nick trade deer-caught-in-the-headlights glances and we endure what seems like the longest awkward silence in the history of wedding receptions. No one knows what to do, so I decide to break the gridlock.

"Genelle, we wouldn't have missed your wedding for the world. It was beautiful," I say as artificially as it sounds. I can tell by the way Genelle squeezes the hydrangea-and-lily bouquet in her garland-withering death grip that she wishes Nick were shorter, uglier, and not so laid-back. The fact that I'm happy must make her want to scream.

I can see the gears turn in Genelle's head. She contemplates a response and opens her mouth to speak, but nothing comes out. She closes it before gnats fly down her throat, but I can see she's thinking hard, trying to come up with something to save face. We're all just letting her hang out there either out of unconcern (Nick), hostility (me), or lack of awareness (Wendell), but anticipation is building nonetheless.

I'm sure it's only a few seconds, but it seems like hours pass. I'm thinking: *This awkward standoff can't last much longer, right?* She's the bride, she has a receiving line, she has to see guests and relatives, hear toasts, dance the first dance. But Genelle seems unwilling to let go of her original goal to humiliate me. So she's calculating, scheming, trying to figure out how to wring just a tiny bit of the satisfaction she had hoped for from the situation. But what can she say? I mean, Nick didn't even seem to notice her name-mangle and Wendell has clearly already grown accustomed to standing around uselessly as Genelle works her wiles. I pity him and the pain of his future marriage, but maybe he likes it or is oblivious, who knows? I'm certainly not willing to alleviate her discomfort.

She opens her mouth again and I'm honestly mesmerized, wondering what on earth she might possibly say.

She takes such a deep breath that her superboobs expand and I worry she'll pop out of her dress. "Well . . . enjoy the glow of our bliss!" she says and smiles impossibly.

I am appropriately speechless.

"Come, Wendell!" Genelle grabs Wendell by the arm, pivots, and flounces off. "I could use a drink," she grunts as they walk away.

I turn to Nick, anxiously awaiting his assessment.

"Wow. Okay. I get it," he says and I squeeze his hand. I really want to fist bump and do the victory dance, but I restrain myself.

"So let's find Marshall and Janet and split this burg," I say, peering about as everyone lines up to give Genelle and Wendell their best wishes. Unfortunately, Mom and Dad are well down the line and I don't think I can legitimately pull them out at this point.

"So you're going to come clean and tell them the truth?" Nick asks. How did he know what I was thinking? Has he added mind reading to his abilities? I kind of don't like the way it cramps my wiggle room.

"Yes," I say curtly, hating that I sound defensive. I feel especially bad when I look over at Marshall and Janet and see how content they seem. Do I really want to interrupt their happiness with something as awful as the truth?

But I swallow my pride and take us meandering to the other side of the receiving line, figuring there's no need to give the bride and groom our best wishes, because, frankly, they aren't going to get any better wish than the wish we just gave them. So we'll wait, ready to pounce on Mom and Dad as they exit, freshly renewed by Genelle's wedding effect. After all, Mom and Dad might be one of the few couples here actually feeling the glow of Genelle's bliss.

We walk around the tables as the guests mingle and look at the swag. There's tons of signage about their website but I suppose every bride and groom has a web link, Tumblr, and Instagram these days. The Fleckersteins have all that and then some.

Her book is everywhere. I understand how writers have to shamelessly self-promote at every opportunity, but it's hard to tell whether Genelle is using her book to promote her wedding or her wedding to promote her book.

Picking up one of the autographed copies that sit on every table and bar, I survey the bright red book jacket of *A Mean Girl's Guide to Change, Love, and Enlightenment*. In the jealous blur of our coffee shop encounter I really hadn't looked at the cover. Upon closer inspection I see it depicts Genelle in all her Photoshopped glory, looming like a giantess. She's holding a miniature guy in her hand. He clings (for dear life) to her fingers while offering a bouquet of flowers in supplication. Genelle has that self-satisfied look of a girl in control, which I'm guessing is what passes for enlightenment in her universe.

They also have plenty of custom-made wedding day plunder scattered throughout the reception area, including a monogrammed canvas bag with Genelle's book cover on the back side as well as a monogrammed four-tiered wedding cake that matches the monogrammed napkin rings. Even the bride's own miniature English bulldog wears a monogrammed bow tie. The Fleckersteins are registered at Neiman Marcus, Christofle, and Tiffany. I called to see if they had a Tiffany butt plug, but no such luck.

The waiters hand out monogrammed water bottles with Genelle and Wendell's names on the label. Don't ask why but I worry mine might be poisoned. I'm hoping we can get this over with pronto and split. The thought of watching Wendell feed Genelle a hunk of wedding cake makes me nauseous—it's an image I hope to avoid at all costs. But overall, for the moment, I'm feeling really good about coming to this shindig and how it's played out.

Nick and I help ourselves to hors d'oeuvres and pluck crystal champagne flutes off a passing tray. We meander, sipping bubbly and making small talk with perfect strangers until I spot my parents breaking free of the receiving line. Dad is wearing the suit he used to wear to client meetings back when he still had clients. Mom's wearing an off-the-rack beige satin ensemble with rhinestone buttons; the skirt hovers indecisively at the mid-calf mark. She looks a decade or two behind the times, but still pretty. With her newly earned riches I thought Janet would have bought something more extravagant, but then again that might have contrasted poorly with Marshall. Besides, moms can get away with that kind of look and Janet has always been frugal.

I'm determined to get my confession out of the way before the endive and goat cheese salad is served. Dad sees Nick and me coming and smiles—but only at me.

"Hey, Sport!" he says and gives me a hug. His expression turns frosty as he nods to my date. "Hello, Nick," he says, as if his name rhymes with "dirt."

Mom gives me a hug. I'm pleased when she hugs Nick, too. I think it's her way of telling him she's rooting for us.

"Look, guys," I say. "There're a few things I'd like to clear up."

"So would I," Dad grumbles, shooting a stern look at Nick, which is completely uncalled for. Nick doesn't even know the whole backstory about my parents observing his "cheater's" kiss with Roxie, so he's not sure what to make of Dad's misplaced disdain, but he keeps his cool mainly because I think he genuinely likes my parents. But it's all the more reason I need to get this over with before the layers of misunderstanding pile even higher.

"Well, when you guys surprised me at, um . . . work . . . that day . . ." I begin, "I was there because—"

"There you are!" we hear, and all four of us snap around to find the source of that overly enthusiastic, utterly affected, upper-crust, mid-Atlantic inflection—Dartmoor Millburn. He insinuates himself into the very midst of our little group, effectively sandbagging my mea culpa before I can say a word to stop him. Who else could make an appearance at a more inconvenient time?

"Well, hello, Clarissa," he warbles and gives me an up-and-down look, ogling me the same way he did that first day when I stepped off the elevator. I guess my dress is making an impression and I wonder where the previously mentioned Aubrey is—Dartmoor seems solo.

Nick takes notice and reaches out to shake Dartsy's hand.

"Hi, my name is Nick. I didn't catch yours?"

"Dartmoor Millburn," he says frostily. Why, I'm not sure. Is his dignity bruised because he's been improperly introduced? Or is it that I'm with a real man as opposed to a man-child like Norm? But it actually seems like it might be something else. There's no way he could be jealous or anything, right?

Nick shakes Dartmoor's hand, but simultaneously slips his other arm around my waist, pulling me closer. The gesture feels so natural and comfortable; anyone watching would think we've had years of practice.

"Oh, right. Nick," Dartmoor says and smiles devilishly. "I do recall hearing about you and Clarissa." A momentary expression of concern crosses Nick's normally tranquil face and I can imagine he's wondering what he's gotten himself into here. I realize that from Nick's point of view, how would anyone I know besides my parents even realize he exists?

But Dartmoor has already shifted focus to my parents. I cringe. No good can come of this. None whatsoever.

"And you must be Clarissa's parents," Dartmoor oozes. "A pleasure to meet you both. I'm Clarissa's boss."

Mom smiles and Dad stands up a little straighter.

"It's great to meet you, Mr. Millburn," says Dad. "Tell me, how long have you been at the *Daily Post*?"

"Beg your pardon?" Dartmoor blinks in confusion. "I've never been employed by the *Daily Post*." At least four entire sets of explanations instantaneously flood my mind, sadly none of them the truth. That's how typical it is for me to lie to my parents, but I hold my tongue.

Dad is outright alarmed and Dartmoor takes note. Before I can venture an explanation, Dartmoor cuts me off.

"Clarissa, dear, haven't you told your parents about your new job?"

A look of embarrassment must have crossed my face because Dartmoor's smile broadens. It doesn't matter because this time, I'm determined to face reality. But before I can say another word Dartmoor beats me to the punch again.

"Oh, you haven't even told them about the last job," he adds gleefully.

Marshall and Janet look at me with strange bewilderment.

Even though this is the least favorable set of circumstances in which to do so, I have an obligation to Nick, myself, and my parents to put all the cards on the table. If there's hope for Nick and me, I've got to come clean, even if it's in the presence of Dartbug.

"Mom, Dad, I've been trying to tell you, that when you surprised me at—" But before I can finish, a uniformed server walks into the midst of our little drama and interrupts my moment of truth by clanging a triangle-shaped bell.

"The newlyweds Mr. and Mrs. Fleckerstein require your presence at the first dance immediately," she demands. I want to scream but I keep my cool.

"Well, I'd love to help you sort this out," Dartmoor adds, gleefully looking my way, "but duty calls." Thankfully, Dartsy dashes away.

"I'm sorry about all the confusion," I say, trying to get Mom and Dad's attention, but they're already distracted. Dad seems ready to listen to me but Mom interrupts.

"Marshall, we have to go," she says, pulling Dad toward the dance floor.

"But Mom, I have something to tell you. It's important," I say, feeling like a little girl again, grabbing her arm to slow her down. "Besides, aren't they supposed to wait until after dinner to dance?" I ask.

"Actually, Clarissa, this is the way it's being done more and more these days. It gives the bride and groom a chance to shine," Mom says, as if she reads bride and wedding blogs all the time.

"Janet, shouldn't we wait to hear Clarissa out?" Dad chimes in.

"If Clarissa has waited this long to tell us what's really going on it can wait a few more moments," Mom replies sternly. "I'd really like to support Genelle on her special day of bliss."

I'm a bit taken aback by how abrupt she is, but I take a deep breath and release Mom's arm from my clammy grip and watch them walk away.

"You tried," Nick says sympathetically. "By the way, you didn't tell me your boss had the hots for you."

"No way," I respond indignantly, but knowing I thought so, too.

I'm too disturbed to say anything more so we gravitate like everyone else to the dance floor as the band strikes up a florid rendition of "If I Were a Carpenter." The band is decent, but the song is cringe-worthy. Especially because Genelle and Wendie have a fully choreographed first dance that includes Wendell on his knees and Genelle prancing circles around him. I scan the audience, certain that someone is recording this for YouTube in the hopes it will go viral as a promotion for her book.

I find Mom and Dad as soon as the song comes to a close, but they are already dancing together to the next song and Mom won't even catch my eye.

"I give up," I say. "I'll tell them another time—let's get out of here."

But Nick is looking at me as if he has no intention of leaving.

"Okay, why are you looking at me like that?" I ask, a little worried.

"Well, as I recall, there was an agreement that left kissing, touching, and dancing open to negotiation, right?" He grabs my hand and walks me to the dance floor and in that moment all my complications and explanations slowly drift away.

I knew we were pushing our luck, but how could I say no?

CHAPTER 29

We easily find a spot on the sparsely populated dance floor near Dr. Hart, my hometown dentist, and his wife, Paula. The band kicks up an old-school song that I've always considered an anthem of romance, "Collide," by Howie Day.

As we begin to dance, three giggly preteen girls take to the parquet wooden floor making duck faces and heart gestures, miming the words of the song.

Nick pulls me into his arms and I am not surprised at how easily I fit. He's a nothing-fancy dancer, but swaying with Nick is like a deep, extended hug and I let him guide me as we cuddle and sweep across the dance floor to the lyrics. His hands drift down to my hips, wrapping his fingers around my lower back, and my heart pounds. He invites me to twirl. So he does have a few *DWTS* tricks up his sleeve. I make a 360 and return finding myself deeper in his embrace.

I can't help thinking, *This is a* Dawson's Creek *moment.* I was pretty young when *Dawson's Creek* was on originally, but over time like a lot of people my age, I caught up with the teen soap and sometimes kicked back on weekends to watch it on Netflix.

Dawson's Creek was the place where I learned about booty

calls, lingering looks, and lip-biting as a form of seduction. Teenagers—those unusually beautiful ones in Capeside, Massachusetts, who had that weird Hollywood growth defect that made them look like they were in their early thirties—didn't fall in love, they "collided" like billiard balls bouncing off each other. Before Katie became Tom-Kat and then Suri-Kat, when Abercrombie zip-up hoodies were all I ever wanted to wear, there was "Collide," the song Nick and I were dancing to.

"Collide" has always meant a lot to me, but the lyrics are enigmatic—is it about a relationship beginning or ending? Will they stay together or just collide? To me, the song was about inexplicably loving someone, even when you're unsure if you complement each other—one's quiet and one's making a first impression, one's open and one's closed. Dancing with Nick, I couldn't help feeling like Howie wrote his song about us.

I'm teasing the shaggy curls at the back of Nick's neck with my fingertips and every so often, he lets his lips brush against my jawline. Things are so dreamy that it's easy for me to forget how the man dancing on the parquet floor a few feet away used to scrape plaque off the inside of my lower teeth with a dental scaler.

"I'm glad you were open to negotiation," Nick whispers in my ear.

I answer by snuggling closer.

As the lead singer croons his way to the big finish, Nick slips his thumb beneath my chin and I lift my face to his. He hesitates, his lips a scant millimeter from mine. In a flash it's like we're back under the bridge and my heart flutters, hoping he won't abandon this kiss like he did the last one. But there's no girlfriend waiting on the tarmac now, there's nothing to hold him back or make him stop. Here's crossing fingers that the tragic spilling curse has passed.

As the song fades, we kiss and I'm swept away . . . away from Genelle's wedding, the preppy country club setting, the perfect brightly dressed little children, and the tacky ice sculptures, away from my recurrently perturbed mom and away from my dad still wearing the suit that he wore for the clients he no longer has.

We're alone in a place that is lush and warm where the gentle friction of our lips makes me tremble deep down inside. Promises hang in a haze around us but our kisses seem to be an investigation without end. My entire body shivers and I'm lost. I breathe him in, kiss him again and I'm found. I don't ever want to leave.

When I hear the sound of rumbling, I honestly think it might be my stomach from the salmon and cream cheese hors d'oeuvres we just ate, but I realize the approaching rumble is a guttural growling, both aural and physical. I look at Nick, but it isn't coming from him. It's originating from outside our respective tummies. I try to contemplate its meaning, this low distant roar, but I come up blank. I find it impossible to leave the enclosed safe place in Nick's arms, but looking over his shoulder, I see the bottles at the bar rattle.

Earthquake? Not likely in Westchester County. Hugh and I reported years ago about fracking in counties north of here, and there's even more hydro-fracturing in neighboring Pennsylvania. But apparently that's not it.

So what is it?

Wait . . . make that, who is it?

Genelle is recoiling in horror by the champagne fountain as a banged-up Harley Davidson crashes through the chairs that surround the dance floor, turning the rental furniture into kindling. At first, I'm wondering how the valet could let someone steal Nick's Harley, but I remember his motorcycle is pristine, shiny, and perfect. This one's not.

Genelle lets out a blood-curdling scream as the rider pops a wheelie and then clutches and brakes, putting the bike into a tire-shrieking circle burn. Oily exhaust smoke fills the tent as the back tire draws a perfect circular black mark on the hand-finished chestnut parquet dance deck, leaving everyone coughing and gasping for air.

I have a fleeting, ridiculous thought that maybe this is part of the entertainment. But I suspect I'm wrong.

Wedding guests scatter and run for cover behind the gift table.

I'm still in a partial love-coma from dancing with Nick, my body snug and warm against his hips. Like a couple of idiots, we keep standing there in the center of the floor. The biker cuts the ignition, drops the bike, and stumbles sideways, almost falling, wobbling in a drunken gait right up to Genelle, who is holding her chest as if to protect those recently purchased assets. She's scanning everywhere for Wendell but he's nowhere to be seen. In fact, everyone is clearing away from her as the driver approaches, leaving Genelle alone and helpless.

The biker rips off his opaque motorcycle helmet and big woven dreadlocks spill out.

"Oh, shit," I hear Nick say beneath his breath. I look at him, wondering what he knows that I don't know.

"Don't hurt me," Genelle pleads almost in tears, looking as if she's going to soil her wedding dress. Nick lets go of me, heads toward the intruder, and it finally dawns on me who has crashed the wedding. There, in all her punk and leather glory, with a nest of wild hair and a whole shitload of eyeliner, is Roxie Buggles.

"You prissy little fashion princess," I hear her say in a drunken slur as she strides toward Genelle as if she's ready to rip her apart.

"Me?" Genelle squeals timidly. I can't blame her, but so much for passing herself off as a mean girl. I guess it's kind of hard to keep up the facade in the face of a true bunny burner.

"How dare you steal . . . Wait a second." She belches big and loud enough to stagger herself. "You're wearing a wedding dress . . . What the fuck?"

Nick puts his hand on her shoulder to turn her around. "Roxie. You have no business being here," he says.

"There you are, stud bucket!" Roxie exclaims with an incongruous smile and lurches to kiss him. He ducks back.

"Roxie, stop this."

"Where is she? Are you hiding her?"

"Cut it out. I told you."

"Yeah and you told me you loved me."

"We're not together."

Roxie scans the crowd and even in her condition, it doesn't take more than a second for her to zero in on me. I'm literally standing a few yards away. "You must be Crasissa!" she slurs and walks right up to me, swaying a bit. She's so drunk her eyes close, confused.

"Now, what was I going to say?" she mumbles. "Oh yeah." Roxie starts again. "You prissy little fashion princess!" she adds as if it's a speech she's memorized for English class. Her breath smells like tequila and Slim Jims; it practically keels me over and she notices.

"Sorry, princess, I should have sucked on a mint before I got here so I wouldn't offend your royal ass. I know I've got one here somewhere." She's so smashed she actually starts digging through the pockets of her leather jacket for a Mentos, I suppose. As intimidating as she may be, she's so daft that this verges on the ridiculous. That is, if she hadn't just destroyed a hundred-thousand dollar wedding. Nick steps between us.

"Roxie, get a grip." Roxie looks up and forgets about the breath mint.

"I did, lover boy, that's why I'm here," she says, and then yells over his shoulder at me, "Hey, Barbie, did you think you could steal my boyfriend and get away with it? You and your uppity Hannah Montana fashions and your little newspaper byline and your stupid brown sugar cubes?"

How the hell does she know about the sugar cubes? And what's wrong with brown sugar cubes? Aren't they better than refined sugar?

"Roxie," Nick says in a low voice, "this is over the top. Even for you."

Roxie flutters her lashes and puts on a ridiculously drunken innocent face.

"But Nicky, baby," she coos, "you like it when I'm over the top." Then laughs. "Oh, wait . . . I mean you like it when I'm *on* top."

I hear a gasp from behind the gift table. Pretty sure it's Marshall Darling.

I look at Nick. He looks back at me, but I don't see what I was hoping to see in his face—not even a crazy laugh or a go-figure kind of expression. That, I could handle. But I see a deep worry, like he's already crossed back over to the Land of On-Again. Like somehow he doesn't know what he wants. Or who. In his eyes I see the last thing I want to see—someone giving up.

"I'm sorry. Denny must have told her, he didn't know not to," Nick says, dragging Roxie away. "I . . . I gotta go." He grabs Roxie's Harley off the ground and pulls her on board. She doesn't fight him. Instead, she throws me a triumphant look, a satisfied little smirk on those dark sangria-colored lips.

I can't believe my eyes. I realize that even in my most paranoid fears, this was a scenario I could never have imagined. At Genelle's wedding, in front of everyone, including Janet and Marshall and Dartmoor, after our dance and that kiss, the kiss I dreamed of, I could never have believed that this could happen to me.

"You have to hold on," I hear Nick say darkly to Roxie, just as he once said to me. He kicks up the Harley and speeds out the way Roxie came.

Before they disappear, Roxie turns back to look at me.

Even from the distance I can see her smiling.

She holds up her hand and gives me the finger.

CHAPTER 30

Driving back to the city cramped in the jump seat of Rupert's Mini Cooper, every part of me, inside and out, is numb or growing that way. I am still wearing Dad's jacket. I hear Jody trying to talk to me and see Rupert checking every few seconds on me in his rearview mirror, but I can't respond to them. Behind my silent facade I am falling deeper and deeper into a pit that I have been digging for so long I can't remember. The last moments of Genelle's wedding keep running through my head like a scene on a defective DVD, playing over and over.

I was standing in the same spot Nick had left me when Genelle started yelling. I'm not sure how long she went on, but she stopped when she saw that I had no measurable response. I was in shock. I could see her and hear her and even though I wanted to say I was sorry for ruining her wedding, I felt so trapped inside my own shell that I couldn't speak. Out of the corner of my eye I saw Dartmoor shake his head and tsk tsk to his buddy Wendell as he took charge of the chaos in the aftermath of Roxie and Nick's departure. It all unfolded in a silent, slow-motion, horror movie kind of way. A fleeting expression of sadness crossed Dartmoor's brow and it stung me. *Even my enemy feels sorry for me*, I thought.

Janet tried to hug me, but I couldn't react.

"Clarissa, shake yourself out of it," I heard Marshall say. "Tell us what just happened."

Humiliation, shame, my foolish heart leaping into another dead-end abyss? Me, faking my way through life, just as I have for the last four years because I don't know any other way to get by? My abject inability to come to terms with reality because I'm so busy charting, defining, making clever comparisons, and fantasizing an alternate reality where everything goes just as I want it to? Unable to deal with the indisputable truth that I can barely support myself, pay my back rent, or pay off any of my loans? Or the fact that I can't find a job that resembles anything that I was trained for or will compensate me with any kind of meaningful salary? Or that the love of my life, my effin' soul mate, Sam Anders, deserted me and I've yet to face the certainty that it destroyed me inside and left me forever wondering what I did wrong? That I seem fated to repeat the mistakes of my life endlessly without interruption until my demise? I knew the answer to Dad's question, but I couldn't open my mouth to reply.

In my collapsed state of mind I just barely comprehended that I owed everyone an explanation. I mean apology. But Nick leaving with Roxie was simply the crumbling of everything in my existence, so I didn't know where to begin. I felt as if I was trying to climb a ladder inside myself to reach my brain and take back control of a nervous system that had completely shut down, as if my body was some giant robotic exoskeleton—like Optimus Prime or some other Transformer—and had stripped its gears and hydraulics. I desperately needed to reactivate myself, to gather enough energy to try to say what I had planned on saying to Mom and Dad before, to confess once and for all to the lies I had told.

"Clarissa, can you hear me?" Dad asked. "Are you okay?"

"I didn't want you to know . . ." I began, but the words were trapped in my throat because the sobs kept choking me. Painfully, I started again. ". . . I didn't have a job and that my personal life is crap. . . ." I couldn't sugarcoat what I was saying or be witty or clever. I could barely spit out the words between my ever-tightening chest and the salty tears flushing down my face. "I lied to you about everything," I said, "and I couldn't stop lying."

When I finally looked up and saw Janet's unease and her pitying vexation, as if I had let her down, I understood why I never told Mom and Dad the truth.

I wasn't trying to save them from the burden of my woes because of *their* problems. I was saving myself from Mom's condescending dismay and disappointment in me. All through my childhood, there had been something about Mom's smug "I don't have that problem" demeanor that never broke down into real feeling. She always saw others through a lens of failure when their lives fell apart, as if it were foreign to her experience. That look, even when she was trying to be sympathetic, has always sucked the life out of me.

With all his faults and challenges, I knew why Dad was barely a shell of his former self. Mom's charming eccentricities aside, no one could touch her. Her ability to manage and never be fazed by those of us less perfect around her is why I've tried to emulate her in my own crazy way. It's why tofu was the perfect symbol for what Mom was all about. Tasteless little squares. Perfectly dependable, predictable, nutritious, and boring. That why it was her food of choice. But of course I didn't say a word of that.

"Come on, sport," I heard Dad say. He put his jacket around me and started walking me off the dance floor. "We don't care about any of those things," he said. "We care about you."

I looked around for Mom and I swear I know she was there, but I couldn't see her. There was nothing about her presence, her expression, anything that registered. But I clung to Dad's words, repeating them like a mantra or an antidote to ward off evil spirits. *We care about you. . . .*

The Taconic State Parkway whizzes by as I finally find the

energy to turn my head and look out the window. I worry how close the guardrails are to Rupert's little red Mini, but I'm not driving, so I stop worrying.

Jody is still trying to talk to me but I can't seem to hear what she's saying. I can see Rupert's eyes in the rearview mirror darting from me to the road. I'm sure they are wondering if they should drop me off at Bellevue or some other institution for the hopelessly insane. I wonder, too.

How will I pick up the pieces? How will I be able to place my fingers on the computer keyboard, tap out a story, and ever again think it worthwhile? How can anything be?

Right now, I just want to curl up in bed and die.

CHAPTER 31

Elvis is gone. I can't be sure because he always comes back. Yet the unalterable fact is he's not here now. I should know—I searched every single corner of my apartment. The devastating possibility that he's gone for good crashes in on my sense of abandonment. As always I blame myself. Yet another omen I've ignored. I'm devastated by the way my bad thoughts fuse with everything that has happened.

I throw open Elvis's window, his magic portal, and hope. The phone calls start coming in from Nick. I ignore them. Every time I see his number on my cell phone, I remember that giving-up look on his face with Roxie sneering beside him and I just can't bring myself to answer.

After a few days in bed, I manage to stumble my way to the kitchen and my laptop. I had gone stone-cold social media sober and blocked all e-mail, texts, Facebook, Instagram, and Snapchats since the wedding. I know it's unheard of but I even deleted Candy Crush Saga from my phone. I might be the first one in history to have done so. I had zero FOMO (fear of missing out) because I knew all I was missing was further humiliation.

I stumble to the corner bodega in my PJ's and robe, shouting

Elvis's name, searching down every alleyway and garbage bin and I know I look like a demented runaway child or a bad reenactment of the last scene in *Breakfast at Tiffany's*. I pull myself together and buy some coconut water for electrolytes and those perfect dark yellow cubes for bouillon. There must be a thousand chickens distilled to their essence in those things, bones and all—a modern miracle, chicken in a cube. I hear they are laced with enough MSG to kill. Well, to kill a chicken, anyway, but I don't care.

Elvis is gone, my life is a wreck, and my imminent work deadline is approaching and there's nothing I can do about it. Once Dartmoor gives MT the report from Genelle's wedding, I am certain no one will want to hear from me at Nuzegeek anyway. But after nights of beating up on myself and staring out the open window wondering how my luck will change, I figure: What's left for me to do?

It takes everything I have to resolve to finish my one story assignment for better or worse as quickly as I can and start thinking about getting some other job. Maybe something in the service industry, like at the Double Bubble Laundromat down the street, or as a Starbucks barista. Time for me to join the rest of the millennial work force and to shelve this notion of being a journalist in an age where journalism is nonexistent or a luxury at best.

It appears as though I had written most of the article before the wedding because by late Monday afternoon, I've finished with most of my notes on Norm's custom skate deck business. I've loaded the finished piece up with lots of nuts-and-bolts money type stuff. I have no idea if I'm punching above my weight class, but I try, that's all I can say. Still, there is the conclusion to write and I just don't see how I can finish in time to e-mail it tonight. I'm just too tired and depressed. I put the article aside and decide to take a tiny nap, long enough to clear my brain, and then get up and finish it in time.

Sunlight is streaming through the apartment windows and I wake up. It's morning. Holy shit. I missed Dartmoor's deadline. My heart sinks. I hadn't realized how long I had been sleeping. I take a quick look at the piece. I just need a conclusion, damn it. I know Dartmoor will use my tardiness as another mark against me, but I have to finish this thing, if only for the sake of my minimal hold on sanity.

I throw together a conclusion. I couldn't help taking an existential approach, since that's how I'm feeling. I know I'm probably getting carried away but I liken the whole DIY concept to the human condition, riffing on the universal struggle for identity and independence in the economic sphere and our innate need to create something unique and individual that will not only please us but also earn the respect of others, i.e., clients, and pay the bills. Life: the ultimate DIY venture, an endeavor at which I feel I am less than succeeding. Who would have thought that I'd get to the point where I envied Norm and his singular focus on life?

A few trims for clarity and cuts to shorten the length for word count and I'm done. Even though it's technically late I'll just hand it in. Chapter closed.

I e-mail the article to MT and crawl back into bed. The act of writing has been a mild balm, a salve that has lifted me enough out of the dark, post-wedding place that I hate having finished. Now, there's nothing to hide behind or wait for. I was protected from facing the tatters of my cracked existence as long as I was in the bubble of trying to complete my article. I curl my pillow under my head and go to sleep.

An hour later, I throw back the covers for some more coconut water and see an "undeliverable: returned" notice pop up on the laptop. The report I slaved over didn't go through. Holy shit. Could MT have blocked me just because I'm such a loser? I consider sending to Dartmoor, then think twice. He'll probably just destroy it and pretend I never sent it in. I try to resend but after a few seconds the same undeliverable message returns.

I can't believe it. Logically, I figure it's just a technical glitch or something, but it doesn't feel that way. It feels like a rejection.

I don't have anywhere to go—except back under the sheets.

CHAPTER 32

It takes a while for me to realize the gnawing feeling in my stomach isn't the regretful combination of coconut water and MSG-saturated broth I made from the bouillon cubes. It's the unfinished business of my article for Nuzegeek. Somehow I can't rest until it's turned in. I know I'm past deadline and still doubtful about the quality of my financial acumen or any acumen I might harbor in my self-pitying state. But after years of working for Hugh, the writer's ethic is too deeply ingrained. I might be past deadline and it may be impossible to avoid running into Dartmoor, but I might as well get this over with.

I stare at the rows of clothes in my closet and realize I have nothing to wear to a firing. Let's face it: I've been swimming upstream on this job from the beginning. The question of the moment is—do I want to dress like a corporate punching bag, demure and sensitive, wearing a meek pair of flats and a high-collared blouse, or do I dress as if I don't give a fuck? Like my leather jacket with Bowie pins, my badly destroyed boyfriend jeans, and my Doc M's?

Everyone knows you need to dress for success, but I believe you also need to dress for failure. When you're about to be fired, you need to make a statement that you'll endure and move on.

Yes, I could wear a wooden barrel with two leather straps over each shoulder and feel sorry for myself. But my wardrobe is not well stacked with barrels and even though I'm not feeling positive, I draw courage from my closet. I decide to go into Nuzegeek as buttoned up and together as possible—with an edge.

I pull a plain blazer with rolled-up sleeves that I bought from Goodwill for ten bucks, a classic button-up white shirt that's slightly see-through, and a pencil skirt. It's definitely too short, but it's a statement. I put on some dark hose and my thrift-store Jeffrey Campbell pumps that make me taller. I'll be businesslike, to-the-point, and get out of there. Hell, for all they know, I have another job somewhere and that's exactly how I'm going to play it.

I do my makeup and decide to wear a light peach nude lipstick for effect. I guess I just like peach. I download the Norm DIY piece onto a flash drive, whip a copy out of my printer, and go outside for what seems like the first time in weeks, but is probably just days, I can't remember. The last thing I want to do is look at a calendar.

I arrive late in the evening at Nuzegeek hoping for minimum face contact. As the elevator doors open on the editorial floor, I'm happy to see there's no one in the halls. Most of the twenty-somethings usually buzzing around the offices have already gone home. I can't help picturing Dartmoor's tsk tsk at the wedding and pray I don't encounter him. I do prepare my stiff upper lip, but it's the lower one I'm worried about. I don't want it to start quivering.

The offices are eerie when there's no one around. As I walk past the employee lounge, I see two people going at it over by the coffee machine, and by that I mean some major make-out action. I guess people start up all kinds of things at start-ups. I look away, but not before noticing the skateboard propped up by the couch where they're snogging.

Shit, is that Norm and MT living dangerously? Don't they have big loft apartments to go home to at this point? I certainly don't need to linger and feel bad about my own joyless personal life, so I hustle forward and decide to make this quick.

Druscilla's not at her desk when I arrive, so I decide to drop my payload there and make my escape. I slip past the executive offices. Dartmoor's light is on, so I walk lightly, silent as a mouse.

There's no way around the employee lounge and they're still going at it. I worry MT will open her eyes as I pass. Luckily, she doesn't. Ah, young start-up moguls in love, getting their DIY on. Maybe a theme for a story someday, if I ever get to write another.

I make it to the elevator and sigh with relief; it looks like I got dressed up for nothing. Fine with me—maybe my look scared off the evil spirits and gave me the courage to deliver my story. In a few seconds I'll be on the street again, free to face my depressing future. I can't help picturing Lou at the Unenjoyment Office snickering at my futile attempt to make it on my own. The elevator doors open—I imagine it's an open shaft and by taking that one step I will plunge to the bottom . . . but there is an elevator there. Oh, well. Can't have everything.

"Clarissa! You're here!" someone yells loud enough that it startles me. I whip around, actually shocked, heart pounding because my mind can only imagine the worst.

It's Drusy. She actually says my name correctly for the first time and she's oddly ecstatic to see me. I absolutely don't want her to ring the alarm.

"Hey, Druscilla, I left the story on your desk," I say and step inside the elevator.

"Wait!" she exclaims and springs to the elevator doors in time to stop them from closing. I forgot about her paramilitary prowess.

"Druscilla, I've gotta go," I protest and start smashing the close button, but you know, that button with those two triangles pointing to each other next to the two triangles pointing away from each other? I always get them confused, and I'm pushing the wrong one.

"But I've been trying to get in touch with you," she says. "We got your story and MT wants to talk to you!"

"I know, I just put it on your desk. It's as good as I can do under the circumstances. Tell Dartmoor I'm sorry it's late but I tried to e-mail it. I can't stay," I say, hating the childish panic in my voice. I find the right button, the one for closing, and I keep pushing it. She looks at me oddly, then finally lets go of the doors and just watches me as they shut. I take a breath and notice I'm sweating.

I have no idea why MT wants to talk to me and I doubt very highly Drusy is telling me the truth. Probably some KGB-inspired trick to get me in front of MT so she can fire me to my face. Or so Dartmoor can swoop in with his "tsk tsk, I told you so"s. Besides, about the last thing I want at this moment is to see MT and Norm coitus interruptus.

On the street, the sun has already gone down. Somewhere on the west side of Manhattan, the darkness is pinching the sunlight into nothing. The city is descending into a darker, more provocative mode, and it fits my mood. The streets are still filled with bustling people who have lives and places to go. People are beginning to think about their evenings and the nightlife a city like New York has to offer. I'm dreading going straight home and back beneath the sheets, so I take a sharp left detour toward Broadway to distract myself from the inevitable depression to come. It's a last-second decision to change my direction, so when I notice a bearded man twenty paces behind me make the same turn, I'm suspicious.

I keep walking, picking up my pace, and decide to make another instant turn by Trinity Church, and sure enough, he turns, too. I consider heading in the direction of the nearest police car, but he's catching up with me fast.

I glance back to look at him and he's just totally weird. My heartbeat quickens. Now this on top of everything. He's wearing a short black hat like a Hasidim but he's not wearing the long coat; he's kind of like an orthodox Jew who doesn't know how to dress properly. It's all too creepy and I prepare to sprint, Jeffrey Campbells and all, when I feel his hand land firmly on my shoulder. I spin, fists ready, figuring I have one chance to disable my attacker and run like hell. I punch him right in the forehead and he goes down. I kick him once and I'm prepared to kick him a second time if he tries to get up.

"Don't! Don't kick me again!" I know that voice.

"Ferguson?" I ask incredulously.

"I knew my disguise would fool you," he says, holding his ribs, propping himself up. "Where did you learn to punch like that? And did you really have to kick me?" I give him a hand. I can tell he's a bit woozy.

"Ferguson—you're in prison. How did you get out?" I ask, brushing him off. "And why did you creep up on me like that?"

He looks around all shifty and I can't help but shake my head, knowing that whatever he says will only be half the whole story.

"I'm not supposed to be seen with family members. It's part of my plea deal with the SEC. I'm on a secret mission: Operation Mighty Hamster."

"I assume they named it after you?" I say, almost laughing. If I were in a better mood I'd go on about it. "The SEC must really be in trouble if they've asked for your help."

"I didn't get to choose the code name, my handler thought it was clever," Ferguson says, annoyed. "But that's not why I'm here. I'm on a mission of mercy. No one can reach you and everyone's worried."

"That's okay, I'm fine. I can take care of myself."

"Well, Mom and Dad will be here tomorrow and want to meet," he says, looking around furtively.

"I'm not ready to speak with them."

"I don't see how you can avoid it," he says. "Hey, sis, I know what you're up against. It's not easy with Dad or Mom. It's not like my record is spotless and I've already confronted them about my situation. They have all these expectations. They don't like how things have turned out but they have to hear it. There's no way around it."

I nod and feel like I should give him a hug or thanks or something, because what he's said makes sense. But he's already stepping away.

"I can't stay," Ferguson says and places a rolled-up piece of paper in my hand. "I've already violated the terms of my release."

"And what kind of new crazy scheme have you agreed to, in order to save yourself from all your other crazy schemes?" I ask.

"Look, I have a chance to atone for what I've done," he says, getting all serious and noble. "Yes, it's dangerous and I never thought I'd ever agree to working undercover to get the goods on those Russian bastards, but if I can pull this off I might get my life back and do something good for the world."

"That sounds dangerous, Ferguson," I say, feeling sad for him.

"Hey, prison is dangerous, standing here is dangerous. You could get hit by a bus tomorrow. You could get that flesh-eating bacteria. Or get mad cow disease. There could be a zombie apocalypse. Life is filled with risks, but sis, you just have to take them."

I'm astonished at how worldly he sounds. Although something about what he says rings familiar. Isn't that the Liam Neeson speech from the end of *Taken 2*? Without the zombie apocalypse reference, of course. But it doesn't matter whether it is or isn't, I know he's right and I give my younger brother the warmest hug I've ever given him. He hugs me back. But after a second he breaks away. I can see he's trying to hold back a tear.

"Sis, good luck with Mom and Dad, I've got to go. It's not nice to keep Vlad waiting. Прощай." He nods silently, turns, and runs off through a side alley. I can't resist taking the few steps to watch. I see him get in a window-tinted black SUV and speed away.

CHAPTER 33

The first two things I think upon entering the coffee shop are: 1) *Wow, Café Angelique is way cooler than I remember,* and 2) *the Darlings are nowhere near cool enough to hang here.*

Yes, I agree we can conclude that my karmic life is built around coffee. But hell, I'm not the one who decided to meet here.

Then I think thing number 3) *Who's the crazy-looking lady with the tortoiseshell spectacles and the chignon hairdo?*

Marshall and Janet are seated, looking very tense. Could the gal in the tortoiseshell be a long-lost relative or could she be Dad's new girlfriend? Or is she the head of a new R&D lab Mom's been talking about, working to increase the bonding efficacy of a new, improved version of ToFlue Glue?

"Clarissa, this is the family therapist, Dr. Leisl Lyman."

No shit.

Dad pulls out the chair between him and the doc for me to sit.

"Clarissa, Dr. Lyman has come all the way from Austria to consult with us today," says Dad, in an uncharacteristically calm tone. He's been practicing for this, I can tell.

"I thought you said you were seeing her in Ohio," I say.

"We were," says Mom. "Via Skype."

Hmmm. I wonder what Dr. Freud would say about transference

in the age of tele-psychiatry? Would Freud still insist his patients lie on a couch? Seems awkward. Where would he put the web-cam? I'm sure Drs. Drew and Phil are fine with it.

"Dr. Lyman is here because we're concerned," Mom says.

"About you, Sport," Dad adds.

An awkward silence falls over our little corner of Café Angelique. Those aren't words you want your parents to say.

"I know," I add at last.

"You've been going on for who knows how long about your pretend job at the *Post* . . ." Mom begins and I sense a note of indignation, which I resent for obvious reasons.

"We used the Google," Dad interjects, "and we learned that the *Daily Post* went out of business a long time ago!" *Okay, Dad, calm down*, I think, *don't have a cow about it.*

"And you've convinced yourself that Nick the coffee-brewing guitarist is actually your boyfriend when, well . . ." Mom's shaking her head gloomily in that Mom kind of way that I dislike that borders on Parkinson's.

"When he's obviously romantically involved with that woman on the motorcycle," Dad adds. Thanks for rubbing it in.

"You've created an elaborate fantasy life," Mom states, looking at Madame Lyman for encouragement. "A made-up world in which you have professional and personal connections that don't actually exist." Ouch.

"Sport, we just want to help you come to terms with that," Dad says.

Gee, thanks, Pop, and exactly how do you propose to do that?

It dawns on me that they've plunged right in here. No "Hi, Sport, how're you doing?" or "Nice to see you! Glad you're feeling better." This is some kind of, I hate to say it, *intervention.*

Lyman adjusts her glasses, pats her stubby hair twist, and looks at me like a frog she just pulled out of a beaker of formaldehyde for dissection.

"Clarissa, dear, may I call you Clarissa?" she asks. *Well, no, not actually, but I don't think I have a choice.* But I don't say that of course, and she takes my silence as agreement. Personally, I consider my silence a kind of protest, but go figure.

"Clarissa, dear, this is a very difficult case. Despite your extraordinary intelligence and functionality, you are exhibiting all the earmarks of paranoid schizophrenia," she says in a clipped Austrian accent that has me wondering if she's going to belt out a chorus from *The Sound of Music.* Maybe we could all sing "Edelweiss" together and be done with this. "Clearly, you must see that your parents are very concerned."

Something wells up within me. Call it defensiveness or mental illness if you like, I don't care. I call it outrage. I feel like I've walked into some inquisition where my brain has been put on the table for everyone to slice, dice, and examine.

In my own personal universe I've known for a while that when Marshall and Janet called my name at the *Daily Post* building and I spilled my coffee that I should have spilled again. I know no one sees the world in the superstition-centric way I do. But whatever you believe in and however you believe it, the outcome is the same. Maybe they think I'm crazy, and maybe I am, but something is rising up within me. Call it rebellion.

"Paranoid?" I say in disbelief. "You betcha. I know I've brought all this upon myself. And I know how hard on myself I can be. But besides some tire marks on Genelle's parquet dance floor and a possibly soiled wedding dress, no one but me was hurt in the process."

"Now, Clarissa, dear," Madame Lyman says and I can see the look in her eyes. She's thinking medication, I know she is.

"Look, Mom, Dad, I tried. You guys are the ones who dropped in on me without warning. I tried to come clean and tell you all about it. I called you, Mom, and you couldn't stop complaining about Dad." There's an uncomfortable moment as Mom looks away and Dad glares at her, but I keep going, plowing ahead. "You want to know what I was worried about? You and Dad. Yes,

I have my problems. What twenty-something doesn't these days? Maybe it's my tendency for hypercritical self-examination, or lack of self-love, or the crazy idea that I'm going to pay back the loans myself and be a working journalist someday, but it's motivation for me to do better. And hell, I haven't had the best luck with the guys I've been with, but that's my business. I know I'm a bit unusual, but who isn't? It's about time everyone faced the facts that human beings, especially the human beings in this family, are imperfect creatures, striving to be more, trying to become . . . *something*."

"Clarissa, we're not criticizing you," Mom begins, "we just felt that this was alarming and excessive and . . ."

"Can't you see? We're all nuts in this family. Mom, you make industrial adhesive out of health food. Dad, you design buildings that resemble fast-food takeout containers, and Ferguson is . . . *Ferguson* . . . a convicted financial trader who is in some kind of witness protection program slash sting operation with the Russian Mafia and the SEC, and you're worried about *me*?"

I squeeze my eyes shut out of sheer frustration.

"Look, Mom, I love you, but you have to understand that everything isn't as neat and easy and perfect for everyone else as it is for you. Some of us struggle, some of us make a mess of things, some of us aren't sure what to do, and a lot of us are sick of tofu." There, I said it.

"Well, I don't see what tofu has to do with this or why you have to criticize me," Mom says. Clearly, I've touched a nerve.

"Janet," Marshall says, trying to calm her, "this isn't about you. It's about Clarissa, remember? Besides, we're all in this together as a family. Right, Dr. Lyman?"

The doc nods and starts to respond, but Mom doesn't let her get a word in.

"Just because I've managed to find a new career and source of satisfaction late in life, that shouldn't make me a target of your or your father's hostility."

Everyone goes silent a moment. We're all stewing inside. I'm getting ready to reload; I mean, she's asking for it. From my point of view, this Roxie thing is nothing compared to Mom's unrealistic expectations of everyone that just suck all the oxygen out of our lives. I'm unemployed and my last relationship didn't work out. So what? Sometimes Mom is so damn faultless and cheerful you want to stab her, which is exactly what I'm about to say without the stabbing part, but before I say a word, a little voice speaks up. It's so soft that it takes me a moment to realize it's Dad's.

"You're so damn perfect," Marshall says, quietly, almost to himself.

Mom has a shocked look on her face. I can't help feeling for Dad. I know what he's been going through and how much guts it takes to say what he's trying to say.

Mom blinks like there's something in the corner of her eye. To my surprise, it's a tear. It makes me want to cry, too.

"Oh, Marshall, how can you say that?" she asks, not angry but all weepy. Marshall looks like he's going to break down, too. He's trying to change gears but he can't.

"I'm sorry, Janet," he says, still practically mumbling to himself, "that I don't meet your expectations. That I've failed."

It's so heavy I don't know what to do.

"Oh, Marshall," Mom utters again, her startled look soon instantly overwhelmed by tears. I'm watching Mom watching Dad, who's looking down at the floor.

But I find myself looking right past Dad through the window to the street outside.

Walking down that street is none other than the one and only bike-wielding, intoxicated wedding crasher and eye-shadow queen.

"Roxie!" I cry out, pointing to the window.

They all whirl to look, but of course, Roxie has already walked by.

"Oh, Lord," says Dad, dropping his face into his hands. "Now she's hallucinating."

Okay, here are my options: I can sit here and continue to be psychoanalyzed by a Viennese Dr. Drew in my own family reality show as Dad finally comes to terms with Mom and vice versa, or I can go after Roxie Buggles and bring to a finish at least some of my own issues once and for all.

"Gotta go," I say, popping up from the table.

"Go?" Mom looks shocked. "We're in the middle of a psychiatric intervention here, Clarissa. We've spent a fortune flying Dr. Lyman across the Atlantic. Where could you possibly have to go that's more important? We know you don't have a job."

Ooof! That was a low blow. I figure I might as well give them what they want.

"Well, Mom, I think you and Dad have a few things to work out. You might consider starting by hugging the man who loves you and find out what's really bothering him. And when you guys are done putting all that stuff on the table, I'll be glad to check back in with you and hash out my problems. But in the meantime, I do have a job," I say calmly. "Didn't you know I'm William Randolph Hearst's personal assistant? I know he's dead and the benefits aren't great, but I'm willing to work with that. Besides I have to meet my boyfriend, Barack O., for drinks, hope Michelle doesn't mind." I take two steps toward the door, and turn back. "Oh, and after that, I'm going dancing with Wolverine from *X-Men*."

What can I say? I'm still a big Hugh Jackman fan even though I know he's tired of playing that part.

Dr. Lyman is about to say something but I don't hear what it is because I turn on my heels and dash out of the café, determined to put to rest the only remaining question I have about the mysterious Roxie Buggles.

CHAPTER 34

I catch a glimpse of her frizzy hair turning the corner onto Lafayette Street. Even following at a good clip, I don't catch up until Roxie disappears down the steps to the subway station.

Down I go, into the bowels of the city, chasing the girl whose boyfriend I unwittingly tried to steal. I'm not sure exactly what I'm going to say to her, but I know if I don't confront her now, I never will, and I'm not about to let her get away. This is probably not the smartest thing I've ever done, but then again, according to one of Austria's greatest medical minds, I'm teetering on the brink of a psychotic break anyway.

"Roxie!" I shout, weaving in and out of the crowd in hot pursuit.

She turns to see me, a little smile creeping across her face. She flips me off just like she did at the wedding, then steps backward through the doors of the 6 train that has just pulled up. I jump, barely making it through the doors, before they seal the train shut and it screeches forward.

The subway rockets through its underground capillaries and this time I don't care about my neurotic fear of subways. I shove, jostle, and shoulder my way through packed cars searching for Roxie's massive woven locks. I find a few Roxie knockoffs and

Roxie-lite types, but the genuine article evades me. As the train arrives at Union Square I catch a glimpse of her dashing for the L. I shove my way through the doors before they close, just barely making it into the nearest subway car before it screeches away and give chase. First Avenue . . . Bedford . . . Lorimer . . . Graham. I think of all the people who live in these places going about their lives in a normal daily fashion while I'm chasing a crazy rocker babe who has given me the slip.

I make it through three cars without getting yelled at too much or punched, but after the next stop it's clear—I've lost her.

The train rumbles on a bit longer, then pulls to a stop.

The sign says I've arrived in Bushwick. I lean out the door, scanning the platform to see if Roxie exits, but there's no sign of her. I give up and slip out of the train as the doors close.

Ascending to street level, I wander around a bit and actually see a few of Norm's custom skate decks rolling by. I wonder whether Dartmoor and MT even bothered to read my story at Nuzegeek. I contemplate calling them and realize I left my phone in my apartment.

I continue meandering, crossing over some invisible boundary into Williamsburg. I'm only half-heartedly searching for Roxie now. My feet seem to have a destination all picked out and I let them go there. Soon, I'm standing beneath that distinctive arch of antique bicycles.

But something's different. The place has that lifeless look that comes from having been recently vacated. Closer inspection shows me that the HeadSpace sign is gone and there's a new one in its place.

My knees buckle under me. It's not as though I thought I still had any kind of chance of making something happen with Nick. It's not as though the real reason I was following Roxie was because I hoped she would eventually lead me to Nick. It's just that I know this place was his dream, that it made his life worthwhile.

And, okay, I wouldn't complain if I got to see him one more time.

But it doesn't matter now.

Because while the bikes and the building remain, one thing is certain.

Nick is gone.

The abandoned studio door opens, scaring the shit out of me.

It's Roxie.

CHAPTER 35

Roxie's locking the place up, carrying a cardboard box, and for one crazy second, I wonder if it contains a sampling of Nick's freshly severed body parts.

"You?" she barks.

"Yes. I want to talk."

Roxie spins and turns away without saying a word. I suppose it's an improvement over the finger. We walk about three blocks at a pretty good clip before she enters a bar, which would be considered a dive even by my friend Rodgers's standards. I linger on the sidewalk a minute, watching Roxie settle into a large window booth already crowded with hipsterish guys who have a tableful of empty shot glasses. She grabs the guy next to her and pulls him into a full-on tongue swapping.

I rap my knuckles against the glass to get her attention. She glowers at me.

But I glower right back. Then I crook my finger at her, not Bruce Lee kung fu–style, but the closest I get to that. "Let's talk," I mouth. "*Now.*"

Maybe Rodgers is right. Maybe I do have a death wish.

Roxie storms out of the bar and in the next heartbeat, we're standing nose to nose. "What do you fucking want? I'm sick of you following me around. You're giving me a bad reputation," she bellows.

"I want to know why you came after Nick and me. And if you're so into him, what's all that in there about?" I spit out, pointing to the guys in the bar.

To my shock, she actually starts laughing.

"You think Nick and I are together?" She laughs. "Nick and I have been shit for a long time."

This brings me up short.

"Then why the big scene at the wedding?" I ask.

"Why? I guess I just wanted to finally see the famous BRB for myself."

"BRB?" I have no idea what she's talking about. I think "be right back," but that hardly applies here. "What are you talking about?"

Roxie finds my confusion amusing. "You're totally clueless, you know that? Blond Reporter Babe. BRB. That's what Nick used to call you before he knew your real name. When he talked to his friends and the studio staff about you, he would be like, 'The BRB this and the BRB that.' You were his favorite topic of conversation. It made me want to puke."

So the CCG had a nickname for me? BRB. I would smile if I weren't so damn stupefied.

"He would yammer on and on about all your crap. From your cutesy wardrobe to your beverage of choice to the fact that you have a really great rack." She grabs a cigarette from her pocket and pokes it between her lips. "The guy has been in love with you since the first time you ordered a cup of coffee from his cart."

I stagger. It's heartbreaking to hear Roxie of all people say it flat-out like that. How could I be so unaware?

"Nick and I, we gave it a shot, but when the record dropped and went nowhere, we both got creeped out. Sure, I got a few benefits from time to time. After all, Nicky boy has a great ass." She smiles in that way that makes me want to punch her.

"I only went to that stupid wedding to see for myself what the hell was so irresistible about you." She lights the cigarette, inhales, and looks me up and down. "He was right about your rack."

I have no idea how to respond to that one.

"I gotta say, for a chick with such a brainy job, you're pretty fuckin' stupid."

I watch her take another long drag as all this new information sets in. After a minute, Roxie stubs out her cigarette beneath the sole of her pointy patent leather boot.

"Now, if you don't have any more questions, I'm busy," she says, glancing back at her fanboys inside.

"Just one," I say. "Why is HeadSpace closed?"

"Because Nicky skipped town. All he left me was that box of my CDs and some other shit."

This news sends a chill through me. "Where did he go?" *Please let it be the Bronx. Or Chelsea. I'll even settle for Hoboken. Just let it be somewhere close by.*

"Fuck if I know. As you can imagine, we ain't exactly talking. He was pretty pissed off after my motorcycle stunt up there in prepster heaven. My best guess? LA. That's where his brother lives. He has great connections in the music biz. He'll probably make it big out there without me draggin' his ass down. Look, if you don't mind, my entire fan base is sitting drinking in there without me," she says, pointing to the boys watching from the bar. "All six of them. And to be clear, I actually like getting fucked up. But for the record, you're *really* fucked up because your head is so far up your ass you don't even know how fucked up you are. So get the fuck out of here."

"Okay, I get it," I say and honestly I do and even in a perverse way agree with her. "But there's one more thing . . ." And using every bit of my body weight and every ounce of strength, I haul off and slug her across the jaw, knocking the cigarette out of her mouth and landing her on her drunken ass.

Okay. I don't do that. But I think about it. Instead, I nod slowly in recognition of my loss and her sorry state. As Roxie turns away I think I see the slightest hint of remorse flicker across her face before she returns to her fan club. Or who knows, it might have been gas and she was about to belch.

Like a zombie, I head back to the subway. *Los Angeles. LA. California*, I think to myself walking down the subway platform.

I drag myself home and drop into bed, slithering back under my pile of blankets—the Clueless Blond Reporter Babe (CBRB) once again in self-pity wallow mode.

LA, huh? Might as well be Mars.

CHAPTER 36

You know when there's a ringing or a buzzing sound coming from somewhere and you're sleeping and it seems to go on and on forever? You have no idea if it's from the alarm by your bed or the doorbell in your dreams or some television show you saw before you went to sleep or your cell phone? It goes on so long, in fact, that you don't even hear it anymore, not really, and you think you're just dreaming it?

I can't sleep anymore anyway so I decide to drag myself to the kitchen and face my morning coffee versus tea dilemma and the fact that Elvis has apparently left the building for good. I'm kind of surprised to hear an actual knock on the door and realize it wasn't a dream at all. I open it a crack and find Norm.

"Hey, Clarissa, I . . ."

But I don't hear the rest because I slam the door on him.

It doesn't take long for him to begin knocking again.

"Come on, Clarissa," he says through the door. "Everyone's trying to get in touch with you."

"Well, I'm pretty tied up right now. What with the sleeping, the moping, the staring out the window, not to mention feeling like a worthless piece of absolute shit—I'm kind of busy being depressed. Do you have any idea how long it takes armpit hair to grow? Come back in three years," I say.

"MT sent me. She really needs to talk to you," he says.

"Well, you can tell her I'm sorry the piece wasn't better and it didn't work out. I still need the kill fee. God knows when I'll get work again." I glance over to the calendar on the fridge and I realize I've crossed over into the dreaded third month of rent delinquency. Gee, I wonder how Mom and Dad will feel about me showing up at their door with my rollie suitcase because I've declared bankruptcy at twenty-six after my landlord kicked me out and I've defaulted on my student loans. How's that for an education in finance? Nothing like spontaneously combusting all your bridges at the same time. I'm so fucked. But I try to muster the last modicum of my goodwill.

"I just can't talk now but I hope you and MT are still good. No hard feelings. I'd love to keep hanging out on the other side of the door with you but I've got a lot of hiding under the covers to get back to."

"MT and I are fine," he says through the door. And my ears perk up. I'm struck by the curious use of the pronoun "I," as if he's finally learned third-grade English. I guess having a girlfriend who hobnobs with the Windsors is enough to straighten you out. Then I realize the article I was writing was about his career and he's probably bummed it didn't go anywhere.

"Look, I'm sorry I got your hopes up with that article," I say, bending over to speak through the space beneath the door so he can hear me. "I did my best to help your enterprise, I really did. And Norm, honestly, you've come a long way. You deserve to have an article written about you, but I've got to go. Or stay, I mean, and you've got to go and leave me alone. I've got wallowing to attend to."

I stand up with effort; my back is killing me. This is the most exercise I've had in a while, but I open the door a crack to be civil and say good-bye when I see Norm . . . wearing . . . like, clothes . . . from Steven Alan or Acne Studio or some other cool store. No shredded cutoffs, no bowling shirts.

"Hey, wait a second," I say. "You're wearing normal clothes."

"Yeah, I've been shopping with MT a couple of times."

"And you're not speaking in the third person."

"Third person? What do you mean?" Okay, he's learned to speak English, not how to write it.

"Your name, Norm. You used to talk about yourself as if you weren't there, remember—'Don't do that to poor ol' Norm'?"

"Oh yeah, that. She made me stop. It was driving her crazy."

Ya think?

"But you *did* stop?" I say.

"Yeah, sure. I don't see what the big deal is."

"It was that easy?"

"Well, no, but she asked me to."

Oh, jeez, why didn't I think of that? Well, too late now.

"The MTV guys got kind of creeped out, too. After the first two shows were taped and it was like 'Norm this' and 'Norm that' and they had a big meeting and decided I should stop or they wouldn't move forward."

"MTV?"

"Yeah, I got my own series. The announcement has kicked up deck orders like crazy. It's been amazing for business."

Oh, great, now I really feel like a total failure. Even Norm has skyrocketed past me.

"Well, congrats, I have no idea how you pulled that off, but it couldn't happen to a better guy. Well, as I said, I have to go visit some of my new friends on *Second Life* who want to see more of me, the virtual me anyway. Besides there's a big sale of some new virtual clothes that will look great on my much better virtual body. Then I have to go cry some tears in my milk. Part of my daily quota." I begin to close the door but he puts his foot in the way.

"It's because of your article," he says. "That's what MT wants to talk to you about. Your pictures and the piece put Nuzegeek on the map. Something about aggregators and click-through syndication. Everyone in the skate world reposted and blogged it. All sorts of other websites picked it up. Even *WSJ*, whatever that is. Your snaps made me look really good. MTV loved it. Something about an option. I don't really understand but everyone else does . . . except you, I guess." He peeks around my shoulder into my apartment. "Whoa, it looks like you've been eating ice cream out of containers for a really long time."

"No! I just started that."

"Well, I'll wait outside while you change out of your PJ's and clean up. MT is waiting downstairs," Norm says like a perfect gentleman. It's shocking what she's done with him. I'm more impressed than ever with MT.

"Really?" I ask.

"Really."

CHAPTER 37

Okay, so let me bring you up to date. First of all, I respectfully declined an offer to appear as the ex-girlfriend on Norm's show. Everyone tried to get me to change my mind—including MT, who is exec-producing, and even my mother. There was actual pay involved but I couldn't even dream of doing it. Besides, the option money for my article was enough to bring me current on my rent and begin to catch up on the loans. I have to say MT was generous; Nuzegeek could have totally screwed me on the deal.

Dad stood by my decision and Mom let it go. Yeah, Mom and Dad, together. They haven't solved all their problems, but Dad's back home in a real and different way. Apparently they continued on for some time after I left the shrink lady in shock at Café Angelique. It was an intervention, all right. Just not mine. Mom and Dad shared lots of weepy hugs and kisses and Madame Schmeud hightailed it back to the airport later that evening completely baffled as far as I can tell, but more than willing to collect her fee, expenses, and take all the credit.

Although they're not remotely the way they used to be when I was a kid, things seem to be working out. Dad's regaining his self-respect and is taking time to explore new career options. Mom is way more considerate about the money situation. Who knew that all those years they kept separate bank accounts? It might have been a good idea when Mom was worried about being financially dependent and maintaining a sense of autonomy, but I see how that definitely could create problems for Dad, who was left with no money and had refused to ask Mom for help.

They worry about Ferguson, but how could you not? Even I do. Once in a while he sends them a secret piece of marzipan from some far-off region of the Baltic or Kazakhstan as a sign that he's okay. I regularly comb the newswire, trying to read between the lines on anything to do with the Russian Mafia and the SEC, looking for hidden evidence of his exploits. Considering the turn in Russia-U.S. relations and all the sanction-bound Russian billionaires in Putin's inner circle, who knows where Ferguson might pop up next. Every one of those Ruskies has to be looking for something to do with their riches. Knowing Ferguson, he might be in the middle of all that. We heard through one source that he even met with Edward Snowden about a proposed business venture. I hope it's not that Internet dating thing for evangelicals in prison. I think more highly of Snowden than that. It could ruin his reputation. Got to admit my little brother certainly gets around in some weird wide circles.

Meanwhile, I've become the queen of DIY. God help me, I've written about so many Indiegogo and Kickstarter entrepreneurs that I really do want to write about the Federal Reserve, the new FICO scores, and Janet Yellen at this point for a change of pace. Janet Y. is totally cool.

And yes, even Dartmoor has begrudgingly begun to show me some respect as my stories have been driving major web traffic to the site. Honestly, I've changed my opinion of him—a teeny tiny bit, anyway. He deserves lots of credit for creating the best financial news site since Ezra Klein set up his own online feed after leaving the *Washington Post.* Beneath his perfectly pressed shirts, his perfectly knotted ties, and his perfectly slicked-back hair, the dude knows what he's doing. Dartsy and I have even collaborated on an article or two. He's even been a bit flirtatious, which I don't mind as long as it doesn't get out of control. I never in fact discovered the gender of the mysterious Aubrey. It's just weird how he only refers to Aubrey by name and never a gender-defining pronoun. I've given up on trying to figure that out for now. I think they've broken up anyway.

Apparently my story *did* go through to MT's e-mail when I first sent it, even though I received that kickback notice. That was why Drusy was so adamant about trying to stop me from leaving. MT had already read my story and loved it. Maybe they were, you know, celebrating that evening in the employee lounge.

It's been months since the day Roxie told me Nick moved to LA. I muddled through a brief bout of self-pity, but my girlfriends didn't allow it to fester. Rodgers gave me one full day of sulking, then a few nights later Piper; her new girlfriend, Hilary; Jody; and Rodgers appeared at my door with a bottle of champagne and an ultimatum.

"Get out of bed and come party with us or we will break into your closet and burn every last one of your accessories, starting with your 1990s Doc Martens," Rodgers said, and I could see they meant it.

I couldn't let that happen. So I partied. Rodgers took us on a series of late-night bright-lights, big-city adventures I'll never forget. Who knew there were amateur molecular gastronomist cooks hosting legally questionable supper clubs and dinner parties in unofficial spaces throughout the Manhattan underground?

"You've been writing so much about DIY, now you get to eat

it," Rodgers said. It wasn't clear how she knew this inside foodie stuff. I figured it might be her Trinidadian pastry chef mom's connections.

On rooftops, helipads, in abandoned restaurants, and Masonic temples, we ate the food of top-notch, not-ready-for-prime-time, up-and-coming chefs from heavy-hitter restaurants.

In one derelict synagogue we feasted on a midnight meal of lamb half buried under snippets of cat grass, sous-vide pork belly, and cheddar fritters. The temple walls were illuminated with massive dripping candelabras and mirrors, and we could see the Milky Way through the broken stained-glass dome. When we discovered the chef was Rodgers's new squeeze, it became apparent how she had become such a gastronaut. Why she kept Bart (short for Bartholomew) Chance a secret I don't know, but he's a very friendly, lugubrious dude with tattoos up to his chin. He's as sweet as his unbelievably delicious chocolate soufflé.

I kept waiting to see if we'd have to know a secret handshake to get in, but apparently knowing Rodgers was good enough. Jody, Piper and Hilary, who's actually a total kick by the way, and I were game to be led around on a crazy week of eating (and drinking) like I've never done before. Here's my list of the weird things we sampled (or were afraid to):

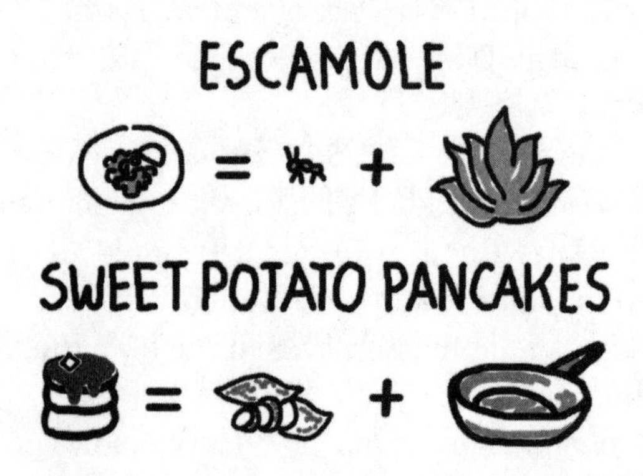

GRILLED BEAVER TAIL

RASPBERRY ICE CREAM

DEEP-FRIED ROCKY MOUNTAIN OYSTERS

? + ? = ...ew.

Okay, allow me to decipher my hieroglyphics. Escamole—which is ant larvae harvested from agave plants. They look like little cannellini beans and taste like really weird cottage cheese with a slightly nutty flavor.

Sweet potato pancakes—way better than you'd think, especially dripping in coconut syrup and ghee.

Grilled beaver tail—a mythical delicacy of Mountain Men—and I'm thinking pretty damn illegal—no comment on this one. I couldn't bring myself to eat it.

Artisan raspberry ice cream—actually changes color when you lick it, part of some mad science, gastronautic engineering experiment.

And . . .

Deep-fried Rocky Mountain oysters—I drew the line on this one as well. If you don't already know what these are, I suggest you look it up yourself.

As night turned to morning we finished up with a breakfast Bart staged with the Bubbles and Brunch Crowd on the actual L train—yep, the subway line everyone takes to Williamsburg, Bushwick, and environs. Breakfast included champagne and banana Nutella crepes.

There was also a massive portable espresso machine on a wheeled cart that kept sliding across the subway car floor, offering anyone on board a killer coffee-and-coconut-oil combo called Bulletproof Coffee. Coconutted espresso was an experience I had never tried before. And there's nothing like going nuts with a bunch of crazy people in bathing suits and bikinis on the L train at six a.m.

I couldn't help thinking about Nick in the middle of it all. Rodgers noticed almost immediately that caffeinated beverages have become a loaded issue for me.

"As my granddad in Trinidad used to say—you've got to get a stiff upper."

"Stiff upper what?" I asked.

"Lip, sweetie—not whatever's on your dirty mind," she said. "What I mean is that Nick is a great guy, but if he can't stand up to Roxie, then he's not good enough for you."

I knew she was right and I had to get over him, but I didn't stop wondering about Nick and how he was doing, and I didn't stop hoping that he'd call now that I wasn't afraid to answer my phone. But as the weeks went by, I kept my chin up per Rodgers's instructions and learned to tuck all that into a tiny place in the back of my heart and let it rest.

Then surprise, surprise: I got a letter from Sam! Unbelievable, huh? I never thought I'd hear from him. It's big, thick, and smells like fish. But I can't bring myself to open it.

That's why I'm standing down here at my spot under the Brooklyn Bridge. I wanted to see how much I've actually healed and how much farther I have to go. I hadn't even considered visiting my secret hideaway since the night I almost killed Nick with a dish of shrimp.

Tonight, though, I decided to test myself.

I've always hated when people deem things "bittersweet." I mean, how can something be bitter *and* sweet? It's like when people say "same difference." Come on, it's either the same or it's different. But I guess there's no other word for the feeling I have standing here, watching the ferries shuttle like gargantuan water bugs across the East River, their lights shimmering in the dusky light turning to darkness as the sun goes down on the other side of the island. Autumn is close and there's a crispness in the air, along with a sad cool whisper coming off the water hinting that summer is over.

I've been thinking about everything that's changed, trying to count my blessings even if I feel like the train tracks never really switched back after the "spill that got away," inserting me into a multiverse not of my own choosing.

The lights from Manhattan's skyscrapers flicker on the water and you can see quite a few industrious souls with their offices in full-on fluorescent glow, working through the night. New York is good for working. It always makes sense to work here. Falling in love, not so much, at least not for me.

As beautiful as my secret, only-view-of-its-kind, Manhattan sanctuary is, it doesn't feel the same. I've worked as hard as I can, writing as many stories as possible and hoping to forget. But I can't stop seeing Nick's slow smile light up his face every time he saw me enter the *Daily Post* building.

Looking down at Sam's letter, I wonder why I don't want to open it. I mean, what can it say after all this time? How can it repair the giant hole in my heart that's been years in the making and that I've tried so hard to overcome?

I realized after my extensive soul-searching sojourn of the last few weeks what Mom and Dad and, yes, even Dr. Leisl Lyman were trying to get me to understand about my wishful thinking. AvPD is what they call it in the *DSM-V*, Avoidant Personality Disorder. Gotta love those shrinks, they have a disorder for every normal thing that happens in life as if it's a disease we all need meds for.

My ego has been bruised and it's taken a lot of hard thinking to see the part I've played in Sam's disappearing act. Here's my unpleasant self-damning conclusion: I believed what I wanted to hear and managed to take Sam for granted when I least should have. Sam may have never wanted to move back to Manhattan. After all, he's a *marine archaeologist*. That means you have to go where the antiquities and water are. You don't see a lot of that stuff down here near Wall Street. I just assumed he'd go wherever I did. He was *always* there before, ever since we were tweenagers. My guess is that Sam couldn't bring himself to tell me or figured I wouldn't listen anyway.

I put Sam's letter back in my pocket. I don't think I can bear to read it right now.

The night seems immense, the stars are luminous, and in the breeze I think I hear Nick's voice:

Funny how you find the coolest things when you're not even looking for them.

He totally understood. He knew why I came to this place without me even having to explain it to him. Maybe things you don't have to explain, and the people you don't have to explain them to, are the ones that matter most.

Time to go home. Time to call it a night and get up early and work again. New York is the place for work and I'm lucky that I have work to do. Writing is the only thing that fills my mind up with enough to think about. That way I don't think about all the other things I can't understand anymore.

I turn to leave.

"You can't go," a voice says in the darkness, and I freak a little bit, worrying I'm imagining the breeze talking again. I dig in my purse for my pepper spray. Generally speaking, in New York, this is the kind of thing that would have you running, screaming for help. The only thing that keeps me from doing so is the fact that I actually *know* that soft voice.

"I've been coming here every night, waiting for you for too long. Don't leave."

Standing by the water in the dark, in the reflected light of the East River, I see a silhouette. I hold my breath and Nick emerges from the shadows. I'm tempted to reach out and pinch him, just to see if he's real.

"Didn't mean to scare you," he says, stepping closer into the half-light, half-darkness beneath the streetlamps. "Sometimes I doze off and, well, you never come down here anymore, so I didn't see you at first."

I can see that behind him, far off in a corner, is his Harley.

"I thought you were in LA. Roxie said . . ."

"I was, for a while. But I came back and I've been trying to build up the courage to find you. I knew calling wouldn't work. I felt sick and pretty confused. I knew you thought I'd lied to you and I let you down. I saw it in your eyes." He sighs and steps closer. I can see his whole face and his downcast eyes, trying to overcome his shyness. I can feel the warmth of his breath in the space between us. "If you'd looked mad, I could have handled it. But you looked hurt. And that scared me more than anything ever had before . . . because I was responsible for it."

He glances out toward the river, gathering his thoughts. "I'm kind of messed up that way. When I think someone feels disappointment, I guess I disappear. Not the best way to deal with it."

Again. Surprising amount of information for such a shy guy.

"I was beginning to think you'd never show up. There's so much I want to tell you." I close the gap between us with one step and place my finger to his lips.

"You don't have to explain anything," I whisper. "And you know what?"

"What?"

I give him the tiniest grin as I go up on tiptoe. "Right at this moment, neither do I."

As he brushes his lips against mine, I understand that sometimes the only explanations that really matter are the ones that don't require a single word.

ACKNOWLEDGMENTS

DEAR READER,

We may have never met face-to-face and perhaps never will, but I am grateful to have been connected to you through the quaint convention of television watching, even if it's a bond that occurred decades ago. It was satisfying enough to hear that you remade your bedroom, improvised your fashion style, doubled down on your Doc Martens, felt empowered to create your own video games, disregarded gender politics, and learned to write your name backward. But discovering that you remembered and thought seriously about all those Clarissa-inspired things in your twenties and thirties was beyond my anticipation. You inspired me to write this book.

I also want to thank my multitalented editor, Brendan Deneen, at Macmillan, who knows how to juggle more balls in the air than I do; Barbara Marcus, publisher of the Children's Division at Random House, who was instrumental in launching my career as a novelist; Myrsini Stephanides, my agent, who loved the idea of this book from the beginning; fashion designer Lisa Lederer, who designed all the original awe-inspiring clothing from *Clarissa*, and who has been my fashion guru and arbiter of everything cool on this book and others; and Nicole Sohl at St. Martin's Press, who has steadfastly navigated this book to publication. I want to particularly thank Demi Anter, for her inspired, spontaneous illustrations.

My thanks for this book extends beyond these pages to many of the people who made the very idea of Clarissa possible, because without *Clarissa Explains It All*, there wouldn't be anything to keep explaining.

First and foremost is Melissa Joan Hart, who continues to embody everything that is forthright, honest, and high-spirited about Clarissa. You can write those qualities in a teleplay or screenplay, but if you can't find someone who truly personifies those values, the character would never spring to life. She was my daughter before I had a daughter, and I couldn't be more proud and astonished at all she has done. Most important, she has kept her humanity and integrity intact in a business that has very little tolerance for those qualities.

Next is Gerry Laybourne, who had the vision, the fortitude, and the moxie to make Nickelodeon happen in those days. It was her directive to explode kids' TV that drove those of us working for her to create highly creative and totally original programming that has endured the test of time and generations. She gave us the chance to reset the clock on television for kids, establishing new paradigms for animation, sitcoms, and other forms. Without that mandate, none of our creative ideas would have made it to the screen.

It's impossible to thank everyone else who worked on *Clarissa*. But know this—you can't make television by yourself. The producers, writers, directors, performers, graphic designers, costume department, editors, and technicians all did their part to make Clarissa come to life. They have all gone on to be highly accomplished people in their own right.

For a long time I've felt that the Clarissa I knew was freeze-tagged before she could really show the world everything she was capable of. Hopefully, with this book, Clarissa is free again, and who knows what's next? As Sam would say, "Yeah, what's the worst that can happen?"